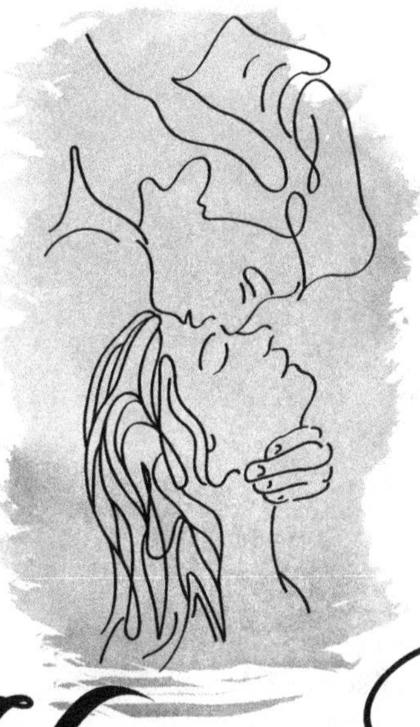

Kismet

A NOVEL

Avagaye Clarke-Heron

ISBN: 978-1-7353069-8-8

Editor: Lena Joy Rose

Layout and Design: Mark Weinberger

Printed in the United States of America

Ordering Information:
Quantity (Bulk) Sales. Special discounts are available on quantity (bulk) purchases by corporations, associations, and others.
For details, contact the author:
ms.avaclarke@hotmail.com
www.inspirepublications.net

Dedication

To my darling husband, without whom this book would still be in my head. Thank you for your unwavering support and for always believing in me, even when I question my abilities.

To mom, just skip over the sex scenes, please.

To all my readers, the veterans, and the newcomers, this one is for you!

Contents

Contents

CHAPTER 1

France

The sound from the phone's vibration against the glass top of the bedside table woke Katie from her sleep. She gently nudged the muscled leg that was still draped across hers, "*Mon chéri,* your phone is ringing."

"What time is it?" Keaton mumbled as he slowly rolled onto his back. He had the look of a sated man.

Katie glanced over at the alarm clock. "Three minutes after 4:00 a.m. I hope nothing terrible happened," her French-accented voice was thick with grogginess.

Keaton reached for his buzzing phone on the bedside table next to him, his eyes half-opened. Katie switched on the headboard lamp on her side of the bed and sat up, her eyes focused on him. He finally managed to grab the phone and struggled to open his eyes to look at the Caller ID. The glaring light from the phone made it near impossible.

"Mom…? Why is mom calling me at this time of the morning?" He looked at Katie as if searching for an answer.

Katie's tense expression eased, but she was no less anxious. "Maybe it's an emergency? Go ahead, answer it."

"Mom…" Keaton answered, waiting for his mom's response.

"Keaton…" she answered, her voice quivering, an immediate indication to Keaton that she had been crying.

Keaton immediately got off the bed; nervousness occupied his demeanor and his eyes filled with worry and concern. "Mom, what is it? Did something happen? Mom!"

"Keaton, Your dad...."

"Mom, what's wrong with dad? Why are you crying?" Keaton's anxiety grew; he paced across the room with the phone fixed to his right ear and his left hand on his head.

"Your dad passed away this morning." The sound of her crying was so loud that Katie could hear it from the bed. Keaton stood still in his tracks, he fell to the floor with the phone still fixed to his ear, and as much as he tried to speak, there were no words, only tears flowed from his eyes. Katie rushed to his side when he fell to the floor; she knelt behind him, wrapping her arms around his chest. The phone fell from his hand as his body collapsed into her arms; the brunt of his weight forced her petite frame to reposition; she sat behind him, wrapping him as tight as she could with her legs and arms. His silent cry turned into deep, loud wails, and although Katie was not clear on all that was happening, it was evident that whatever he had heard was bad news, and she could not help but cry with him.

"Keaton...Keaton...are you there?" Katie heard the voice coming from the phone. She grasped his chin, tilting his head back. "*Mon chéri*, your mom is still on the line; you need to talk to her." She picked up the phone and held it to his ear. Keaton managed to pull himself together for a moment.

"Mom, how did this happen, when..." he sputtered. "I mean, I spoke to dad two days ago; how could this happen?"

"Keaton, I need you here; you need to come home. There is so much to talk about, and I cannot do it all by myself. We cannot discuss it over the phone. I have sent the plane for you. Jaxen will text you the arrival time. Give him your address to transport you to the airport when they land. I'll be expecting you home by noon tomorrow."

"Mom..." She had hung up before he could ask another question. Keaton wiped the tears from his eyes and tried to calm his elevated heartbeat and breathing.

Katie moved and knelt in front of him; she lifted his face to look into his eyes. "*Bébé*, what is it. What just happened?"

Keaton looked at her, his eyes blood red and still wet from his tears, the tip of his nose, his ear and cheeks flushed.

"My dad...my dad passed away." With the words coming from his mouth, the sudden reality seemed to hit him. The veins in his neck and arms grew larger; Keaton leaned forward, placed his head in his hands, and sobbed. Huge body-shaking sobs racked his body, each coming in a wave, and, with every groan, he let out a low whimper.

Katie held her hands to her mouth in shock at his response. She could not believe it herself, and the thoughts of him telling her two days ago that he had spoken to his dad and that he was doing fine flooded her mind. The same question weighed heavily on her heart; how could this happen? She tried her best not to speak, not to ask the questions racing in her head; instead, she laid on the floor with him and hugged him as tight as she could.

About twenty minutes had passed when a text message came in on Keaton's phone. Remembering what his mom had said earlier, he checked his phone. Jaxen had texted the airport location and landing time. Keaton checked the time on his phone and realized his plane would arrive in two hours.

Katie sat up beside him. "Is that your mom again?"

"No…I have to return home today. I need to be at the airport within the next two hours." He stared into the distance. Katie gathered her thoughts before responding; she needed to be selective in what she would ask next. "Do I need to book a flight for you? What can I do?"

Keaton got up from the floor before responding. He glanced around the room, figuring out what he needed to do next. Noticing his obliviousness, Katie asked again.

"*Bébé*, do I need to…."

"No need, mom has sent the plane; you can help me pack a few things."

Katie stood still, in a state of confusion. As far as she knew, Keaton was a grad student, and his family worked in real estate. They live a decent life but are middle-class in society at best. At least, that's what Keaton had told her.

Keaton looked over at Katie and could see the confusion on her face; knowing her for almost three years, he could tell what questions she wanted to ask.

"Katie, I know that I'll owe you an explanation; there are some things I have withheld for personal reasons. Just know that I have not lied to you; I have just omitted a few things, waiting for the right time to tell you. Believe it or not, I had planned to tell you everything on your birthday in two months, and I still will."

He walked up to her and held her two cheeks with both hands, slightly lifting her face to look into her eyes. "Please just wait for me. I can't get into the details right now, but I promise you that as soon as I get back home and settle things with my dad's funeral and with my family. I will be back, and we will have that special surprise I have planned for your birthday. Please, just trust me."

Katie nodded in agreement, but her eyes could not hide her thoughts or her feelings. Keaton kissed her forehead and hugged her tightly; his tall 6ft-3inch-body towered over her 5ft petite frame. She hugged him back, laying her head mid-way up his chest.

"Take me with you," she sobbed. "You promised I'd meet your parents soon, and now…your dad…"

Keaton pulled himself from their hug so that he could look at her. "Katie, I know I promised, but now is not the time. With the news I just received, and what I can imagine is going on now in my family, it's not the best time to introduce you to them. I had no idea that my dad had any life-threatening condition, or else I would have formally introduced you to my family before this."

He paused, not wanting to repeat the heart-wrenching words. "Katie, I will come back, and if I can't, I will send for you. Please let me handle this first; I still want to introduce you to my family in the proper way I have planned. Please trust me, it's just not the right time."

Katie reluctantly nodded in agreement. She moved to the closet and took out his travel bag and packed what he would need to travel on a short trip. Keaton looked at her, packing his things, and could feel her sadness. He wanted to take her with him, but it was not the best time. He grabbed his phone, walked to the bathroom, and texted Jaxen his apartment address.

Katie placed the packed travel bag on the bed and stood outside the bathroom door, listening to the shower running. She wanted to join him; her thoughts were feral, he was leaving, and though he said he would return, there were now uncertainties brought on by what she had learned earlier. He was certainly not an average guy, and everything she thought she knew about him for the past two years and nine months was now questionable.

She stood outside the door at war with her thoughts, and before she had a chance to enter, Keaton opened the door, bumping into her.

"Katie…?" He held her hand and led her to sit on the bed. He lifted her chin to look into her bold, blue-gray eyes. He wiped the streams of tears flowing down her cheek and tucked loose strands of her deep-wave blonde hair behind her ears. His heart was in shambles from the news of his father's passing and knowing he also had to leave Katie behind with doubts and questions. He needed time to tell her everything, to clear all misunderstandings, time that he did not have at that instant.

"Katie, I love you, you know that right? I promise, once I sort things out back home, you will know everything you need to know, and you can ask me anything you want to; please just don't ask me now." He kissed her, lingering with desperation for her understanding. She pulled away and wiped her eyes and nodded with a forced smile. "It's okay, I trust you, I understand." Her words contradicted the feeling in her heart.

Keaton got dressed and went back to sit beside her on the bed. "Do I need to take you to the airport?" She asked hopefully.

"No, I've arranged pick-up; neither of us is in the right frame of mind to be driving." Katie agreed with a slight smile. Keaton pulled her closer to him and laid her head on his chest. He kissed her gently on the top of her head. Knowing the meaning of her silence, he comforted her. "Don't worry too much, okay? I promise, you and I will be fine…."

His phone rang. Jaxen was outside his apartment. Katie had raised her head from his chest when the phone rang. "Your ride is here?"

"Yes, Jaxen, a family friend, he's outside."

Katie stood up and lifted the packed travel back from the bed; Keaton held her hand and took the bag. "Can I walk with you to the car at least? She asked, staring up into his face with a feeble pout." Keaton smiled at her with a quick snicker and pulled her in to kiss her on her forehead. "Of course, do you even have to ask?" He took her hand, leading her beside him as he walked towards the door.

Exiting the elevator on the ground floor, Keaton could see Jaxen waiting by the car outside the building's main entrance. He held on tightly to Katie's hand as he pushed through the rotating glass door exiting the building.

"Mr. Dawson." Jaxen greeted Keaton with the right rear car door open. "Cut the formalities, Jaxen," Keaton snapped as he handed Jaxen his bag. He pulled Katie to the front of him. "I'll call you as soon as I land. I should be in New York in the next eight hours or so. Do not stay up too late, and please remember to eat. I know you are booked for competitions for the next two months. I can't say for sure now that I will be back in time to be at every one in person, but I'll send my support in any way I can."

He lifted her chin and kissed her gently on the lips, which turned into a fervent interlock. She stood on tippy toes, wrapping her arms around his waist. It was the first time in almost three years that Keaton would leave Katie without knowing when he would return. And almost simultaneously, both their hearts fluttered at the thought.

"I love you," Katie whispered as their lips unlocked. "I love you too, now go back inside and be safe." Katie stepped away, allowing Keaton to enter the car. Jaxen closed the door and walked around to enter from the driver's side. As the car pulled away, Keaton and Katie kept their eyes on each other with aching smiles on their faces until they were no longer in sight.

Keaton sat motionless in the back seat for a few minutes, in a blank state of mind. He looked up in front of him, and his eyes caught Jaxen's gaze in the rear-view mirror, and his brain buzzed with information about the past few hours.

"Jaxen." He uttered, inhaling deep. "What the hell has been happening back home? Was dad sick? Is there something you all are not telling me?"

"Sir, I learned of the news this morning. Your mom's assistant contacted me around 3:00 am to pick you up...."

Keaton maintained eye contact with Jaxen through the rear-view mirror, his brows now knitted and a puzzled look on his face. "3:00 a.m.? So how did you get from New York to France in two hours?"

"Sir, we were in Leicester in the UK, assigned to travel with and transport the CFO on his three-day business trip. We have been in Leicester since Monday, scheduled to leave back to New York tomorrow."

"Oh," Keaton responded, his shoulders fell to a more relaxed position. "Mom called me around 4:00 a.m. this morning, which would have been around 11:00 p.m. in New York, so whatever had happened to dad must have occurred around that time yesterday, and suddenly too.

I can't wrap my head around it, Jaxen. As far as I know, dad was healthy; I spoke to him two days ago on a video call, and he was playing tennis...." Keaton played through the thoughts in his head, scanning his memory for any fragment of information or occurrence that could justify his dad's sudden passing. But there was nothing. As he drifted away again, consumed with his thoughts, Jaxen spoke, snapping him back to reality.

"We're here, sir," the car pulled into Paris Charles de Gaulle Airport towards the private jet terminal. Jaxen exited the vehicle to open Keaton's door, but Keaton was already on the pavement. Jaxen took the travel bag from the trunk and walked behind Keaton to the waiting jet plane.

Keaton sat down, putting his earbuds into his ears while sending a mental goodbye to Katie. The following eight hours would be a grueling battle between anxiety and disconcertment.

CHAPTER 2

New York

"Sir, we're about to land." Keaton felt a gentle nudge from Jaxen.

Keaton secured himself for landing, then checked the time on his phone screen, *10:00 a.m. Wednesday, September 19, 2018*. The realization triggered a knot in his chest; it was no longer Tuesday morning in France. For the first time in nine months, he was back home, in New York.

Within two hours after landing, Keaton arrived at the family home in Lenox Hill, Manhattan. He was more than excited to return during his last two-yearly visits and always had pleasant thoughts on the drive home. However, this time was different; the knot in his chest tightened as the car entered the property.

The exquisite estate basked in over nine acres of verdant, enclosed landscape, offering the Dawson family complete privacy. The family home sat in the estate's center, a grandeur hallmark that beautifully preserved its authentic details with a hint of modern flair. Though Keaton is an only child, he grew up in this masterpiece of home design with over 18,000 square feet on three floors. The home featured twelve primary bedrooms, twelve full and three half bathrooms, and separate staff quarters. There were outdoor and indoor pools, a spa, grass tennis court, paddle court, two pavilions with full kitchens, arbors, a fountain, a carriage house with its connecting greenhouse, and two detached four-car garages.

As a child, Keaton would often get lost running around inside, and at one point, he would question his parents about the need for such a big house. However, as he grew older, he began to understand. His father, Keegan Dawson, was the founder of TrueTek, one of the most extensive technology multinational conglomerates headquartered in New York, involved in the invention, production, and distribution of specialized hardware, software, internet infrastructure, cloud computing, and biotechnology. TrueTek's industries, corporate offices, and retail sites situate in over eight hundred locations within the USA and Asia, Canada, the United Kingdom, and the Caribbean.

Keaton's parents would host mega business parties that would run for days. Depending on the partnership's success, some foreign partners would often lodge at the Dawson's home for short transactional periods. Consequently, Keaton was always surrounded by non-relative 'uncles and aunties' of the business world.

Without realizing the car had stopped, Keaton sat inside staring at the main entrance door of the house. Jaxen opened the car door and waited. "Sir?" Jaxen hinted politely; Keaton took a deep breath and stepped out. He walked hesitantly towards the front door. The thoughts that he would not be seeing his dad when he entered occupied his mind, and the reality sent a sudden shudder all over his body.

"Welcome home, Young Master Dawson." Jared, the family butler, greeted Keaton by the door. Even though Keaton could see Jared standing there, the sudden absence of conscious awareness made him unmindful of the fact that Jared had welcomed him. He walked past Jared into the main hall. He closed his eyes and raised his head, inhaling deep, almost trying to clear the overdrive of thoughts in his head. "Mom!" he called, his voice radiating the pain he was feeling.

"Keaton? Is that you? I'm in here."

Keaton followed her voice to the sitting room by the fireplace; she sat by the fireplace wrapped in a throw surrounded by albums and loose paper and files.

"Mom…."

"Keaton…" their voices ladened with pain and grief. Keaton hurried towards her, he dropped to her side by the fireplace. They both broke down into tears, evidence of sorrow was all over her face. Her eyes were red and swollen as she had been crying for hours. Her body quivered in Keaton's embrace as she shrieked in anguish. He knew he needed to be strong for her, but his will was shattered. He became a sad five-year-old boy in his mother's arms, broken, grief-stricken and bereaved.

As an only child and the sole heir, Keaton and his father shared a tight-knit relationship. Though he was the founder and president of one of the largest tech conglomerates, his title and work responsibilities never took precedence over his family. From the moment Keaton could understand things as a child, it was clear to him that he and his mom were his father's priority and that he was their most important investment.

Keaton was groomed to take over from his father one day, but he never felt pressured in the process. He knew every step of the way that his father was his advocate, and his love was always abiding and unconditional. Keegan had made sure that Keaton was knowledgeable about all the functions and operations of TrueTek. He spent hours after work every evening with Keaton in his study, analyzing TrueTek's performance indicators, financial statements, and operational activities. Keaton was involved in the development process for the majority of the products and services offered by TrueTek.

Keaton spent the bulk of his childhood, adolescent, and young adult years in the care of his parents and only left New York at the age of twenty-three to study for his MBA at Oxford University in England. Even then, his father would visit him at least twice every year during the two years of study, and Keaton would return home at least once each year during breaks. When Keaton graduated from Oxford with a master's degree in advanced computer science, he went on to live in France to study for a second master's degree in Complex System Engineering from the University of CentraleSupelec. After his graduation in 2017, his father offered him a year free from responsibilities, a "*Leisure Year*," where Keaton could do as pleased, live wherever he pleased, before taking his place in the company. Keaton chose to remain in France because he had met Katie Crozet, a witty, sophisticated, and high-spirited French figure skater.

He pursued her during his first year in France. He dated her during his last year of grad school and they moved in together after his graduation during *the leisure year*.

As Keaton sat embraced with his mom on the floor, he could not help thinking of the plans he had made: (a) To return home at the end of *the leisure year*; in three months. (b) To propose to Katie on her birthday in two months and take her home for introduction to his parents as his fiancé. Now his dad was gone, and he did not know how to accept it. Keaton felt blindsided by roller-coaster emotions of shock and disbelief, sadness, fear, and anger, He tamped down his feelings of anxiety and guilt because he was not home when his father passed, and the pressure he felt to provide the strength, support, and comfort that his mother needed.

Keaton glanced around at the scattered objects on the floor. His eyes rested on an opened photo album holding a picture of his father embracing his mom in a back hug. The photo triggered a distant memory from when he was sixteen. Having just received his driver's license, he had gone driving with his father. It was his first time on the open road; he felt anxious and nervous and, he swerved to avoid hitting a deer and ran into a parked pick-up truck on the other side of the road.

Keaton remembered being scared to death and went into a panic attack when he got out and saw the damage. His dad had embraced him tightly in a back hug, securing him until he had settled. The experience left him feeling weak and vulnerable. His father continued to hold him and told him that no matter what situation he should find himself in, he should always know that his father would protect him from anything.

Keaton realized then that he had to be strong for his mom; she must be feeling worse than he did, weak and vulnerable, losing the love of her life. He had to let her know that he would be there for her, just like his father would if he was there.

Their embrace unraveled, and he helped her up to sit on the sofa. He handed her the box of Kleenex from the coffee table and began gathering the scattered items from the floor. He went to the kitchen and poured her a glass of water.

"Drink this, mom," he said as he handed her the glass. "I'm here now; everything will be okay." She looked up at his face with a comforting smile as she took the glass and sipped a couple of times. Keaton sat next to her and held her hands.

"Mom, I hate to ask, but I need to know what happened? "How did dad die?"

Celia positioned herself to sit forward on the couch; she looked at Keaton, trying to find the words. Her voice brittle, she responded, "that day I called you, we had a perfectly normal day, he never went into the office, but he was in his study for most of the day, approving contracts and proposals that his assistant had dropped off earlier."

Celia paused before continuing, trying to halt her sniffles; Keaton squeezed her hands gently as a reminder that he was with her. "It's okay, Mom…." Celia nodded and continued.

"We retired to bed around 9:00 p.m. Shortly after I fell asleep, I felt him turning on the bed as if he were restless. As you know, I'm a light sleeper so I had a hard time falling back to sleep because of his tossing and turning. Finally, I asked if he was alright and I distinctly remember him saying, "I'm fine dear, go back to sleep, I'm going to get some water."

"He got up from the bed shortly after and left the room; I was still awake, so I could hear his footsteps leaving and heading down the staircase. Then suddenly there was a loud thud that lasted for a few seconds. I remembered being frightened and I rushed out of the bedroom and when I got to the staircase...." Celia's voice began to quaver, and her eyes became glossy again with tears. She sputtered the rest of the tragic moment in broken words. "Your—...dad was lying... motionless at the bottom...of the staircase." Celia burst into tears. Keaton pulled her in, hugging her, resting her head on his chest, trying as best as he could to conceal his anguish.

"Mom, are you saying dad died from a fall...?" Celia raised her head from Keaton's chest, repositioning herself on the couch; she pulled a few sheets of Kleenex from the box and attempted to dry her tears.

"At that moment that is what I thought. I was so frightened. I began screaming for help from the top of the staircase, and when I got to him, I was frantic, I didn't know what to do. He was not moving, he was not breathing, he was just lying there, I screamed his name. I held him to me, but nothing. She inhaled between sobs, "—I remember seeing the servants rushing towards me, and I can recall hearing someone calling an ambulance. I laid over him until they pulled me away. Catherine, the house manager, had pulled me up when the paramedics arrived. I remember I kept asking them, is he going to be alright and insisting that I ride with him in the ambulance. The paramedics questioned me on the way to the hospital, and I told them exactly what had happened."

"So, he was still alive?"

"I don't know. When we got to the hospital, they rushed him to the emergency room, and they asked me to wait in the waiting area. Not long after, the doctors came to me and told me he was dead...." Celia's words cracked and faded to a desolate whisper. Her breathing intensified and her eyes revealed the deep pain she felt as if she was reliving that night.

"They then escorted me to an office where I was introduced to the hospital's administrator and the head of oncology. Keaton, that's when I learned that your father was diagnosed three years ago with inoperable Glioblastoma."

Keaton's heart jolted, his eyes widened. "Mom, what do you mean? Are you saying dad has had cancer for over three years and none of us knew? —How?"

Celia inhaled a deep breath, tears streamed down her face. "Your father found out and kept it from us. He signed a nondisclosure with the hospital's administrator and the oncologists. His diagnosis was never to be revealed until the day he passed."

Celia shifted and took a file from the coffee table. "It's all there," she said, handing him the file. Keaton took the file; disbelief etched on his face. He tensely flipped through the contents of the folder, his breathing became quick and uneasy, he looked up at his mom with bewilderment in his expression. "Mom, this is not real? It is showing different treatment centers around the world that dad has visited in the past years since his diagnosis, he was trying to get treatment which kept failing, how could we not know about this…?"

Celia sniffled before answering, "Keaton, how would we know? It wasn't unusual for your father to travel for months at a time on business. In the past year, all those frequent 'business' trips to Europe were for treatment, and yet he told us each time that he was traveling on business. When diagnosed, some of the best doctors in the world told him that he would have another three years to live at most. He never intended for us to know and tried to prolong his life as long as he could so that he could make the necessary preparations for you to take over. Don't you see, he gave you that year free from responsibilities because he knew he would die soon, and he wanted you to live your life as much as time would allow before his passing. He knew we would be worried, anxious, and fearful for him; he never wanted that, knowing his cancer was inoperable. He kept it from us so that our lives could go on as usual. He never wanted us to suffer while he was here; he's always trying to protect us. I want to hate him for not letting us be there for him, but I can't because I understand why he did it." While she talked, Keaton took out his cell phone and typed furiously the word, "Glioblastoma + symptoms" into the search engine. His eyes popped when he read the list:

- Headaches.
- Loss of appetite.

- Loss of balance or trouble walking.
- Mood swings.
- Nausea and vomiting.
- Personality and behavior changes.
- Problems speaking.
- Problems with memory.

He read them off loudly, his voice rose an octave with each symptom that he read. He looked askance at his mother. "Didn't you notice any of these mom?"

Celia hung her head and wrung her hands. "If he had those symptoms that you are reading, he hid them from me or was away when he exhibited them." Keaton nodded his head in understanding.

Celia tapped her fingers in her lap as if summoning her thoughts and memories. "Now, when I look back, I understand the reasons behind all he has done in the past three years, to realize his vision with the expansion of TrueTek in the European markets, he risked everything to complete the project within a relatively short period. Things were unfavorable in the early stages of the partnership. He never revealed everything to me. But from the little that he told me, I understood that he came under fire for the decision. Some opposing shareholders tried to remove him from his position as president on some baseless accusation that he intentionally placed shareholder interest at risk with the European partnership. He told me that he had to make drastic decisions to avoid being voted out of his own company. Now I know the reason he did so much and took such a risk; it was to fortify the company for you. He knew what expansion into the European market would mean for the future of TrueTek, for your future, and he made sure to make it a reality in what little time he had left."

Her eyes gleamed with a sense of comfort behind her tears. She patted Keaton's cheek, and her lips slowly managed to shape a half-smile. Keaton held onto her hand on his cheek, resting the file back onto the coffee table. "Mom, I miss him, there is so much I wanted to say to him, to…."

"It's okay," Celia interjected, comforting him." It won't be easy, but we will be okay, we have to be, that is what he would have wanted. I am happy you are here; we can cope together. You must be tired from such a long flight, why don't you go and freshen up? I'll have the kitchen prepare something for you to eat, then try to get some rest. We will have a lot to handle in the days to come.

CHAPTER 3

That night Keaton laid in bed scrolling through photos on his phone of him and his dad, there were so many memories they had made, and he was still in disbelief that his father was gone. He went to his call log and called Katie.

"*Bébé*," she answered, almost immediately as if she were impatiently waiting for his call. "I was just about to call you; you had me worried all day. I wanted to wait for you to call because I know you are dealing with a lot but at the same time I…."

"I'm fine, or trying to be," Keaton responded. He laid in bed, flat on his back with the phone to his ear and his left hand resting slightly above his forehead.

"So, your dad—what exactly happened?" Katie asked cautiously.

Keaton inhaled; his eyes closed. He exhaled with a tempered sigh before he answered. "In a nutshell, dad was diagnosed with inoperable brain cancer three years ago, given another three years to live at most. He hid his diagnosis from mom and me until he finally succumbed to the illness.

Katie went silent for a moment, "Whaaaat?"

"Can we not talk about it any further;" Keaton asked in almost a gentle plea "—I really can't right now. I just want to be distracted. That's the only way I'm coping."

Katie could hear the pain in his voice, and she tried her best to understand his feelings and changed the subject. "I'm leaving for

Japan on Saturday. The committee finally confirmed our itinerary for the figure skating championships. We will leave two weeks in advance to participate in the qualifying competitions in October. Then I'll be back in France in November for two weeks, which is great because I'll get to celebrate my birthday at home and hopefully with you. After that, I'll be off to winter championships in Canada in late November through to December."

"I wish I could be with you," Keaton responded. "You'll be away in those foreign countries without me, having the time of your life, doing what you love, I'm jealous." His words were wistful, and the expression on his face was brooding. "Hopefully, I will get to be with you on your birthday," he continued. "I would love nothing more."

"I hope so too," Katie responded. "I'll let you get some rest; you must be tired. I love you, and I miss you. Whenever you need to talk, I'm just a phone call away."

Keaton managed to form a soft smile. "I love you too; we'll talk soon, sleep tight."

The days that followed were solely for funeral arrangements. Celia wanted to give her husband a funeral befitting his status, which meant Keaton had a lot to manage to ensure his mother's vision came through. He also needed to be her pillar of support. As things became harder for her during the funeral arrangements, she started to suffer from severe migraines brought on by lack of sleep, anxiety, and stress.

Keaton was also dealing with his fair share of stress, which he had to suppress to appear strong for his mother. By Saturday,

Keaton became inundated by the number of phone calls, financial decisions, dreaded paperwork, and every other detail he had to handle while grieving. Writing his father's obituary was incredibly daunting. He knew once the obituary was released, he could no longer elude the reality. Everyone in the company would become aware of the fact, and the pressure for him to fill his father's position would be overwhelming.

His only escape was talking to Katie. Now that she was on her way to Japan for competition, reaching her at the right time would be nearly impossible. Not only would she be busy competing, but the thirteen-hour time difference did not help at all.

Though infrequent, they still managed to keep in touch. He would wake up to her video messages or a simple, "I love you, or I miss you" text messages helped Keaton through to the following week.

On *Sunday, September 30th, 2018*, they laid Keegan Dawson to rest. Close to one thousand persons were in attendance, relatives, business partners, foreign dignitaries and affiliates, employees, and subsidiary representatives, not including the hundreds of people who lined the street during the procession. The expected turnout and admiration from everyone, even total strangers, and the outpouring of support towards Celia and Keaton, had touched them more than anyone knew, which made it even harder for Celia as she stood over her husband's corpse during the church vigil.

At the graveside, Celia piteously sobbed as they lowered her husband's corpse into the earth. Keaton held her close to his side;

he was numb from deep sadness and acted on autopilot throughout the ceremony, not allowing himself to think or feel.

On the drive home, Keaton and his mom sat in the backseat of the limo in silence. Mother and son sat on opposite sides, staring out the window into nothingness. They never saw the stately Italian cypress trees or the abundant crepe myrtles in an array of colors that lined the drive home. They could only feel the emptiness of their great loss. Now and then, Jaxen gazed back at them through the rear-view mirror; he could almost feel their misery as it permeated the car like an imperceptible odor. He, too, was mourning the loss of Keegan Dawson. Jaxen had been the family's driver and head of their security detail for over ten years and was treated as part of the family. He coped in silence, remaining professional throughout the ordeal. Though Keegan never uttered a word of his illness to Jaxen, he had long drawn his conclusion after the numerous hospital visits and appointments he had taken Keegan.

Keegan never tried to conceal the reason for his hospital visits from Jaxen because he knew even with the knowledge, Jaxen would never utter a word to his family without consent. Their relationship shared an uncompromisable degree of loyalty, unspoken and otherwise; it was safe to say that Keegan trusted Jaxen with his life.

The car pulled into Dawson's Estate at 7:40 p.m. that evening. Keaton led his mother to her bedroom and requested a cup of unsweetened chamomile tea for her. He then had her take a single dose of sleeping tablets that he had gotten her earlier in the week and sat by her bedside until she fell asleep. As Keaton got up to leave the bedroom, his eyes glanced at a framed photograph of his father on her bedside table. He picked up the frame for a closer look, making him reminiscent and nostalgic, as pleasant memories flashed across his mind. He returned it to its position, kissing his sleeping mom's forehead before turning off the lights and exiting the room.

In his bedroom, Keaton undressed for a bath and unburdened himself under a long cold shower. Other than talking to Katie, this was one of the only things that seemed to improve his somber mood. An hour later, he walked to the bedroom wrapped in a towel from the waist down. He stood in front of the full-length mirrors that formed the doors of the large walk-in closet. His reflection stared back at him. He was the spitting image of his father, only younger. Statuesque, with warm skin tone and an athletic build, perfectly sculpted face with sharply contoured jawlines, and inviting brown eyes that became almost luminous when he smiled, complemented by a subtle Grecian nose, and coiffured warm honey-brown hair.

Like Keegan, Keaton was also sagacious, academically accomplished, confident yet humble, which meant physically, and from a view of personality, he was more or less a consummate man.

He slid the closet door open and entered, retrieving a white T-shirt and a pair of boxers in which he got dressed and sauntered back to the bedroom, where he sat on the bed. He looked down at his phone on the nightstand that he had intentionally left home for obvious reasons. A tap at the screen revealed eighteen missed calls from Katie. Keaton immediately redialed her, but it rang for minutes without an answer. He checked the time, "Forget it," he grumbled, tossing the phone to the other side of the bed. "It's already 11:00 a.m. in Japan; Katie should be on the ice by now, and her phone in a locker somewhere." Bummed that he had missed her calls, he turned out the lights and laid still, desiring sleep.

CHAPTER 4

"Keaton—Keaton, are you up?" At the sound, Keaton sprung up abruptly from a trivial rest, with a sharp tension headache. He sat up, hanging his legs from the bed, pressing his palm against his forehead in a futile effort to alleviate the ache.

Another knock at the door, "Keaton…."

"Mom?" He answered, his brain still in a fog, "What is it?"

"Oh good, you're awake," Celia responded, "Wash up and meet me in the garden for breakfast. Your father's estate attorney will be joining us, please be quick, he should be here in an hour or so."

"OK…" Keaton responded, reaching for his phone. It was a few minutes to eight in the morning. He had barely slept and was awakened suddenly with a now nagging headache, which made him jaded and irritable.

A few minutes later, he joined Celia in the large pergola at the center of a magnificent rose garden in their backyard. Celia smiled at him as he walked towards her. She signaled him to sit in the chair across the table from her.

He kissed her on the cheek before he sat down. "Good morning, mom."

"Look, I've asked them to make all your favorites," Celia said, looking at Keaton with gleaming eyes. Keaton acknowledged the careful selection of homemade pastries and fresh fruit, served alongside his favorite *Croque Madame*

Muffins, cinnamon brioche French toast as well as freshly squeezed orange juice and a pot of black coffee, at the center of the casually set carriage house breakfast table. He looked up at her and gave an agreeing nod and smiled; he could see that she was in a better mood, much better than the days before, which made him pleased and a bit relieved, though he knew her sorrow was still there. His gaze lingered on her for a moment, watching as she gleefully plated a few of his favorites.

Celia was still lovely and looked a lot younger than her actual age. She wore her full-bodied russet blonde hair in a stylishly messy bob that hung just below her jawline, complimenting her delicate features beautifully. Keaton inherited her sweet and luminous brown eyes. At fifty-four, she kept herself in shape, though naturally slender; it was noticeable that she was physically active, keeping her muscles toned and her skin firm.

"Why are we meeting dad's attorney here?" Keaton asked, pouring himself a cup of coffee.

"I prefer to have the meeting in a more relaxed setting," she responded, placing the plate in front of him. "You know I feel at ease in my garden, and with laying your father to rest yesterday, I don't think I can handle being outside of the estate for a while."

Keaton's eyes agreed with her reasons. He shared those sentiments, being at the estate made him feel like his father was still alive, and even in the sadness, being home provided solace.

Jared, the butler, approached the pergola announcing the arrival of Stefon, Keegan's estate attorney, who was following closely behind. Keaton stood to greet him with a firm handshake. Celia welcomed Stefon with a friendly *La bise* and showed him where to sit. The three made casual conversation over breakfast, which offered Keaton a relaxed occasion to get more acquainted with Stefon and the nature of his visit.

After breakfast, the three moved to a banquette sitting area at a corner of the pergola, accented with an arrangement of warm-colored pillows and cushions, which harmonized effortlessly with the rose garden.

Stefon went through the legal formalities, discussing the transfer and distribution of assets and estate as set out in Keegan's will. It all seemed straightforward to Celia and Keaton as they both knew what the family owned, and they understood and validated Keegan's wishes. At the end of the reading of the written will, Stefon revealed a video recording left by Keegan pertinent to the company's takeover. Stefon retrieved a laptop from his briefcase and set it on the coffee table in front of them; he injected a flash drive and proceeded to play the video recording.

In the video, Keegan sat behind his desk in his office at TrueTek. He bore a peaceful smile that immediately brought tears to Celia's eyes at sight.

"My dear sweet wife Celia, my beloved son Keaton, if you both are watching this, then it means I have passed away and left you both in unintended grief. I must first apologize for withholding my diagnosis from you; please know that I did so with the best intention. I would never have lived as long as I did if I were to spend the rest of my dying days witnessing the sadness, anguish, and anxiety that I knew the knowledge of my diagnosis would have caused you both. IT WAS INOPERABLE when I discovered my cancer. There was nothing anyone could have done to save me; believe me, I tried. I then decided that it would be pointless and inconsiderate if I allowed you both to suffer with me because I knew neither of you would accept my fate and would try aimlessly to find a cure. I do hope by this you understand my reason and forgive my pragmatic selfishness.

Keaton, I am incredibly proud of you. I cannot say that enough. I consider myself extremely fortunate to have shared in twenty-seven beautiful years of your life, creating unforgettable memories, watching you grow into the brilliant man you are today. I am incredibly grateful and proud that you are my legacy. As the new president of TrueTek, I am confident that you will undoubtedly champion the company to greater heights.

There are some important matters that I failed to discuss with you before. It wasn't convenient to discuss this with you during your studies, so I withheld this information pending your return home at the end of your *leisure year*. I wanted to discuss this matter with you in person. If you are now learning this information from this video recording, unfortunately, I passed on earlier than I thought I would. Forgive my inadvertent negligence.

Three years ago, after learning of my diagnosis, I entered a partnership with SANCORP, a biotechnology manufacturing corporation in Europe, to establish TrueTek's products and biotechnology in the European market. This partnership has been a life-long vision of mine, which I know you supported and is significant to the future direction of TrueTek for the next generation. Knowing my diagnosis and my limited life expectancy, I had to make some hard and fast decisions to realize this vision for us before I died.

The partnership sought to invest in constructing and developing new state-of-the-art technology and manufacturing facilities throughout Europe, equally owned by SANCORP and TrueTek. The facilities would be advantageous to the seamless production of TrueTek's new genetically engineered products.

Working on a strict timeline for the completion of the project doubled the risks. It required a vast portion of TrueTek's equity, which made most of our shareholders unreceptive to entering the partnership. They did not share my vision and were unwilling to take the risk; being the majority shareholder, controlling more than half of the company's voting interest, I decided to enter the partnership, overriding their resolution. In the first year of the alliance, we experienced an enormous deficit, our stock price plummeted, negatively impacting shareholder interests. I made some enemies in TrueTek. The stakeholders conspired to remove me as majority shareholder on the grounds of violating the shareholder's agreement, stating that I had intentionally and irrationally subjected the company to irremediable peril.

I assumed all the risk to avoid this, which cost me twenty percent of my controlling shares; this meant that I went from owning sixty percent controlling shares to forty percent, which left the ownership of TrueTek in a vulnerable position. I anticipated that sooner or later, those who opposed my decisions in the company would use this as an opportunity to coalesce or purchase shares from those willing to sell to usurp my presidency and take control of TrueTek. I would never allow it, so I made a shrewd decision.

I signed a new contract with SANCORP's founder Bill Paton. An agreement where he would anonymously purchase the shares of those minority shareholders willing to sell, offering a price we knew they would not resist, and an offer that those in TrueTek who wanted to remove me could not afford. Based on my insider knowledge at that time, Bill was able to purchase a collective thirty percent of available shares from three willing minority shareholders, each owning ten percent voting shares.

TrueTek will realize a substantial ROI on the SANCORP partnership in four years, doubling returns on our initial investment.

At that time, the deal is to sign over twenty percent of my ownership rights in the SANCORP project to Bill and install SANCORP as the sole manufacturer of TrueTek's products for the European market. In return, Bill would transfer the thirty percent TrueTek shares to me, essentially a share trade.

However, late last year Bill experienced significant health complications that left him bedridden. He transferred the shares purchased in TrueTek to his daughter Lia Paton, currently the Project Management Director for SANCORP, handling the projects between SANCORP and TrueTek in the European market.

With my diagnosis and Bill's deteriorating health condition, we recognized the high probability and, in my case, the indisputable fact that we would die before the end of the contract. As such, a contingent amendment was added to the agreement, binding you and Lia to honor the contract terms. Another primary concern that gave me sleepless nights is that you would still only hold forty percent voting shares until the end of the four years. This means that those opposing me could still find loopholes that could prevent you from taking over my position. With the limited time I had left, I made sure to leave no stone unturned, ensuring nothing would threaten your take-over. However, early this year, my legal team found one such loophole within the company's articles of incorporation. As president, you would have a fiduciary duty to the company and its shareholders. As such, there is a strict stipulation in the articles that whoever assumes the presidency at TrueTek, be extensively experienced, an expert in all areas of TrueTek's operating industries and subsidiaries.

It turns out I had made such handover stipulations in the articles of incorporation back then to protect the company and shareholder liability. I also thought I would be around to mentor your take-over when the time came.

Unfortunately, I will not live long enough to follow through on the protracted legal process required to make any significant amendment to this stipulation. I am afraid that others will use this loophole to question your ability to lead TrueTek effectively. With this ambiguity, the other stakeholders can petition the board to subject you to a mentorship program within the company, putting you in a position befitting your academic qualifications. You would then need to work your way up to acquire the skills and experience outlined in the article to be deemed eligible to assume the role of president.

The board would appoint a more experienced officer or director as acting president until you have met the requirements.

However, meeting the requirements through the mentorship program may take years. During this time, the acting president would have the power to make significant business decisions with or without the influence of the shareholders. With this power, I am sure the resisters will take the opportunity to terminate the SANCORP contract they initially opposed. If the board were to make this decision, you would have no significant control to fight it without being the majority shareholder. Not only that, if they terminate the SANCORP partnership then you lose the thirty percent shares they hold forever.

The only solution I found that will secure TrueTek's and SANCORP's vested interest. Immediately ensuring you gain majority voting shares to override any such decisions and eliminate the loophole is a marriage between you and Lia for the remaining term of the contract.

Your marriage to Lia will mean that you can become joint shareholders. With Lia holding thirty percent of TrueTek's voting shares and you owning the forty percent I have transferred to you; you would become a majority shareholder. TrueTek would remain under our family's control, and we could safeguard the continuation of the partnership with SANCORP, as well as ensure that the terms of the contract are met…"

Keaton's eyes protruded at the latter, and a sudden feeling of anxiety and uneasiness washed over his body. He sat speechlessly; a running conversation was going on in his head. *There must be another way,* he thought to himself. *How can dad expect me to marry someone I have never met? How would I explain marrying someone else to Katie? Oh my God, Katie, this would ruin our relationship? There has to be another way.*

Keaton turned to look at his mother; his expression unveiled onset panic and disbelief; Celia's countenance revealed she had no prior knowledge of her husband's decision to arrange a marriage for Keaton.

"Mom, did you know about this?" Keaton asked frantically. Celia was also dumbfounded; she stuttered, trying to find words to respond to Keaton. "I—I had no idea. I mean, I knew he had to make some drastic decisions related to the European partnership, but the nature of those decisions was unknown to me, until now."

Stefon interjected, indicating that there was more to the recording; he replayed the video picking up from the areas they had missed in their state of sudden unrest.

"Keaton, I know this marriage will come as a shock to you; you have every right to question my decision, but please know that I would never subject you to something as serious as this without conclusive reasoning. Please, I urge you to understand.

I know this will be hard on you. I have considered your feelings and believe that the best way to approach this is a contractual marriage. You both only need to be and remain married for the term of indenture. We are now in year three of the contract, which means only a year remains. You and Lia would need to get married before you take over my position in the company, that way, you would have the security of controlling shares. At the end of the remaining year, Lia is bound by the contract terms to transfer the shares to you. And you are specified by the agreement to relinquish twenty percent of your ownership rights in the European biotech facilities to Lia and approve SANCORP as the sole manufacturer for TrueTek's products in the European market. By then, ROI from the investment would have doubled, earning billions for TrueTek and SANCORP, a win-win situation.

At the end of the year of your contractual marriage, if you remain incompatible and without intimate feelings for each other, you may separate amicably, as you both would have honored the terms of the contract. If you both found that you are compatible, developed intimate feelings for one another, and wish to remain married, then you may do so. The future of TrueTek and SANCORP would have limitless possibilities. Either way, there is a favorable outcome for both parties.

Though this marriage would be considered contractual, certain aspects will need to remain traditional. Lia is Bill's only child, and he is very protective of her; as such, he is adamant that her terms for the marriage agreement be fulfilled. Lia's only condition is that the traditional aspect of marriage takes precedence over the contract. Lia wishes to hold a formal wedding and live together as husband and wife until the end of the contract. Take what time you need to think it through. Bear in mind though, that if you wish to carry on the legacy of TrueTek and remain its legal successor, preserving the heirloom for your generations to come, you must go through with this, there is no other way. Son, I only want to protect you and secure your future; I trust you will see reason and do what is best."

CHAPTER 5

A bit uneasy from the now tense mood, Stefon ejected the flash drive, closed the laptop, and cleared his throat. "Keaton, Mrs. Dawson, as Keegan's estate attorney, I believe it's my place to validate this decision. We spent months trying to find alternatives but failed miserably. Without majority voting shares, Keaton will be in a vulnerable position in the company. SANCORP holds thirty percent of TrueTek's shares through Keegan's efforts; however, these shares are held anonymously in TrueTek's legal documents and are of no use to Keaton until the end of the contract term. The only option available now to access those shares is as a joint holder, only possible by marriage.

Keaton's jaw clenched. He felt hot and flushed, he refused to believe there was no other option. His thoughts were racing and ready to flare. "With everything I have heard, I understand the importance of having majority shares before assuming dad's role. I get it; he made enemies who want to take over the ownership of TrueTek, and I agree, we cannot allow that to happen.

However, what I do not understand is why marriage is the only option. Fine, I am supposed to marry this woman to have legal access to the shares, so the marriage is about the stakes, then why not repurchase them from SANCORP?" Keaton sputtered, pressing his right fist into his left palm which had become sweaty.

"Keaton, that would have been possible if the funds were available; Keegan went against the board on the SANCORP partnership and lost a lot of shareholder equity which he had to replace from personal funds, including losing twenty percent of his controlling shares in TrueTek.

With the current market value for TrueTek's shares, repurchasing the thirty percent from SANCORP would cost around thirty billion, give or take. With the SANCORP project yet to realize significant ROI, at this point, there are no liquid funds available to repurchase the shares. From a financial perspective, TrueTek's fiscal stability is linked to the success of the SANCORP partnership. In another year, you will reap the benefits of the investment; before then, I have to advise against any other elaborate investment."

"What about liquefying personal assets to generate the funds?" Keaton asked in desperation. "We have properties and other assets that we could sell, right?"

"Again," Stefon replied, adjusting his posture. "I must advise against this; as I previously explained, your dad had to replace the company equity he lost with a large portion of personal funds. He generated those funds by collateralizing his most valuable personal assets, including properties. Until the loan amounts are repaid, those assets cannot be liquified. The bottom line is the repurchasing of the shares is not an option at this point unless you want to run into bankruptcy. The returns from the SANCORP deal will be vast and is guaranteed based on the current financial reports. The finish line is close. It's just a year away; you only need to do your part to secure your position and hold the mold together so that your father's efforts will not be in vain.

Though Keegan never mentioned this in his video, I must inform you of all the possibilities. The shares currently held by SANCORP are legally owned by its successor, Lia Paton. You need to bear in mind that SANCORP has the upper hand in this contract. Keegan and Bill shared a similar vision for the future of their companies and valued preserving their legacy for their children. As such, it was in good faith that Bill was willing to purchase the shares to secure Keegan's position in TrueTek. Keegan is out of the picture, and so is Bill. Lia may decide at any point to refuse the initial terms of the agreement because, in this partnership, SANCORP has less to lose. They legally own a thirty percent stake in TrueTek and can keep those shares or sell them to the highest bidder.

Though this would be a breach of the contract and would mean that SANCORP would have to relinquish their rights to any of the incentives previously offered, it is possible and attainable with the proper litigation. So, you must gain access to those shares as quickly as possible to avoid such a scenario. It would be best to safeguard against all the things that will work against you, or else, there is a possibility you could eventually lose TrueTek.

At present, marriage is your best option, not only to gain access to the shares legally but to further connect SANCORP's and TrueTek's interests in such a way that Lia will be less likely to break the contract. You need to see this marriage from an objective point of view; a year of pre-arranged marriage is a small price to pay when compared to the benefits."

Celia glanced over at Keaton. Agitation overwhelmed him, his jaw still clenched, and his right fist pressed tighter against his left palm in a grasp resting under his chin. She placed her hand on his shoulder, an attempt to settle his seething emotions. "Stefon," she said, followed by a shallow exhale. "This is a lot for us to take in, certainly, Keaton will need some time to process it. As a mother, I believe it's easier said than done to look at this marriage agreement objectively. Though I understand my husband's position, I cannot disregard my son's feelings and the emotional upheaval he is experiencing right now. Give him some time; we will get back to you when Keaton has had sufficient time to decide, unrushed." She returned her gaze to Keaton, applying a gentle squeeze to his shoulder. Their eye contact made an unspoken consensus.

Stefon gathered his belongings in a neat stack in preparation to leave. He turned to Keaton; his voice laced with empathy. "I recognize that this request is a lot for you to process, and I completely understand your need for time. However, time is of the essence. The marriage needs to occur in less than three months before TrueTek's next annual general meeting, scheduled for January 1, 2019. The board members and other stakeholders will be present at this meeting, and undoubtedly, the primary focus on the agenda will be the replacement of TrueTek's president. You must be prepared as much, or even more than they will be. With the absence of your father, others will be gunning for the current vice president to resume the role of president. However, you will have the power to overrule that decision if you have majority voting shares; and that is only possible if you get married to Lia, and in time for you to gain joint access before the AGM.

In essence, today is…." Stefon paused mid-sentence to verify his thought by checking the date on his phone. "…today is October 1st. I'll need an answer no more than two weeks from today. That way there will be sufficient time for us to prepare the marriage contract, which will then need to be reviewed and signed by Lia and confirmed by both parties in time for the marriage ceremony to take place by or before the end of the year." Stefon stood up with his briefcase and files in hand. Keaton and Celia followed suit.

Keaton extended his right hand to Stefon for a handshake and gave an agreeing nod, "I'll be in touch," he said, releasing Stefon's hand. Celia gave a parting smile as Stefon took his leave from the Pergola.

Keaton remained standing minutes after Stefon had left, just staring out into the garden. His mind was bombarded with thoughts of the marriage and what it would mean for his relationship with Katie. Celia stared at the back of his frame for minutes, not uttering a word, considerate of his need for silence, to process all that has happened, unbothered.

He was now emotionally exhausted; no matter how much he tried to process it, there was no resolve, no reasonable way that the arranged marriage and his relationship with Katie could coexist. He turned to face his mom with hopelessness in his eyes, almost like a young child in need of his mother's solicitous attention.

Celia got up from the banquette seating and walked towards him. "Let's go inside first, shall we? I think it is best not to think about it any longer, at least not for today. Tomorrow is another day, and we will start fresh. I will contact some of your father's trusted advisers. We will go through the company documents together, whatever we need to do to find an alternative solution. Let us do that first before thinking about it any further." She gazed into his eyes with maternal compassion; all she wanted was to get him out of this quandary.

Keaton took a deep breath followed by a sharp flutter of his eyes, giving Celia an approving headshake. Agreeing felt disingenuous, as Keaton knew it would be virtually impossible to escape the involuntary need to contemplate, especially since there was so much at stake, all dependent on an irreversible judgment. What was the right choice in this situation? Whatever decision he made would end up hurting someone or his future. It was a tough call with no visible way out; he left the pergola with Celia feeling trapped and dejected.

CHAPTER 6

Keaton and Celia spent the next few days meeting with one adviser after the other, trying to find an alternative solution to Keaton's predicament. They reviewed all the relevant company articles, files, and policies relevant to the voting shares and the presidency. However, their efforts were futile. He had a choice between love and legacy, Katie or TrueTek.

When he spoke to Katie in the past two days, he felt guilty, as if he was already deluding her. To make matters worse, he had previously hidden from her facets of his true identity he had yet to clarify. Now he was facing an unavoidable contract marriage that he would soon need to disclose to her. He felt that he was having a surreptitious affair, making his last two phone conversations with Katie awkward and strained.

The middle of the week was approaching, and there was still no viable solution; Stefon would be expecting a response in three days. The decision was clear, he had no other choice but to accept the marriage, but his heart was reluctant for obvious reasons. That evening, Keaton stood outside on the wrap-around terrace of his second-floor bedroom, overlooking the verdant backyard. There was something eternal about the yellow-brown sunset that kept him riveted and commanded his attention. Yet, he knew in the blink of an eye that the sky would change and plunge into darkness; much like his life right now.

He stared into the distance for hours, long after the sun went down, a fixed expression on his face. He was lost in the silence of the evening, burdened by the weight of the inevitable task before him.

"Keaton…Keaton," the sound of his mom calling, suddenly freed him from his transfixed state.

"Mom, I'm out here." He answered, turning to face the direction of her voice. His eyes followed her like a bewildered child as she approached the sliding glass door that opened to the terrace. Anticipation overcame him as if she were bringing the solution he so desperately needed.

"I knocked," she stated, as she exited his bedroom onto the terrace, "I knocked twice before I entered your bedroom when I did not hear your answer, I figured you were on the balcony; you'd always try to escape your troubles here, even when you were much younger. Standing out here always seemed to help you cope with whatever it was you were going through. However, I would not be your mother if I did not say this. Standing out here torturing yourself for hours, lost in a minefield of endless despairing thoughts, will not resolve this matter. You cannot escape this inexorable ordeal. As much as I hate to say it, this marriage is inevitable.

I understand your reluctance, you are in love, and I believe that one should be partial when it comes to heart affairs, guided by core feelings and emotions. However, in this situation, heart matters are trivial compared to what it is up against, your future. There is no room for emotions here, Keaton you must be objective on this matter. You must ask yourself the question, is she worth giving up on everything you and your father have labored to build all these years? If she is, why have you never brought her home? Why haven't you made your intention towards this girl known to us? And why have you kept your true identity from her till now?" Celia probed, making intense eye contact.

"Mom..." He responded, with a sharp exasperated respire, "You are fully aware of the reasons I took my time getting to know Katie before I brought her home. All the others I introduced to you and dad in the past showed their true colors shortly after getting to know who I am and who my parents are, they were all opportunists, and you know this. I took a different approach when I met Katie; I wanted to prove that I could find true love, someone to love me unconditionally, without prior knowledge or influence of my affluence.

When I was in France, I met Katie at Vegapolis, an indoor ice-skating rink in Montpellier. A group of friends from the same systems engineering cohort had convinced me that ice-skating was an excellent weekend pastime in France, so I decided to try it. And since it was my first year living in France, I took the opportunity to get familiar with the recreational side of the place.

I tried ice-skating for the first time, and I was terrible at it. I can vividly recall the countless times I fell, and my friends hooted with laughter at my expense. Even though they were having a whale of a time jeering me, I was relentless, you know me, I am implacable in my pursuit when others believe I will fail. So, I kept going, or I should say, I kept falling.

I think it was about the hundredth time that I had fallen, and just as I was about to get back up, someone skated up before me to lend a hand; I looked up and saw a wide-eyed splendor, with shiny- halo white teeth that shone through a bubbly smile. I remember; clearly, she wore all white with a panther-face beanie on her head and gray mittens." Keaton's eyes gleamed as he recalled the events of his first encounter with Katie.

"She smiled at me with assurance in her eyes, in some way an unspoken affirmation. She spoke in French to me as she helped me up, "*Continuer à essayer.*" I became speechless; I never responded to her; I just stood there staring at her mindlessly until she spoke again in English, "Keep trying," she said. My mouth was still agape, so she giggled and skated away. When I think about it, I still can't believe that I, Keaton Dawson, who since a senior in high school, renowned for being forthright and glib tongued concerning the opposite sex, became speechless and mindless at the sight and sound of a woman.

I went to that skating rink every night since that day to see her again. It took months of describing her to everyone at the skating rink who would listen until I finally found out that she was a professional figure skater and then I found her practice rink. After that, I pursued her for an entire year, she was unwavering in her decision that she was not interested in a relationship at the time, but I kept chasing. At the beginning of year two of my pursuit, she decided to give me a chance. I found out then that the real reason why she refused my courtship for so long was that she was wary of having romantic relationships with foreigners. She thought foreigners were incapable of true love; she believed that people like me just wanted to experience 'the French fling,' and when the time came, we would leave for our home country with no strings attached. She had experienced this before.

I spent most of year two of my pursuit convincing her that I was not that type of person, that I too was looking for true holistic love. By doing so, I omitted my affluence from her, in some ways not to scare her away, and a point of validation that true love can exist outside of wealth.

When dad gave me that *leisure year* after graduation, it was the year we moved in together. That is when I started mentioning her to you and dad. At that time, I had confirmed that she was everything that I was looking for in a life partner. I planned to propose to her on her birthday this year in November and tell her every detail I had intentionally omitted about myself. I bought a ring and had everything planned. I had every intention to introduce her to you and dad after the proposal. However, before that could happen, dad passed away, and now this." Keaton sighed in aggravation.

"So, you see, mom, it is not that easy for me to accept this marriage as everyone is making it out to be. I have invested so much time and energy in my relationship with Katie; we have practically been together for almost three years. I am genuinely and wholeheartedly in love with her, and I know she feels the same way about me. So how then must I tell her that I am getting married to someone else, just like that? No matter my reasons, do you honestly believe that with everything I have told you about her, she will understand, or that she will believe me? She is going to be heartbroken and what's worst is that she is going to believe that I am truly one of those foreign guys she was wary of, who have used her and dumped her with a ludicrous story of a 'contract' yet 'traditional-like' marriage. I do not even believe me, and it's coming from my mouth."

Keaton turned away, turning his back to Celia, returning his sightless gaze into the now moonlit distance. Celia walked up beside him, resting her hands on the panel infill railings. She kept silent for a moment, matching his gaze into space.

"I honestly had no clue you were this serious with her, and I am almost certain that your father was also unaware. I am not saying this would have changed the circumstance, but there is a high probability that he would have handled this differently, maybe informed you earlier, if he knew you had such feelings for her. I believe he thought you would use that *leisure year*' to have transient escapades and live carefree until it was time for you to return home to take his place in TrueTek. I think falling in love was the farthest thing from his mind when he came up with that idea."

Keaton shook his head in despair.

"Keaton, you must know that your father is far from being a dictator. He would never force you to do anything against your will; from what we both can see; this marriage decision was his absolute last resort. He tried to find other alternatives just as we did, but the truth is, there are no other practicable options. I understand this is not what you want to hear right now, but I also know that you have realized it is your reality, and I trust you will do what needs to be done. If this girl loves you as much as you say she does, then go to her as planned, explain your circumstance to her, and if she loves you, she will understand, and she will wait for you. You are both young; one year is not too great of a time to wait for the one you genuinely love. You said it yourself, you pursued her for an entire year without her reciprocation, so I believe she knows deep down what you have invested in that relationship and that you love her, and for that reason, she will understand."

Keaton turned his head to look at her with a strangled expression on his face. Indeed, what Celia had said was not at all what he wanted to hear, but in some respects, she was right; this was his reality, and there was no escaping it, he thought to himself before responding.

"Thanks, Mom," he replied with a wistful smile. "I will do what needs to be done." Celia initiated a hug and held him in a fleeting, benevolent embrace.

"Don't stay out here any longer; go get some rest, and tomorrow morning, contact Stefon and get this marriage agreement process underway. Remember who you are; you have a conglomerate to run and a legacy to preserve." She cast him a final affirming glance before leaving the terrace.

Keaton exhaled deeply in her absence as if he had been holding his breath the entire time. He walked back to the bedroom, closed the slide doors, and ambled over to the bed, where his cell phone laid angled on top of a pillow. He tapped the screen, which showed a new message notification from

Katie. With fervid hands, he unlocked his phone to read the message.

Hey Bébé, I wanted to call, but I didn't know if you were up, so I decided to send a text message instead. If you are up and need to talk, you can call me; I am available today. Coach decided to give us a break for sightseeing today, but I decided to stay home. I would much prefer to talk with you. I miss you so much it is driving me crazy. I hope you are awake. I will be waiting for your call; if not, we will find another chance. Love you, Bébé (heart eyes emoji).

Without hesitation, Keaton dials Katie, but before allowing her phone to ring, he immediately cancels the call. *She has a day off today.* He thought to himself. *She's not rushing out for practice or to compete. She'll want to make use of this free time to have a long, meaningful conversation. If I speak to her now, what will stop me from spilling, especially about the marriage?* No, I cannot do that to her; I cannot risk telling her this over the phone; it's best if I do not call her tonight. I need to keep our phone conversations minimal until I see her in person for her birthday.

"This is what's best under the current circumstance," he said, trying to convince himself.

He placed the phone down on the nightstand, sitting at the edge of the bed, his head hung, and both hands lengthened, gripping the edges of the bed on either side of his legs. Heartsick and crestfallen, he sank deeper into a disconsolate state.

CHAPTER 7

In the days that followed, Keaton had no other choice than to come to terms with his new reality. He spent days reviewing the marriage agreement drafted by his and Lia's legal representatives. It was clear what Lia wanted, a contract marriage that would come with all the perks of traditional marriage, which meant Lia would move to and live in New York during the term of their marriage. They would have to cohabitate as husband and wife; Keaton must agree to allow their marriage a realistic, fair, and unhindered chance to progress into something authentic or not. Keaton decided to start a 'happy' marriage whether or not he wanted to.

Early the following week, Keaton signed the final draft of the marriage and prenuptial agreement and sent it off to Lia for her signature. The only thing that kept Keaton's mind at ease throughout this entire ordeal was the terms of the prenuptial agreement. Neither could lay claims on assets outside of the contract terms between their fathers. Keaton somehow felt relieved that Lia could not trick him out of other assets at the end of the marriage.

Lia's legal representative returned the signed marriage contract and prenuptial agreement by the end of the week. He removed the documents from the sealed, oversized envelope in his father's study, a final testament that his fate had been sealed. He emptied the envelope's contents onto his desk; a flash drive with a 'play me' label was among the documents. Keaton inserted the flash drive into his tablet at the far right of his desk; he was subtly surprised by the image on the screen that spoke.

"Hello Keaton, I am Lia Paton. Like me, I can imagine these past few weeks have been a roller coaster for you. We are preparing to enter this marriage contract, corresponding back and forth through legal interceders, and we have never met each other. So, I thought before my move to New York; I should send you this video. Providing a simple introduction before we officially meet in December will help break the ice and ease us into the task ahead.

Like you, I agreed to this marriage because I understand its value to SANCORP'S business relationship with TrueTek, and I know the importance of safeguarding the legacy our fathers have labored to build. Primarily this marriage is contractual, so I know you may have questions as to why I wish for this marriage to maintain most of the aspects of a traditional nuptial; So, I will clear that up now."

At this point of the video, Keaton sat up straight in the chair; undoubtedly, this was something he wanted to know. In the video, Lia paused for a beat, her piercing green eyes repositioned with a direct stare as if they were looking right through Keaton's soul. She quickly ran her fingers through her thick blonde hair that rested just along her shoulders in a bob, styled with soft waves, elegantly sparse with caramel highlights.

"Keaton," she continued, resting clasped hands on the top of the desk she sat behind. *"When it comes to marriage, you can say I am a purist. I grew up in a traditional home where my parents were married until death did them part, I may be only*

twenty-five, but I have been around long enough to witness this generation's degradation of the marriage institution. I do not wish to be a part of it. Ever since I was a little girl, I have envisioned the day that I would get married, and I have kept myself, preserving morals and upholding my values, waiting for that day.

I know the reason behind this marriage is unorthodox; however, if I am to be married to you on paper for one year, with my character and what I value, it means I am committed to you for that year. This also means any intimate relationship or romantical encounter before this agreement would now be non-existent; that is my nature. Contractual or not, this marriage is legal, and when we separate, it will be documented legally as a divorce, so what happens after the fact? I would have spent one year lawfully married to you, only to become a divorcee with no effort to know what could have been. I do not believe I can genuinely watch my first marriage experience waste away like that.

The way I see it, we will be legally married, so why not use it as an opportunity to see where it takes us? What if we find that we are compatible within that year, what if we are meant for each other, and if we find that the universe created this dilemma only to bring us together? How amazing would that be?

I might be getting ahead of myself, but I choose to look at the glass half full. And if during that year we find the opposite, that we cannot exist as husband and wife, then at least when we are divorced, I can look back and say that for my first marriage,

I gave it all I had, and it just was not meant to be. I would rather that than look back and wonder what if.

Keaton, I have agreed to this marriage against all I hold dear, and I believe that wanting to experience this as traditional marriage is a modest request; I hope you understand. I appreciate that this was not an easy decision to make, especially with my terms, but please keep in mind that we were both placed into this situation against our will; it is just that I am choosing to make lemonade out of lemons. Let us give this a fair shot and see where this road takes us, and no matter what happens, I hope we can remain lifelong business partners, as our fathers intended.

I have included my card in the folder; if you wish to speak on personal matters before the marriage commences, feel free to give me a call. The road ahead of us is by no means straight, but if we get a good start and work together, I believe we can make it a lot smoother than it looks now.

Until then, take care of yourself."

Keaton ejected the flash drive, vaguely more frustrated than before. He braced back in the chair almost like a recline, with both hands slightly rested on his head, an enigmatic expression on his face. More so, because he understood that Lia was not the enemy, as much as he wanted her to be the focal point of his frustration, she was just as much a victim of responsibility as he was. Who was he to dictate to her what this marriage can and cannot be? If he was honest with himself, he had no right because she was doing him a favor; he is the one who needs access to the shares she legally owns. She was going against her beliefs, giving up her first experience of fairytale matrimony to enter a contract marriage. In return, all she wanted was a reasonable chance to experience some normalcy of traditional marriage for the contract term. Was it too much to ask? Keaton thought, *if the circumstances were different, Lia's request really would be a fair condition*, but other parties are involved, Katie will be the one to get hurt, and there was nothing he could do now to avoid this.

He recomposed himself and sorted through the envelope's contents to locate Lia's business card; then neatly stacked the rest of the documents and pushed them to the far left of his desk. He then placed the flash drive in the small top right drawer. As he made his way out of the study, his phone rang; a glance at the phone screen immediately revealed Katie's bubbly smile on the photo attached to her caller ID.

Keaton took a shallow breath, swinging his head back, and uttered a stifled "fuck" under his breath, the timing was less than perfect, but he could not keep evading her calls when his mood was not convenient. He stepped back inside the office, closed the door, and answered the call, camouflaging his tone to conceal his dispirited mood as much as he could.

"Katie..."

"*Bébé*, I hope I haven't gotten you at a bad time," she responded in an anxious tone.

"No, it's fine; I just finished up on my commitments for the day; how about you?"

"Well, for starters, I miss you like crazy. I keep re-convincing myself that I'm going to see you in a few weeks, and that's the only reason I haven't gotten on a plane to New York; if it's even for one night, I want to hold you, kiss you, make wild passionate love to you," she giggled sheepishly at the latter.

Keaton unbuttoned the first few buttons of his slim-fit, Polo Ralph Lauren button-down denim shirt, scrambling to sit back in the chair. The eroticism in Katie's tone instantly aroused him and he knew what she wanted.

"Being away from you these past months has been hell," he responded, switching the cell phone into his left hand as he got more comfortable in the chair. "There's nothing I would love more now than to kiss those supple, alluring lips of yours, to bend you over our kitchen counter, slowly sliding my hard-on inside the pool of moisture my fingers would have conjured between your thighs."

"Are you doing what I think you are doing?" Katie questioned with a sensual gasp, exhilaration, and lust in her voice.

"Isn't that what you want?" Keaton responded, matching the yearning in her tone. "You need me, and I need you; we can't be together now, but there are other ways we can satisfy our carnal desires; we are no strangers to this," he asserted, biting the bottom of his lips.

"Besides, I can only think of one reason that my Katie is up at...what time is it now in Tokyo? Like 2:00 a.m.?" He teased, with intensified desire in his voice.

"I'm all for it," Katie responded, affirming her desire. "I'm switching to Facetime, I need to see your face when you tell me what you want to do to me."

"Sounds good," Keaton said in a silky voice. Keaton checked the door, quickly securing the lock, and walked towards the oversized accent armchair to the corner of the office.

"Could you be any more beautiful?" he complimented, admiring her sensual blue-grey eyes on his phone screen.

"Hmm…God, I've missed you" Katie said, moaning and staring back at him with a yearning smile.

Her response was stimulating; the greenlight Keaton needed to induce and satisfy her libidinous nature. Katie placed her phone in the gooseneck phone holder mounted to the night table next to her bed, tweaking the angle of her phone so that Keaton could see the length of her, from head to toe.

He set the scene with a sensuous tone: "Imagine, you are back home after an exhilarating championship. You dominated. I pour you a celebratory glass of wine in the kitchen. After a few glasses, I am ready to reward you. I lift and sit you down onto the kitchen island countertop, your legs spread and wrapped tightly around my waist. My lips meet yours, and the flutter of our hypnotic desire intensifies."

Katie's heartbeat elevated as her hands found their way beneath her blouse and up to her chest. They functioned on autopilot, sensually groping each breast; with eyes closed, she could only focus on how soft Keaton felt against her mouth, how addictively his voice invaded all her senses.

His eyes devoured her while his voice penetrated the speakers of her cell phone…"My lips make their way to the sides of your neck, then to the cusps of your shoulders. I remove your top, making my way down to your waiting rose-red nipples. I tease them with the tip of my tongue as I hungrily fondle the mounds of your breast. My right-hand makes its way down to the throbbing flower between your thighs. You are already wet, so wet that I can feel the moisture on the length of your inner thighs. I slid two fingers in with ease, gently stimulating the surface of your g-spot while my thumb feverishly taunts your pulsing clit."

Katie moaned in mounting ecstasy; one hand under her shirt probing her conical breast while the other rhythmically prodding her sensitized clitoris.

Keaton's erection grew more prominent and rigid at the sound of Katie's sensual moans. With one hand, he freed it from the restraints of his slim-fit trousers. He gripped his erect shaft, systematically gliding the flesh against the palm of his fist; his stomach flinched from the titillating sensations that immediately catapult over his body. His breathing remained steady and shallow; he swallowed and recomposed himself, his shaft growing in his fist as he continued:

"You grind on my prodding fingers between your thighs as your desire heightens, you're in a frenzy, zealously you remove my shirt, you hop off the counter to kneel before me. Maintaining eye contact, you unzip my pants, and without hesitation, you put my dick in your mouth. I can feel myself growing **big** and **firm** in your mouth. Your warm and soft tongue wrapped around the length of my dick. You look into my eyes as the length of my dick disappears to the back of your throat. You slurp from the buildup."

A titillating spasm ran through the pit of his stomach as he watched Katie sucking on the bottom of her lip, her hands exploring the most sensitive parts of her petite body. He breathed in hard as he continued ...

"My body jerks involuntarily, moving my dick back and forth in your warm wet mouth, and just as I am about to come, I pull my dick from your lips, pull you up, and bend you over the kitchen counter. I take you from behind, you push back, forcing more of me into your dripping wet pussy, it sucks me in. I press on the middle of your bareback with one hand and a handful of your hair in the other. I straddle you like a wild stallion; you beg me to go faster and harder, and I oblige. With every feral stroke, your knees buckle, and moans heighten into rapturous screams. I show no mercy; I want you to come. **Harder...faster...,** I stroke until you scream my name, you're coming. I'm coming too; my back muscles arch in spasms, I cum deep inside you, filling you up. I can feel you climax, gushing all over my soaked dick; I fall onto you. Your legs collapse beneath me, your belly supported by the countertop; I pull my emptied dick from your gushing pussy."

"Je viens! Jeviens! ...I'm coming...." Katie screamed in ecstasy; she began to move her hand faster, spreading her legs wider, leaning back against the pillows.

"I'm almost there...." Keaton moaned in sync, his eyes focused on her face, contorted in the grip of ecstasy. His fist glided faster and faster over his rock-hard shaft. Almost simultaneously, they climaxed, Katie's hips bucked, and her legs twined as she climaxed all over her fingers. Keaton exploded like a loose cannon, his fist coated with viscous fluid, his belly spasmed, and his shaft uncontrollably throbbed until it had run dry. Katie's body collapsed on the bed, her heartbeat still elevated, her mouth agape releasing shallow pants. Keaton reached for the box of Kleenex next to him and wiped himself off; his overly sensitive shaft throbs to the touch as he wipes. He catches his breath, inhaling and exhaling deeply to calm himself.

He managed to speak, "Katie, are you okay?"

"*Très bien,*" she responded, panting between breaths. "I think I'm falling asleep...."

Keaton chuckled at her response, "get some rest; I love you..." He ended the call and laid back in the armchair; his brain had gotten a much-needed reset, and just like that, he fell asleep at the peak of the afternoon, exhilarated and content.

CHAPTER 8

The month of November came faster than Keaton wanted; he no longer had time on his side. Katie was leaving Japan to return to France in two days, and he had to get ready to meet her a day before her birthday, as they had agreed—a trip he anticipated would be bittersweet. He wanted to be with her more than anything, but at the same time, he was more than anxious trying to decipher what her reaction would be towards his big 'not so good' news.

On the other hand, Lia was due to arrive in New York by December 1st. Their wedding date was set for; *Sunday, December 16, 2018,* printed on blush pink and grey invitations sent to his residence by Lia. "Close friends and Family invited; however, his side of the invitation list was still blank. He had declined to submit names to Lia when she had requested and was adamant that only his mother would witness the less than an auspicious affair.

On the business side, Dawson's legal team had ensured that everything was ready for his takeover of the presidency in TrueTek, come January 2019. Previous Annual General Meeting minutes had been reviewed; relevant proxy documents checked. Keaton spent the majority of the last month getting abreast of TrueTek's operations, ongoing projects, and financial position, as well as a discrete background check on all the relevant stakeholders, directors, and officers he would be working with once he resumed.

He was already experiencing workplace politics, with the circulation of the news to the board of directors that he would be assuming the presidency come January. He had received several letters of objection over the week with illogical explanations why the board believes the Vice President, currently acting as President, should remain in the role for a 'strategic' timeframe. As advised by his legal team, Keaton had refrained from responding to the ludicrous objections before the AGM. So, he remained silent in observation, preparing the element of surprise.

On November 5th, five days before Katie's birthday, Keaton had to make the disheartening call to his event planner in France to cancel the proposal plans he had made for Katie's birthday. The proposal was to take place in the romantic little city of Bonifacio, Corsica, situated on a stunning cliff overlooking picturesque seaside scenery following a romantic dinner at the modish restaurant, L'Archivolto. Canceling the proposal was on Keaton's list of the top five most complex decisions he had to make since his return home. It seemed as if that list kept growing. For the most part, nothing was going entirely in his favor since his return, at least not without heart-wrenching sacrifices.

He sat at the edge of the bed after the grueling phone call, staring at the little black box in his hand that kept the engagement ring he had gotten for Katie. He was knee-deep in anticipated regret; every decision so far has only sunk him deeper. What was he to do? He was caught in a helpless situation, a precarious web from which he was incapable of freeing himself without daunting repercussions.

At dinner, Keaton sat at the dining table, picking at the steak on his plate; Celia sat at the other end, observing in silence. In a feeble attempt, she tries to break the silence; "So you will be leaving for France in four days…?"

Keaton raised his head to look at her and nodded, his expression bearing the appearance of a compelled child.

"I saw the ring—" Celia continued, "The one you got for her, you left it in the study the other day, it's beautiful, I'm sorry you won't get to give it to her this time around. What do you plan on doing with it?"

"I still plan on giving it to her" Keaton responded, slightly aggravated. "It belongs to her; I plan on letting her know I was going to propose before all this happened. I want her to keep it, whether or not she will agree to wait, to love me through all this."

He dropped the fork, making a clinking sound on the plate; his face instantly flushed. He knew he was being passive-aggressive, as he struggled internally to repress his feelings of frustration and anger.

"Look, mom, can we not talk about this? I can't handle it right now; I just can't".

Celia took a sip of red wine from the oversized wine glass; her left hand raised in an apologetic gesture. "Fine, let's not talk about her." Celia responded warmly, "But what about Lia?

When do you plan on purchasing the rings? If I remember correctly, that's your task. You will be in France in a few days; I have a trusted jeweler there. I'll make contact and place an order; I have all the specifications; you could take them home on your return, wouldn't that be lovely?"

"For goodness sake, mom!" Keaton snapped, "what makes you think I want to talk about Lia or anything concerning this onus of a marriage. I am going to France to try to salvage whatever I can of my relationship with Katie. Which undoubtedly will be impossible after she learns about this. And you expect me to go 'ring' shopping for Lia! GOD DAMN IT!" Keaton flared, pushing his chair backward, ejecting himself from it. He tossed the napkin on the table and flounced out of the room. Celia's earlier wholehearted expression retracted; she set the wine glass down on the table, wide-eyed. "I was only trying to help," she countered, picking up the glass again for another sip.

Keaton stood outside the terrace of his bedroom, his haven. He felt embarrassed lashing out at Celia like that; God knows his frustration was not directed at her, but he had reached his limit, and the conversation only fueled his annoyance.

He texted Katie before she called. *Hey baby, I'm just letting you know I love you and am thinking about you; I can't wait to see you in a few days. Today, I had a rough day, so I am retiring to bed early; text me when you land.*

For some reason, as the time drew closer for his trip, the thought of it seemed to ease his frustration somewhat. The reason was Katie, he could not deny that he had thought about running away with her more times than one would consider normal, but he also could not gloss over what was at stake.

As the evening grew darker, he fetched a bottle of Dalmore 15-Year-Old whisky from the wine cabinet, a whiskey tumbler, and some ice. He went back to the terrace and sat down, pouring himself a glass. "Fuck it," he grumbled, "this is my life now, deal with it—it is what it is. I am off to France in a few days. Essentially to **destroy**...my near three-year relationship and back to marry a total stranger, isn't that just **fucking** peachy?" He gulped from the glass and continued to grumble. "All in the name of preserving the legacy, all for TrueTek, **Thanks, dad**! He ranted sarcastically, raising his glass in a cheers gesture to the imaginary image of his father sitting before him.

One glass after the other, he quaffed them down; another attempt to Band-Aid his predicament. Hours later, he was now sitting on the terrace floor, peering at the empty whiskey bottle, cock-eyed and woozy. Shakily, he got up and staggered back to the bedroom. His gaze drifted about the room to locate his bed. Once locked in, with a few more stumbles, he lurched his body face down, and sprawled across the bed, one leg hanging over the edge. "I'm sorry, Katie," he slurred as he drifted into an intoxicated slumber.

The next day he was awakened by a sudden flood of light hitting him directly in the face; his face squinched in reaction, and his right hand reflexed as a shield covering his eyes. "Do you know what time it is?" a voice said, coming from the path of the bedroom window. Keaton turned his head in the direction, his eyes straining to open against the harsh light. He sat up on the bed, his hand slightly above his eyelids, trying to gain focus.

"Mom?" He said as Celia's image became clear, "What are you doing here?"

"It's 2:00 p.m." Celia affirmed, sliding the plantation shutters to either side. "You've been asleep all day; your room is a mess, broken tumbler on the terrace and an empty whiskey bottle. Is this your life now?" She scolded, in a chastising tone, making eye contact with her piercing brown eyes. "Look at you; you are still hungover; what would your father think of you if he could see you like this?"

"He's the reason for all this," Keaton mumbled under his breath as he grappled to put his T-shirt back on.

"What did you say?" Celia questioned, her voice raised.

"Nothing, mom," Keaton responded, slightly irritated. He got up from the bed after a few wobbles and started to pick up the items he had knocked down and stumbled over during last night's drunken attempt to find the bed. The lowering of his head immediately made him nauseous triggering a pounding headache. He staggered back to the bed, where he sat with both palms pressed against his forehead.

Celia looked at him and shook her head, releasing a disheartened sigh. "I'll ask the kitchen to make you some ginger tea," she said, picking up the rest of the items, "and take a shower; it will help."

As she left the room, Keaton nodded, his hand shuffled over the bed searching for his phone. Twenty-five miscalls all from Katie, and a text message that read, *"I'm home, call me when you get this."*

He tossed the phone back on the bed with an exasperated groan and sat there for some minutes with eyes closed, both hands gripping the edge of the bed, his back slightly arched as his upper body rocked back and forth, self-castigated and contrite.

After a shower, he returned to the bedroom to find the cup of ginger tea on the end table next to the button-tufted sofa. He ruffled his hair a few more times with the towel before picking up the cup to take a sip. As the afternoon transitioned into evening, so did the after-effect of his intoxication gradually shifted into total sobriety.

CHAPTER 9

On Friday, November 9th, Keaton boarded the family jet at 7:00 a.m.; to arrive in France the same day at around 9:00 p.m. An overzealous Katie sent him more than a dozen voice messages the night before, after their brief phone call, unable to contain her genuine excitement to see him the following day. Keaton was equally thrilled, but at the same time, perturbed by the uncertainty of Katie's imminent reaction to his impending revelation, and he just could not shake the daunting feelings that coursed through his body, which made him near sick to his stomach.

When the jet landed in Paris at Charles de Gaulle Airport, Keaton took a deep breath before exiting, his anxiety level rose even higher, and his heart was palpitating wildly. He stuck his earbuds in his ears as he walked towards the waiting car.

After a quick text message to Katie: *Just landed, will be at the apartment in 20 minutes.* He restarted his playlist and zoned out during the drive.

When the car pulled up at the curve outside the apartment building, a bouncing Katie was standing at the entrance waving frenetically. Keaton's face involuntarily relaxed with a smile. Katie's vivaciousness always had that effect. He exited the car and Katie leaped into his arms, her petite figure nestled perfectly in his muscular arms, and her legs wrapped tightly around his waist.

She kissed him deeply, her eyes closed; he dropped the travel bag and wrapped his arms around her waist. She was refreshing, soft, scorching, and tender, almost like she was pulling the anxiety out of him while refueling his virility.

When she came up for air, their eyes opened instantaneously, fixed on each other in brief stillness; they both smiled. "I've missed you," she said, in a purr-like whisper, wrapping her arms tighter around him.

"I've missed you more," Keaton replied, pecking her amorously on her lips. He bent to pick up the bag with Katie's legs still locked around him. She giggled as he straightened up, tucking her face between his neck and shoulder. Keaton walked towards the rotating glass door of the apartment building with Katie still on him, one hand around her waist for support and the other carrying the travel bag.

"How long have you been standing out here?" he asked teasingly.

"Since I received your text message," she responded with a soft chortle.

"You're crazy," he jested, using the supporting hand to press the elevator button.

"Only for you," she responded, staring passionately into his eyes.

As the elevator door closed behind them, Katie kissed him again, this time a little more intense, the pressure of her lips pressed against his, Keaton tightened his arm around her waist.

Katie's hands moved along his shoulders and onto his chest, then to the back of his neck. They had each other mesmerized.

"Press the floor button," Keaton whispered in between kisses. Katie stretched her hand from the back of his neck, her head slightly raised so one eye could guide her fingers to the elevator buttons; she pressed number 9 and slid back into their kissing trance, their tongues vehemently caressing each other.

By the fifth floor, she was dying to take Keaton's shirt off. Their breathing deepened, her body movement was fierce and hungry. His smell was her natural aphrodisiac, and his apparent virility intensified the sultriness between her legs. Everything Keaton was anxious about earlier was slowly dissipating. He could not bring himself to worry because she was in his arms, her lips were parting, her hands were coiling around his neck, her tongue was in his mouth, and for the moment, he was in rhapsody.

At the *ding* of the elevator stopping on the 9th floor, Katie hopped off Keaton and rushed to unlock their apartment door. She pulled Keaton in as she opened the door, closing it behind them. The fire was now burning red hot between them.

Keaton dropped the bag, stepping forward, aligning himself in front of her; their bodies were close, barely any space between them. He cupped her head with both hands, gently lifting, so her lips could meet his once more. He kissed her again with greater force in a vibrant tongue lock, each time with increasing urgency, cupping her face between his flaming hands.

On tippy-toes, Katie's hands fiercely unbuttoned his shirt, raking it off his body in frenzied passion. Keaton's hand found its way under her skirt. She was wearing nothing beneath; his middle and index finger gently slid into the inviting orifice between her legs.

Katie gasped, her head jerked back, and her hands swung around his shoulder. He glided his fingers intensely, spreading a sensational thrill to her sensual soul.

She unbuckled his belt, unbuttoned his pants, and forcefully pulled it down to his knees. His legs assisted in the removal the rest of the way, as he ripped open the buttons of her sexy slim-fit crop top and unzipped the zipper to the side of her black, asymmetric faux-leather mini skirt that fell effortlessly to the ground.

He stepped out of the pants below his ankles, and hoisted her to his chest, his muscles rippling—exuding sheer masculinity. Her legs spread evenly across his face, each resting on his shoulders. He used his hands to support her back while his mouth immersed into the heart of her femininity. His tongue caressed her clitoris, making her entire body shiver; she locked her legs over his back, her hands squeezing hard on both her breast, her moans intensified, her hips moved in a frenzied motion. He increased the speed and flexibility of his tongue, driving her to the point of insanity. She screamed his name and gripped his hair, forcing his face more between her legs, "Oh God! *Bébé*, I'm coming!" she screamed, as she dissolved into convulsive spasms.

Keaton moved her down to his waiting manhood that was sprouting firmly upward. He held her gaze as he gently slid inside her, securing both her legs over his solid arms, her hands wrapped firmly over his shoulders. Already stimulated, he was plunging madly into her wet heat; her warmth consumed him, scorched him, caressed him, drove him near delirious. His groans tore out deep from inside his chest as he thrust faster and harder; each jab immersed his shaft deeper, and deeper inside her. She was equally on a pleasure high, loudly moaning as she neared climax again. "Oh fuck, Ah God!" he howled, as his release swelled through him, expelling from the tip of his member deep into her, hurling him briefly into a place full of light and sound before leaving him gasping, trembling, and shaken. He quivered inside her, prolonging the moment until she had her release. She collapsed her weight into his arms; her limbs hung limp like a life-size rag doll.

He was undone. She was spent. Both wholly torn to shreds. He trudged on shaky legs to the bedroom with her in his arms. As gently as his weakened knees would allow, he laid her carefully on the bed and plopped down beside her. They were both breathing heavily, their chest visibly moving up and down; Keaton turned his face to look at her, their eyes met, a gratified expression on both their faces. He moved his head closer to hers and kissed her lingeringly on the forehead, "I love you," he whispered, gently pulling away. "I love you more," she replied in delight, holding onto his arm. They laid flat on their backs, lost in bliss, completely unaware of anything else but their existence at the moment. As their bodies cooled and their heart rates tempered, they dozed off.

CHAPTER 10

"Morning sunshine," Keaton smiled at her as her eyes opened. Her beauty was natural and effortless; he missed this, her, those sultry blue-gray eyes that sucked him in every time, just as the first time he looked up at her at the ice rink. She smiled back blushingly, pulling the covers up to her nose.

"Happy Birthday," he effused, kissing her on the forehead. She moved the covers back below her chin, exposing her supple rose blushed lips. "Thank you," she replied, smiling coquettishly, her eyes flirtatiously batting at him. "And what an amazing pre-birthday present that was last night," she stated, smacking her lips in pleasure. He simpered with a swift shake of his head; he was pretty pleased with himself.

"How about round two?" she said, moving closer to him.

"You're insatiable," he joked, pecking her on the lips.

"One of the reasons you love me," Katie grinned, rolling onto her back.

"Maybe later," Keaton smiled, getting up from the bed, I have a lot planned for you today, starting with the surprise that is about to arrive in ten. Wash up and join me in the sitting room; he winked at her, walking away from the bed butt naked. She smirked at him with lustful eyes, goggling his butt as he walked away.

"Aren't you going to join me?" Katie asked, walking towards the bathroom door. "I already took a shower," Keaton replied, grabbing a white T-shirt and grey jogger pants from the closet.

"Was I that passed out?" Katie laughed.

"Yes, you were; I tend to have that effect," he teased.

She giggled and trekked off to the bathroom.

Moments later, she walked into the sitting room to find Keaton waiting with an entire glam team. "What is all this?" she said in shock, as she ran over to him. Keaton received her in a bear hug, kissing her on the forehead.

"This, my love, is a full spa day for you in the comfort of your own home. I have prepared a full body massage, manicure and pedicure, hair and make-up, and your stylist for our outing this evening." Keaton declared, pointing to each station and their respective massage therapists, aestheticians, nail technicians, stylists, and assistants.

"Oh, mon Dieu!" she screamed, jumping up and down, "*Bébé*, you shouldn't have; when did you plan all this? You arrived last night," She asked, peering animatedly into his eyes.

"I've been planning for your birthday since the start of the year," he replied, playfully stroking her cheek. Now, get breakfast; it's plated on the table, and then enjoy your spa day. I will be running out to finalize the rest of the plans for today. I will see you in a few hours. She wrapped her arms around him, and on tippy-toes, she puckered for a kiss. He kissed her warmly.

"Thank you," she whispered.

"You deserve it," he whispered back, shooing her off to the dining table. He kissed her again on the forehead and slipped out the door.

He had to check out the new location he had booked; canceling the venue for his earlier plans was devastating to him, but he had to ensure that the new one was just as perfect, even if it was not for a proposal. He pulled into the open parking lot across the venue, parked, and exited the car. His phone rang.

"Hey, mom..."

"Keaton, you promised you'd call me as soon as you land; I was worried about you. Did you not see my missed calls? Why haven't you returned my calls?"

"Mom, …last night was a bit inconvenient to call you; I know you're concerned, but I'm okay."

"Fine, so have you told her yet. What was her reaction?"

"I haven't gotten to that yet mom, today is her birthday, and I won't ruin it; I want her to have a great day like I initially planned. It is bad enough I am not able to propose to her today. I will not ruin anything else. I'll find the right time to talk to her."

"I'm just concerned about you, that's all," Celia responded in a worried tone. "I know this is hard for you, and I know you might end up not telling her in fear of breaking her heart, but Keaton if you do that, things may turn out worse than it is now, it's best to lay it all out on the table and see how it goes."

"Mom, you think I don't know this! I have to tell her, I will tell her, I just can't do it today. Just let me handle this my way."

"Fine, so when will you return?"

"Well, it depends on how Katie will handle this revelation. I will let you know in time. I have to go. I will call you tomorrow. Love you."

“Okay, remember to call.”

Keaton hung up the phone, tucking it in the pocket of his jogger pant. He stood beside the car for a moment; it was hard to deny that he still had some scruples about revealing the contract marriage ordeal to Katie. Everything was going so great; she was so innocent in all this, the thought of what the information would do to her pierced him deeply, but he had to suppress the feeling, at least for today.

In some ways, ensuring that her birthday was beyond spectacular and unforgettable was a kind of preliminary restitution. Keaton released a deep breath as he walked off towards the venue, determined to make the day a success. He spent hours at the venue meeting with the event coordinators, making sure every detail was perfect, from colors to decorations to music and food selection; he made sure there was a personal touch; besides, he knew Katie best. All her close friends that he knew received a text message, reconfirming time and change of venue. All set.

He even had her lunch delivered to the apartment on schedule, with her favorite snacks and desserts. He knew he was doing something right because Katie texted him that he was the “best boyfriend in the world” and that lunch was “delectable”; her exact words, with a face savoring food emoji; which made him flush after reading it.

He returned to the apartment later that afternoon to find a relaxed and alluring Katie, sitting upright in the center of the bed, in an extremely short black robe, with her legs crossed and tucked in front of her, savoring a pint of butterscotch ice cream. He smiled at her as he walked in. "You look beautiful," he said, taking in her enhanced beauty, full makeup—tastefully done, and hair extensions that gave her hair more volume and a youthful, sophisticated vixen appearance. Her skin was glistening in the natural light; it was hard not to desire her.

"You are spoiling me," she snickered, looking in his direction, "I had such a great time, especially that massage, *Oh mon Dieu!*; my body needed that. I feel so light and calm." She exclaimed, twirling the ends of her hair.

Keaton walked over to the bed and sat beside her; he looked sincerely into her eyes. "You deserve it, and even more, I want you to enjoy yourself; you've been competing for weeks with no break. I know how hard you train and work for these championships. I regret not being with you in Japan, but I'm here now, and I promise to make this birthday unforgettable. Besides, you only turn twenty-five once," he said as he kissed her on the forehead.

She placed the pint of ice cream on the bedside table and threw her arms over his shoulders, pulling him in for a succulent kiss, lightly tugging on his bottom lip with her teeth.

Keaton swallowed, then pulled away playfully, "You better not start what you can't finish," he teased, unless you want me to mess up your hair and make-up." Katie giggled.

"Speaking of which, the stylist was quite the character; I had a bit of a tiff with him. He practically wanted to ignore my choices, forcing me to choose what he selected from the rack of dresses. He said my sense of style was "rakish." She scrunched her face imitating the stylist's 'snobbish' facial expression.

Keaton guffawed at her expression, "I bet you dealt with him" he said, with an impish grin, "next time, he'll know not to mess with my Katie," he laughed and playfully tapped the bridge of her nose.

"There won't be a next time for him," Katie responded, reaching for her ice cream. "But *Bébé...*" she continued, taking a spoonful. "Those dresses I saw on the rack today were all designers and awfully expensive. Not to mention the homecare pampering; all of this must-have cost you a small fortune. Do not get me wrong, I am grateful, but I am still a bit curious. You can't blame me, your mom sent a private plane to fetch you when you left, and I believe you still owe me an explanation for that." She peered at him with probing eyes.

Keaton took the ice cream and held both of her hands up to his chest, looking into her eyes. "Yes, I do owe you an explanation, and I'll make that clear to you now. Just promise to hear me out, and you'll understand."

Katie nodded in response and held eye contact. Keaton took a deep breath and proceeded to explain. "My parents aren't particularly realtors as I had said before," he paused, clenching her hands a little tighter. "Neither are they average or middle-class. My father is the founder of TrueTek, one of the largest technology conglomerates headquartered in New York. We do everything from the invention, production, and distribution of specialized hardware, software, cloud computing, internet solutions, and biotechnology. We have subsidiaries all over the United States, as well as Canada, Asia, the United Kingdom, the Caribbean, and most recently Europe."

Katie's eyes widened with more curiosity, but she remained silent.

"When you were in Japan, you told me that your coach made you install a new software, SPORTFIC, for your training logs, right?"

"Yes," Katie nodded.

"Well, SPORTFIC is one of the many software that is invented and manufactured by TrueTek, and that's just a small example. Now, why I kept this information away from you before is primarily for two reasons. One is quite personal; I grew up in the prime light, always known for my affluence. For as long as I can remember, whenever I would meet someone new, whether it be a friend or otherwise, once they'd learn of my background, everything would change, and relationships became insincere.

Knowledge of my affluence always seems to influence the people I attract, often opportunist, shallow, and vain. What I was worth always took precedence and seemed to be more important to others than getting to know the real me. I am the guy who wants a genuine relationship with a foundation built on pure love, not materialistic and not conditional on what I can offer. I am also the guy who worked my butt off to achieve two master's degrees by the age of twenty-six without my father sponsoring any of the schools I attended or paying for a pass.

But others don't always see that side of me. They get to know my background, and they immediately think I'm a "trust fund baby" whose father bought my way through Ivy League schools, or they immediately want to be my friend or be in a relationship with me for all the wrong reasons.

When I moved to France for my studies, I wanted to take a different approach with my relationships. I was tired of being in relationships that were going nowhere because the person I was with was either vain or a fortune hunter. And that is why, when you decided to give me a chance, I did not lead with my true identity. The more I got to know you, the more I saw that my affluence did not matter to you; you were never that kind of person. You also wanted a genuine relationship, and we gave that to each other. The second reason is that I admired your humbleness; you are a lauded figure skater here in France, have won many championships, and gained many accolades. Still, no one would ever know from your personality. You have never let that take precedence in the way you treat people or the way you love me, and for that reason, I found it irrelevant to talk about my affluence because it genuinely didn't matter in our relationship."

Keaton looked deeper into her eyes with earnestness, begging for her understanding; she held his stare, and a smile formed slowly across her face. Keaton could see it was a genuine smile, an *I'm-not-mad-at-you* kind of smile.

"You're smiling. Does that mean you understand and you're not mad at me?" He asked nervously.

"Why would I be mad at you?" she responded, with affection beaming in one eye and understanding shining out of the other. "I mean, I would rather you had told me sooner, at least when our relationship had gotten more serious. Because you know how much I value honesty. But at the same time, I understand where you are coming from because I too have encountered similar situations in previous relationships, so I get it."

A weight lifted off Keaton, at least for that moment. He hugged her tighter than a vice grip. "Thank you for understanding, I promise, I had plans to tell you, it is just that before I had gotten around to it, I received the news of my father's passing, and I just couldn't explain everything at that time, I'm truly sorry for not telling you sooner."

"It's fine," Katie replied cheerfully, "It's not like you're a serial killer or an obsessed fan," she joked. They both laughed.

Keaton looked at her with complete admiration. That was just who she was. He could expect her to make the best out of any situation. Her bubbly personality was infectious; he always believed that meeting her was his luck, to be her boyfriend was his blessing, and to be with her forever was all he wanted. At that moment, he questioned everything. Would she have the same reaction towards the news of his arranged marriage, was it at all possible for her to be this understanding when the time came, was he willing to take the chance of possibly losing her forever?

CHAPTER 11

With one secret out in the open and a positive reaction from Katie, Keaton was even more eager to celebrate her for being an extraordinary woman. He whisked her off to the venue later that evening, and she was in for another fabulous surprise. He led her down a deliberately circuitous pathway, revealing an ideal setting overlooking an exclusive French Riviera, panoramic and luminous. Her mouth dropped as she took it all in. The scene was a picture postcard, with a magnificent lucid night sky accenting the venue like an illusory backdrop.

Katie gasped, holding one hand over her heart, her expression overcome with astonishment and delight.

"How did you find this place?" She exclaimed, looking at him with glistening eyes. "It's magical!" Her smile broadened in astonishment, baring her dazzling white teeth, an infectious smile that traveled telepathically to Keaton's lips.

"Come with me," he beamed; taking her hand, they walked through an alley flanked by gardens on either side to a dark dining area under the stars. An instant flood of light came with a chorus of "surprise!" from their close friends, her family, and her teammates. Katie's hands went up over her mouth; her eyes glinted with joyous tears. She was smothered with pure love and hugs from everyone, one after the other. She cried, laughed, pranced, screamed; she laughed some more and cried some more. A roller coaster of emotions that sincerely expressed how genuinely happy and excited she was in the moment. Surrounded by the people she loved the most, the night could not get any better.

But it did; it was perfect, like something from the Hallmark channel. From dinner to cake cutting and the hilarious off-key birthday singing; each moment came with a unique snippet of felicity. When they had all had their fill of cake and bubbly, her friends and family each took turns to give a heartfelt narrative of how Katie had impacted their lives over her twenty-five years of life. Keaton's speech brought her to tears, especially the part where he said: "It was your bubbly personality that bewitched me. Your unconditional love captured my body and soul. Being a part of your life is the fulfillment of a dream. If I could have one wish come through tonight, I would wish never to be parted from you from this day on."

She ran into his arms after that speech; her eyes welled with happy tears. His mind teleported into wishful thinking, holding her in his arms at that moment. A hopeful prayer that after his revelation, she would remain his forever. He discretely sniffled as he tried to hold back his tears, a smile formed across his face, a smile that disguised his fear, a smile of falsified contentment.

The DJ made the rest of the night energetically wild, with a flair of sophistication. On the dance floor, Katie unleashed her inner vixen. Her once elegantly curled extensions were now windswept, and perfectly applied makeup had naturally dissolved throughout the night by the electrifying thrill she was experiencing.

Her form-fitting, jewel-embellished, short dress, with sheer bodice and delicate long sleeves, was still sitting pretty on her size two body; but her silver shimmer, ankle-strap stilettos were abandoned in a corner somewhere. When her girlfriends joined her, their rave was joyful and untamed. For a while, Keaton watched from the sidelines giving the girls time to themselves. They jived to a timeless remix of French Polynesia, Hollywood, Bollywood-mash-up, and by midnight they were euphoric.

It was past midnight when Keaton left the party with Katie after everyone else had gone their separate ways. He drove her on what seemed like a lonesome road in the opposite direction of home.

"Where are we going?" Katie asked, rhapsody splashed across her face.

"We are ending the night with one last surprise," Keaton replied with a beaming smile.

They pulled up to the entrance of an amusement park; the outside was dark and solitary.

"What are we doing here?" Katie asked, a thrill of curiosity in her eyes, "it's after midnight; this place is closed."

"Closed to the public, but open to us," Keaton replied, giving her a quick glance.

With a single beep of the car horn, the giant entrance doors of the amusement park began to open, and the grounds flood with light. Keaton exited the car and walked around to open her door. Katie stepped out barefooted, her mouth agape and her eyes fixed on the still, opening, metal doors.

"No, you didn't!" She yelled, emitting a lilting scream.

"I thought I'd end the night with you on top of the world?" Keaton gushed, "You have always wanted to come here, but we have never gotten around to it, so, what better time than tonight.?" He gripped her hand and walked hurriedly towards the park, pulling her eagerly behind him. She followed, giggling like an enlivened little girl. Keaton gave the curator standing at the gate a confirming nod before whisking Katie over to the Ferris Wheel.

"After you," he said with an elaborate arm gesture.

Katie gawked, stepping onto the platform with Keaton's support. She sat in the double-seated pod, and Keaton followed suit. He secured her and himself before the operator powered the wheel. Katie released an exhilarating shriek as they gradually climbed higher.

At the top of the Ferris wheel, the stillness of the night heightened the sound of her excited giggles and the jingling from the amulets on her bracelet. They shared a grin as she kicked her feet out in the open air. "Best night ever!" she screamed as they reached the pinnacle of the rotation. She pulled in a deep, clean breath, eyes closed, she was indeed at the top of the world, and at that moment, everything seemed so clear, so full of life. They both felt alone in the world, in a good, free, whimsical way. While Katie was undoubtedly having the time of her life, Keaton secretly hoped that the night would go on forever. The wheel shuddered to life, pulling forward and then down, and as they sank toward the ground, his mind returned to the secret inside. Lower and lower, he was closer to the reality that the night would indeed come to an end.

CHAPTER 12

"Katie...Katie", Keaton whispered, tapping her on the shoulder. "I made you a cup of coffee."

"What time is it?" Katie mumbled, lifting her head slightly upwards with foggy eyes.

"A few minutes after 1:00 p.m.", Keaton replied, gently pulling the covers off her.

"Is it afternoon already?" Katie exclaimed, her voice still groggy, she sprung upwards, rubbing her eyes, her hair messy, and her cheeks slightly flushed.

"I didn't want to wake you earlier. You were sleeping so peacefully, but I thought you might be a bit hungover, so I made you some coffee. It's Sunday afternoon anyway; you can go back to bed after having something to eat."

"Oh my God!" she screeched, covering her face with her hands as flashes of the after-birthday party escapades sped across her mind. "Last night was so crazy, wasn't it? I cannot believe I pushed you to have sex with me in the open on a ***Tilt-a-Whirl***. You must think I'm such a freak," she pulled the covers over her head, shamefaced.

The enunciation of the word *freak* with her French accent made Keaton unintentionally chuckle. He playfully pulled the covers, slowly uncovering her face. "What is so wrong with you being a freak? On the contrary, I find that side of you extremely endearing, and I'm quite fond of it. I like the untamed passion that you emanate when your freak comes out." He stared reassuringly into her eyes, giving her a genuine you-are-everything-that-I-want, kind of smile.

She blushed, holding on to his gaze. A warm, comforting feeling washed over her, and it's as if she read the secret thought in his smile, and without words, she affirmed, you are everything that I want too.

Keaton handed her the cup of coffee that was sitting on the bedside table. "Here, drink this; I'll go make you something to eat." He tenderly stroked her hair then left the room. Katie took a few sips, then got off the bed. She met her reflection in the mirror of the closet doors and released a ghastly gasp. "God, I'm a hot mess," she shrieked, running her hands through her hair before hurrying off to the bathroom.

Moments later, she joined Keaton in the kitchen, wearing a waist apron over his boxers, flipping blueberry pancakes. "Hmmm," she tittered, leering at him with lust-stained eyes. "You see what you do to me. How can you be so sexy making breakfast?"

Keaton laughed at her comment and walked over to the breakfast counter to stack three pancakes on her plate.

"Down, girl," he teased, pecking her on the forehead. "I made scrambled eggs too," he said, returning to the stove for the skillet. He spooned some in both plates and sat down beside her. Katie looked at him gleefully, pouring maple syrup on her pancakes.

"Thank you, *Bébé*," she said, beaming after she took the first bite.

"You're welcome," Keaton smiled, "I hope I didn't burn the pancakes."

"They are just fine," Katie replied, looking down on her plate.

A few minutes in, Keaton walked over to the refrigerator to get a bottle of orange juice and two glasses from the cupboard. Katie's eyes followed him, a rather curious expression on her face.

"What is it," Keaton asked, meeting her stare.

"Can I ask you something?" She replied wide-eyed.

"Of course, anything," Keaton replied, setting down the bottle and glasses as he stood at the opposite side of the counter.

Katie made a sharp sound as if to clear her throat a little and released a shallow breath.

"I—I saw it by accident. I wasn't searching or anything; it just happened..." she blurted out, her hand gestures a bit skittish.

"What are you talking about?" Keaton asked in a quizzical tone. Katie's response came out in a blather, as she tried to lay out what she wanted to say in a way that vindicated her from appearing intrusive.

"Yesterday, when you left to finalize my birthday plans. I was looking for some items in the closet when I saw your traveling bag still packed, so I started to unpack for you, and that is when I saw it, at the bottom of the bag...you know? the ring," she said, stating the latter in hushed tones, her eyes beaming and a sudden radiant expression on her face.

The blood suddenly drained from Keaton's face and the thoughts in his head unexpectedly twisted into a scramble. Something flickered through his eyes so quickly. Though Katie's focus was on him, she had a hard time deciphering the expression in his eyes. Was it guilt?

She stuttered to break his silence, "*Bébé*, I'm sorry…did I ruin the surprise? —I did, didn't I? I swear it was a total accident. I thought you were going to propose yesterday, so when it did not happen, I became a little curious, and that is why I brought it up…*Bébé*, if you are planning an elaborate proposal, you do not have to; yesterday's surprise was enough for me. You do not need to go through all that. My answer will be yes, no matter where or how you propose." She rambled on with sincerity in her voice.

For a moment, Keaton's mind was distant, even though his eyes were fixed on her. He was brooding, a battle within himself, wanting to speak but not knowing how or what to say. He knew this moment was coming when he would have to tell her everything, but he had never imagined that it would have happened like this. Caught off guard and unprepared, he stood fixed across the counter from her, dazed.

"*Bébé, Bébé!*" Katie said, snapping her fingers in front of his face. Blood suddenly rushed back to Keaton's face as his mind regained focus. His eyes could see her once more; his mouth opened and shut alternatively in a split second, but nothing came out.

He looked at her, his eyes downcast, as he gathered his nerves to summon the few words that were conveniently available for his imminent confession. "Baby, there's something I have to tell you."

Katie's eyes became wary with concern, "What is it?" she questioned, moving her head down to catch his downcast gaze.

"Can we go to the sitting room?" He asked, walking around to her side of the counter.

"You are scaring me," Katie muttered, getting up from her chair.

Keaton took her arm and led her into the sitting room. He sat her down on the couch and sat beside her.

"You are making me anxious," Katie continued as she tried to read Keaton's still facial expression. It was perplexing enough that she could not understand why he was nervous and worried about something, but how it all connected to her discovering the ring was even more baffling.

"I, I did get that ring for you," Keaton stuttered. "I had every intention to propose to you on your birthday, before…." He paused, a taut expression on his face.

"Before what…?" Katie asked eagerly.

Keaton shuffled uncomfortably beside her; he grabbed both of her hands, positioning himself to face her directly.

"For you to understand, I need to go into details, so please bear with me," His eyes showed vulnerability as he held her gaze. Katie nodded, still perplexed.

"I did plan on proposing to you on your birthday; that is how serious I take our relationship and how much I want to spend the rest of my life with you, but ..." He adjusted himself again before he continued. "When I went home after I had received the news that my father had passed...shortly after, I started to discover a lot of things that I previously was not aware of, with my father's health, the company, and some projects he had been working on."

Katie's expression deepened with even more anxiety. Keaton continued.

"The day after his funeral, my mom and I had a visit from his attorney. My dad had left a will, including a video, pertaining to my takeover of the company, assuming the role of president. In that video, my father explained that he had made a risky investment, launching TrueTek's biotechnological facilities and products into the European market, against the objection of the stakeholders.

"He was working to finalize the project in a shorter period than usual, based on his life expectancy. It was virtually impossible, and as a result, the project ran into some difficulties within the first year of its launch, and the company lost billions. Because dad went forward with this project against the stakeholders' decision, he was solely responsible for compensating the stakeholders for portions of equity he had lost. And in so doing, he had to sell the majority of his voting shares and other assets to recover the sum. By doing that, he found himself in a compromising position within the company. The stakeholders who were against his presidency, infuriated with his decision to go against them, were now gunning to accumulate majority shares to outvote my father and remove him from his position.

Katie pursed her lips, a slight furrow between her brows as she focused on his words.

"My father convinced his European business partner to purchase all available outstanding shares he could get his hands on to avoid this. Enough to ensure that no one else within the company could accumulate enough to overthrow him. Dad's business partner purchased the shares on his behalf based on a contract where he would hand over the shares to my father at the end of the Biotech project in return for some special incentives. However, because of his deteriorating health condition, he later transferred the shares to his daughter, the sole heiress of his company.

"Dad feared that I would face the same unfavorable company politics with his passing, where others would fight against me assuming the company's presidency. The only way that I would be able to take possession of the company after his passing with the power to overrule any objections; is if I assumed the role with majority shares. The only problem is that the percentage of shares he signed over to me in his will would not be enough to make me a majority shareholder. I would also need access to the shares held by his European partner's daughter. However, there was no easy way to recover the shares from his business partner, he could repurchase them, but the money was not readily available. He was banking on the predicted returns from the European investment, which won't materialize until the project's completion, not until the end of next year. With no other readily available option to access the shares, they came up with the only other viable solution...." He paused again, clenching her hands a little tighter; the buildup of anxiety and tension caused his throat muscles to constrict, giving him the feeling of a lump suddenly wedged in his throat. He swallowed; it was almost excruciating.

"...They, ...they, came up with the solution of a contract marriage, between the daughter of dad's business partner and me."

In reflex, Katie immediately pulled her hands from his grip. Her lips formed a smile, an uneasy, sort of uncomfortable smile, *my- brain- does- not- know- what- to- make- of- the- information- I- just- heard-, so- I- am- awkwardly- smiling- while- I- get- my- thoughts- together-* smile.

Keaton kept looking into her eyes, waiting for a response, puzzled by the smile on her face. The smile didn't dither for some seconds. It didn't waver or fade in the least. But the smile in her eyes, the genuine part of a smile, evaporated.

"Say something, please," Keaton begged, holding on to her hand again. Katie's mind rushed into a dark place as if she was now suffering from a moment of tinnitus, a high-pitched buzzing in her ears that drowned out all other sounds in her reality, including Keaton's voice.

He gently tugged at her hand, his eyes yearning for her response, "Baby, please say something."

The awkward smile vanished from her face. She looked down at her hand in Keaton's grip, almost as if she were waking up from a coma. Unaware of the person in front of her. She pulled her hand from his grasp once more and stood up abruptly. With her back turned to him, she spoke, "Are you saying that you are getting married to someone else?" Katie's voice quivered while her hands visibly shook.

Keaton stood up immediately and walked towards her, his arm outstretched to touch her.

"Baby, I promise you it's not like what you are thinking. I have no other choice. These past few months have been hell. I have tried so hard to find an alternative to this nightmare. But to no avail. The marriage is provisional, a contract; it means nothing. I only need to be married to her for a year, until the end of next year, and then it's over."

He wrapped his arms around her waist, acting on impulse, hoping to hold her in place for fear of her leaving. She started to pull away from him, but he grabbed her wrists, his grip impenetrable, his eyes warped with remorse and helplessness, yearning to be pitied, yearning for forgiveness.

She swung her body around to face him, her wrist still in his grasp. Her breathing was heavy, her body convulsing, a tear broke free from her eye's reservoir, and the rest followed in an unbroken stream. Keaton's heart sunk, not knowing what to say to comfort her. His worst fear was happening right before his eyes. Unintentionally, he had broken her heart.

CHAPTER 13

It was painful seeing her like this. All Keaton could do was stand there, helplessly watching the torrent of her tears cascade down her cheeks. He clenched his fists, asphyxiated by his heartache, knowing that he directly caused her pain. He could hear her silently screaming, suffocating with each breath she took, holding onto her pride.

She staggered towards the sofa, almost in a limp, her body weakened from the ache within her heart. She sat down, both palms pressed to the sides of her face, an attempt to silence the noise inside her head.

"All this while, you knew that this was going to happen, you knew you were getting married, and not once did you ever mention it! All the time that we spoke over the phone, you knew...!" She screamed at him with every breath that her debilitated lungs could muster. Her palms still pressed against the sides of her face, her voice breathy and wheezy from her cries.

Keaton knelt before her, his hands on her knees, his voice brittle, as he tried to explain.

"Baby, I could not have told you all this over the phone. You were in championships. How could I have told you this then? It was just not the right time. After I learned about it, I spent weeks seeking an alternative, any other option but this. I failed.

I know you're hurting, but I'm begging you to understand. I have no other choice. I stand the chance of losing everything, our future if I can't secure the leadership of the company while I still have a chance."

He groveled on his knees, lightly pulling her hands away from her face, lifting her head to meet her eyes.

"Baby, please, this marriage means nothing. It's just a contract, one that will be over in a year. I know nothing about this woman, and I don't want to know. It's just that I have a responsibility, to my family, to TrueTek, to myself, for our future—, an obligation to preserve my family's legacy, and right now, this is the only way to do that. I beg you—, please— don't let this get in between us.

"I only love you. You are the only one that I want to spend the rest of my life with, and I will. I need one year, and I promise you that I will spend the rest of my life making it up to you as soon as it is over. I will spend the rest of my life making you happy. Please say you will wait for me…please."

She tried desperately to wipe her eyes with the back of her palms, aggravated by his presumptuousness. Her mind was screaming, *how dare you agree to marry another woman and ask me to wait for you. How can you not see what this is doing to me? How can you be so heartless?*

"No wonder you were so indifferent when you were in New York," She sniffled.

"For all the times I felt like you were ignoring my calls, this was the reason…. Then you came back, made love to me, more than once! You threw this elaborate birthday party, all for what! Was it all to make me feel less hurt when you impale my heart?

Was it pity? Was it guilt? Was any of it even real!" She let forth a rapid stream of French invectives in her anger and despair.

Her wildfire gaze burnt through his raw skin, torching his heart. His mind spoke what his lips hesitated to say. *Katie, your thoughts could not be further from the truth. It was all real. My love for you has never wavered, not once. I was indifferent because I feared hurting you. I didn't know how to speak to you without exposing the guilt, the secret, the burden I was carrying. I made love to you because it was right, it was real, and it made sense. You are the only one in the world that brought calm to my frustration, to the raging storm this quandary has caused in my life.*

He hesitated to reconcile her thoughts because he could not blame her for thinking that way, for doubting his love. She was speaking from a place of anger and hurt. He told himself she did not mean it. His eyes, his body, his soul pleaded with her.

He would have extracted his heart from his chest and handed it to her at the moment if it meant she could see how much he loved her and how badly he, too, was hurting because of this.

He could no longer hold back the tears he had been trying to blink away. In agony and sheer hopelessness, he bared his vulnerability, defenseless before her. He blubbered in gut-wrenching sobs that tore through his chest.

"Please, tell me what you want me to do, and I will do it. Just don't leave me. I cannot lose you. I can't." His face sank into her lap; a tremor overtook him that wracked his body with an onslaught of sobs and tears. Katie placed her shaking hands on his head; a great cry escaped her, tightening her throat, shortening her intake of breath. They sat there entangled as their hurt poured out in a flood of uncontrollable tears.

Katie raised his head, her hands still shaking, her eyes glazed with tears. "I need time to think about this," she sniffled, "I need some time alone."

Keaton's head shook in a disagreeing motion; his expression bore emotional fear.

"What—what do you mean?" he stuttered, searching her eyes.

"I need time to process all of this!" She shrieked, "You want me to wait for you, you want me to understand, you want me to be fine with all of it; you want all these things from me at this moment! Without giving me a chance to think! You asked me to tell you what to do, and you will do it; well, I am telling you that I need time alone to process this, gather my thoughts, decide what I want, and what's best for me in this situation. I cannot do that with you here," Katie said with a snivel. Each time I look at you now, the pain, the heartache, it goes on repeat. Keaton, I am stuck in this emotional rut. I can't breathe; I can't think straight. I need a little time. I want you to leave, please, please! please, go."

She pushed against him, thrusting past to stand on her feet. She meandered towards the breakfast counter, holding on to it for support; constant sniffles escaping her as she tried to resist her tears. He stood up in reaction, but he did not move towards her. He remained close to the couch, giving her space.

"Okay," he answered, his tone racked with defeat. "I'll leave, but only if you promise me that as soon as you calm down, we can talk about this, about moving forward." He lingered in pause for her response, his expression somber and pale.

She nodded, her back turned to him; he could feel her suffering from across the room.

"Okay then…" he muttered, breathing in deep as he turned to walk towards the door. Walking out the door was the most harrowing few seconds of his life. His misery had melted into a languishing wound deep inside him, and the hurt in his heart escalated to a burning, glaring pain that seared through his veins.

CHAPTER 14

For Keaton, the next three days was a mush of anxiousness and agonizing wait, overwhelmed by thoughts of what-ifs. What if Katie never calls? What if she decides to leave him? What if she never gives him another chance? Over the last three days, he kept his distance, staying at a nearby hotel. He knew he needed to give her space, to wait until she was ready to discuss it on her terms. But it was not easy waiting in silence, not being able to call her, out of fear that he'd anger her even more. Not being able to know how she was coping, was she still crying, was she eating. Considering her schedule to leave for Canada in less than a week, was she mentally prepared to travel, to compete?

All these questions lingered in his mind, circulating like a bad horror movie on replay. He thought about his father in the passing days. How great of a father he had been. He had never done anything but support him, be there for him. But these last days, Keaton couldn't help feeling like his father's decision for the arranged marriage was the worst thing his father had ever done to him, which stirred an instance of resentment deep inside him. But he later felt guilty for his fleeting resentment, knowing the circumstances that led to the decision, but in a way, it was a way of coping, of channeling his hurt, his frustration.

On the fourth day in the hotel, with no contact from Katie, Keaton called his mom, the only person who understood what he was going through. Though Celia was happy he called, she was disheartened listing to her grown, twenty-seven-year-old son break down, whimpering like a baby. She understood even more how in love Keaton was with Katie and wanted to help. Celia begged Keaton to let her speak to Katie; he objected at first, but then he thought what else could go wrong? Out of desperation, he gave her Katie's phone number as he needed all the help he could get. Maybe if Katie heard from someone else, she would understand his vulnerable position in the situation.

Following the phone conversation, he took Celia's advice to get out of the hotel room, so he took a walk to clear his head. He had stayed cooped up in the hotel room for the entire time, not letting any sunlight in, sinking in literal darkness and depression. Celia questioned how he had survived on coffee, alcohol, and muffins from the mini bar for so long. She was even more worried about his physical and mental health, taken aback that such a love existed among the "younger generation," causing her son not to eat or sleep properly for days.

On the morning of the fifth day, Keaton was out for a walk when his phone rang.

"Mom," he answered intently, "Did you speak to her? What was her response? When will I hear from her…?" His anxiety was bursting through his questions, so much so that he didn't realize he wasn't allowing his mom to get a word in.

"Keaton! Calm down," Celia snapped. "Will you allow me to speak?"

He replied in a subdued apologetic tone. "Sorry, mom. I'm just a bit anxious, she still hasn't called, and it's driving me crazy. I don't know what to do."

"Just listen to me," Celia asserted. "I have spoken to Katie for almost an hour; she is a nice girl, but…." she paused for a beat. "I found her to be a bit fickle; I don't know if she's like that because of the situation, but…."

"Why do you say that, mom?" Keaton asked with eagerness in his voice.

"Initially, she sounded happy that I had called; and was very respectful throughout the entire conversation. But halfway through, I could sense that she no longer wanted to hear what I had to say." Keaton let out a long, dejected sigh over the phone.

"She claims she loves you, but at the same time, unsure of whether she loves you enough to go through this with you. I get from our conversation that she is a free-spirited young woman, aggressively independent. There's nothing wrong with that, but she wants you to be the same, live on your terms. She doesn't understand why you have to accept this marriage. In her opinion, you are under pressure to conform to our ideas for your future, and that isn't the case. Haven't you discussed how important this company is to you and how hard you have worked to take over after your father? Haven't you explained that the decision to be the president of your father's conglomerate is not by force; instead, it's what you've been dreaming of doing ever since you were a child?"

"Not in so many details...." Keaton responded hesitantly. "But I have tried to make it clear to her as to why I have to accept this marriage.... Then, does this mean that she's made up her mind not to be with me...?" His face fell, not sure if he wanted to hear the answer.

"I tried my best to make it clear to her," Celia continued, "to make her understand that TruTek is not only your father's life work or legacy but yours as well. She didn't express to me what her decision would be. However, she did say she'd decide by the end of the week, that's in two days. I'm confident that I have given her a new perspective on the situation. Now that she has a more precise understanding, all that's left to do is wait."

Keaton did not respond; somehow, he didn't feel at ease with the outcome of his mother's and Katie's conversation. Plus, he had to wait another two days to know Katie's decision. This response was not what he wanted to hear.

Celia broke his silence. "However, I know this is not what you want to hear, but I'm going to say it anyway. Have you considered at all that it might be best for both of you if you went your separate ways? I mean, I completely understand what you both have invested in this relationship, but things and circumstances change, and sometimes it is for the best. Have you thought of the possibility that even if Katie decides to wait for you, the distance and lack of or limited communication that the marriage will cause between you might just be the breaking factor of your relationship? What if during the marriage you fall for Lia? What then happens to Katie if she decides to wait for you? Have you thought about any of this?"

His face suddenly turned red, and he snapped, "Mom, don't go there. I am in love with Katie, and nothing will change my feelings for her. I can't see myself spending the rest of my life without her, let alone falling in love with a total stranger during a contract marriage that means nothing but business. How could you even say that…?"

"Son, I'm only speaking reality. If I'm anything, I'm a realist, and I have been around long enough to know that emotions and feelings can be erratic. Sometimes it's best to accept and deal with things as they are instead of pulling the wool over your eyes and being impulsive. If your feelings change towards her along the line, don't you think she'll be even more hurt then and even more unforgiving? Asking her to wait for you is riskier than breaking ties with her now, while you have a bit more control over the situation. All I'm asking is that you think about it before you end up making a decision you will live to regret."

Keaton wasn't having any of it. As far as he was concerned, he and Katie were soulmates. It wasn't possible for him to love anyone else, so he refused to acknowledge Celia's advice in his requited response.

"Look, Mom, I appreciate what you have done, interceding with Katie on my behalf. I can't thank you enough. However, when it comes to my love for Katie and her love for me, I'd appreciate it if you did not question our relationship because you have no idea how deeply we love each other. Please don't ask, suggest, or even mention ever again that I break up with her; as long as she's willing to have me, I'll be hers forever."

"Fine," Celia responded, "as long as you believe you are making the right decision, I'm okay with it, you are my son, and I only want what is best for you. If you want me to stay out of it, I will. I sincerely hope things work out with Katie the way you wish. At least I will be comforted knowing that you are happy. I have got to go now, be sure to take care of yourself. You are all I've got. I love you."

"I love you too, mom, take care." He hung up feeling less agitated over Celia's and Katie's conversation but more worried about his relationship; subconsciously, he questioned himself. *Was I too selfish, wanting Katie to accept my predicament and wait? If I genuinely love her, shouldn't I be willing to set her free ...and if she's mine, then eventually she'd find her way back to me...right?*

Waiting for the end of the week seemed like infinity, the days lasted forever, and the nights were not ending fast enough. It took all of Keaton's self-control to resist the urge to text or call Katie. Not to mention on the sixth day, in a moment of weakness, he had stormed out of his hotel room and drove to their apartment building. It took complete restraint to stand outside and not go up.

On the weekend, he sat in his hotel room staring flint-eyed at the phone, his face hardened in concentration. When a text message notification finally came in, he near twisted his leg in the rush of a wild scramble to grab the phone from the coffee table. It was a message from Katie that immediately formed a blooming smile across his face before he had even read it. She had invited him over that evening in the text message, which sent him springing into the air like a hyperactive bunny.

He finally took a long shower, appropriately dressed, and got her flowers before heading to the apartment that evening. He prayed in hushed tones, "God, please let her not hate me," and repeated it about ten times before getting off on the elevator on the ninth floor.

Outside their apartment door, he pressed the doorbell and stood there in a nervous jitter. He felt like a sudden hot flash had overtaken his body. It felt highly intense over his face, neck, and chest. Keaton's hands quivered so much that the petal cups on the bundle of yellow tulips were visibly vibrating in his hand. He used his left hand to grab the right, intending to calm the shaking. When the door opened, he flung his left hand to his side, trying to conceal what he had been doing, but Katie had already noticed, which made her smile pleasingly.

"Come in," she said, widening the door. "The…these are for you," Keaton stuttered, handing her the bundle of tulips. Katie took the tulips and closed the door.

"Tulips show new beginnings," she remarked, walking over to the dining table, "Is that what this is, a new beginning?"

"Well, I hope it will be…." He replied apprehensively, following closely behind her.

She placed the tulips in an empty vase and added water from the kitchen. Keaton stopped at a close distance in the sitting room waiting for her.

“Sit,” she said with a hand gesture. Keaton sat. She sat arm’s length beside him. For a moment, there was an awkward silence, as neither spoke but stared at each other in a silence rich with words unsaid.

“So, your mom called,” Katie averred, breaking the silence, “I must say it was a pleasant surprise. It is funny, though, how I’ve never spoken to her before at length, but it’s a situation such as this that would spark an hour-long conversation between us.” She snickered.

However, I am happy that she called. It helped me put things into perspective. I can tell she loves you and wants the best for you.

“I hope that’s a good thing, your new perspective.” Keaton queried, interlocking his fingers on both hands to make a fidgeting clasp.

Katie looked at him and uttered an inaudible, brief grunt. He looked back into her eyes, searching for the answer, but the look on her face gave nothing away, and the panic clawed at his gut.

She took a deep breath and placed her hand over his, looking intently into his eyes. “I won’t lie and say that I agree with this decision, but after speaking to your mom, I understand why it is necessary. With that said, I—I am willing to wait for you, but only if you can promise me today that my wait will not be in vain. I love you,” her voice broke on a sob, her gaze packed with truth. “Too much to walk away from. I have found something special with you, something that is worth this sacrifice. So, I have decided to focus on my training and my competitions in preparation for the Olympics. Training will keep me occupied for the majority of next year while you focus on what you need to do to keep your end of the contract and come back to me when it's all done."

Keaton's clasp dismantled beneath her palm, his shoulders relaxed as the tension subsided. He grabbed her hands bringing them to his chest, his eyes carrying a mixture of shock and barely containing his joy. "You don't know how happy I am to hear you say that" he whispered as his eyes welled with tears.

"I ***promise*** you," his tone emphasized the promise, "your wait will not be in vain, Katie; you mean the world to me, and I want to spend the rest of my life with you. When this problem has passed, I ***promise*** to spend the rest of my life making it up to you. I love you so much," he sobbed, kissing her hands between his grasp. "I promise to love you forever, every single day of eternity."

He pulled her body in closer to him, his arms wrapped around her in a tightening embrace. He repositioned his head to look at her; their eyes initiated the kiss before their lips met. They wedged into a passionate lip lock, and everything seemed to go oddly quiet. It was an unfamiliar kiss, one that spoke silently to their hearts, that revealed how empty they were apart, how badly they needed to be together. And for the first time, they were both completely yielding; nothing else in the world mattered. The tension surrounding the contract marriage had dissolved entirely, and in that kiss came an unspoken promise of forgiveness and new beginnings.

CHAPTER 15

Now that they had resolved the tension surrounding the marriage agreement, it was time to decide on a plan to move forward. The next hurdle was maintaining the passion in their relationship over a year of distance and limited communication. Keaton had made clear to Katie—Lia's terms in agreeing to the marriage, which required Keaton to be committed to Lia during the year, which meant that Keaton and Lia were both restricted from having any other intimate relationship or partners during that year.

Keaton was adamant that this was one of Lia's rules that he would have to break. Though he had signed this agreement in Lia's proposal contract, he decided with Katie that nothing would stop them from communicating with each other during that year. They would find a way to make it work. It was a sour topic for Katie, agreeing to sneak around with her man, but she later found it exciting and joked about being the "side chick" for one year. It became easier for Katie to agree to do whatever it took to maintain their relationship, more so when she thought about what Celia had told her during their phone conversation —"*It is easy for anyone to say they love and are in love with someone. But the measure of absolute love comes when you must prove your love through unfavorable circumstances. Great trials and tribulations without condition, without waver; when you are willing to go through everything designed to tear you apart from the one you claim to love, that's when you have an unrefuted right to say you truly love someone, unconditionally.*"

And so, they both decided to view the marriage predicament as a test of their love and relationship rather than an insurmountable obstacle. With that approach, they planned their new beginning, determined to overcome, to triumph, and, if possible, be more in love than they were before.

On the eve of Keaton's return to New York, they drove to a corniche along the enthralling coastline between Marseille and Cassis for hours. They sat on the bonnet of Keaton's silver-grey 2015 Chevrolet Camaro LT, overlooking charming firths of majestic limestone cliffs and rocky peninsulas that plunged brilliantly into the turquoise waters of the Mediterranean Sea. Katie sat in front of Keaton, who had his hands wrapped around her.

"How beautiful is this?" Katie said in an awestruck voice, beaming at the pine trees clinging to the gleaming rock of the cape. When mixed with the majestic sunset over the coastline, an enchanting view ignited their amorous mood.

Katie leaned her head back on Keaton's right shoulder; her face turned to his. Their eyes locked on each other's like magnets, lingering in an alluring gaze that pulled their lips closer together, in subtle, slow motion, an electric force.

He kissed her, once, twice, and then some more, fiercer, and richer, fervently sucking the air from each other until they were forced to pause for breath. He pulled away, shifting himself from behind her, and steadily got off the bonnet of the car, picking her up in a one-person lift, his left hand under her knees and the right hand around her back. Their eyes met in shared awareness, hers' giving him unspoken permission to rock her world. He sits her down on the left side of the backseat; she scoots on her butt to the far right, giving him room to enter the car. He creeps into the car, over her legs, up to her chest, with the posture of a silverback in heat.

His body aligned over hers, his weight supported by hands pressed against the seat. She reaches up, running her fingers along his well-defined chest, as she starts to undress him in a heated tussle, pulling the T-shirt over his broad shoulders then off over his head.

He pulled backward, resting on his knees, to unbutton and remove his shorts. He reaches under her sundress and slides off her plum-colored thong. Swiftly he maneuvered himself so that he sat beneath her, pulling her onto him in a straddle, her groin perfectly positioned over his member.

She used her hand to slip him inside her. Her head swung back in reflex, and her eyes closed, deeply inhaling as he entered her, forcefully extracting a soul surging gasp.

She began a slow rotation of her hips, gradually increasing the speed as her stimulation amplified. The edges of her yellow dress caressed his naked thighs as she ground into him. Ripping open the top buttons of her sundress, he exposed her slight slopes. He groped her left breast, just a handful, taking it into his pleasantly, warm mouth, and nibbled on her rose-pink nipple, caressing it with his tongue until it was hard as a rock, making her yearn for the completion his tempting brown eyes had promised.

Keaton assaulted her senses for several minutes, utilizing mouth, tongue, and hands with intent to rile her wild side. He was quite successful, but then, he usually was when it came to handling her. It was a kenotic connection between them; their bodies were entirely receptive to each other's will.

She threw her arms around the back of his neck; her hips grinding then transitioning into brisk bouncing, her moans grew louder. Her warmth shrouded his manhood. It vigorously drew him in and, at the same time, pressed him out to the rhythm of her bounce. As his erection swelled to an eruption, he gripped both her hips in a firm hold, forcing more of him deeper inside her, thrusting harder, faster, wilder, till he reached the peak of explosion. "Oh…Fuckkkkk!" He groaned, deep from the pit of his stomach, tightening his grip on her waist as his release slammed through her, undone by her passion. She followed suit, screaming his name, digging her short nails to the back of his neck, pressing her forehead into his, exploding in orgasm, melting into him.

Unable to catch a steady breath, they stayed in position, gasping in shallow pants. "You do not know what you do to me," Keaton uttered between breaths, placing his head onto her bare chest. "I am completely yours forever." She pressed her chin into the top of his head. Her heart fluttered at his words. "You already have all of me," she sniffled quietly, tears threatening to spill from her eyes. "Tomorrow, when you leave, you will be taking a part of me with you, a sacred part of me that I have never trusted anyone else with—my heart. The agony of parting with you, no matter how short or long of a time, still steadily eats away at my core. This time the pain is more significant, but I am comforted by your promise, by our love. I'm looking forward to the insurmountable joy of our reunion. I am confident it will surpass the pain. I love you, Keaton Dawson, more than the bad days ahead of us. I love you more than any fight we will ever have, more than the impending distance between us, more than any obstacle that could try and come between us. So, hurry back to me, and make me whole again, because the person I am when I am with you will never be the same without you".

Her words quietly made an engravement on his heart. Her love and sacrifice only confirmed what he knew from the beginning; she was his soulmate. He reached into the pocket of his shorts, retrieving the little black box. Their eyes shared meaningful contact. He removed a flawless princess cut diamond ring and took her hand, sliding it ardently onto her ring finger as his eyes flickered upward to capture her gaze. "No matter what happens, no matter where I am, no matter who I am with; no matter what trials we undergo, this ring is my promise to you that I will always love you. I will always find my way back to you. Because you are mine, and I am yours forever."

What else was there to say? The moment said it all. They wrapped each other in a tender embrace, one that meant goodbye but promised forever.

CHAPTER 16

December 1st, 2018

"Mom, what are you doing?" Keaton asked in an irritated tone. He had exited his bedroom and caught wind of Celia bustling with a stack of decorative pillows and cushions heading to the guestroom directly across from his bedroom.

"She arrives today!" Celia responded anxiously, pushing her way through the guestroom door, with the stack of pillows and cushions hindering her view. "By the way, why aren't you dressed? Aren't you picking her up from the airport?" She unloaded the mound of pillows and cushions on the bed and turned to face Keaton, who was now standing at the guest bedroom doorway, looking at her with a querying expression.

"Mom, why are you doing this? Why do you need to do this? You have been fixing this bedroom for weeks now. What else do you want to put in here? If I did not know any better, I would think you expect a dignitary of some sort. You seem too excited to welcome a total stranger into our home, considering the circumstance. Are you on my side or hers?" His eyebrows knitted.

"Keaton, stop being childish. There are no taking sides in this situation. You are getting married to Lia for an important reason. She deserves a warm welcome, considering what she's sacrificing to agree to this marriage. I mean, she is leaving her home, her family, to move here and live with you for an entire year, to make this marriage believable, to the press and all the other speculators in the company. It would be best if you gave her a break. As badly as you want her to be, she is not the enemy." Celia flashed him a reproachful look, then turned to arrange the decorative pillows on the bed.

Keaton scoffed, folding his hands, casting her a skeptical look. "Mom, I don't believe you. Is she the only one that's making sacrifices? What about me, what about your son, aren't I making sacrifices to accommodate this marriage? Something that I didn't even ask for in the first place, I…."

"Enough, Keaton!" Celia snapped, resting one hand on her head in an 'I've had enough gesture. "You are giving me a headache. Look, I do not wish to argue with you anymore on this topic, this marriage is happening, and we all must be adults about it and accept it. I am trying to do that, and you should at least make an effort to do the same. I am anxious, not because I am happy about the situation, but as a mother, I do not have the heart or reason to be callous or cold towards this girl. She has been placed into this situation against her will, just as you were. However, unlike you, she has chosen to make the best out of it. She wants to experience this marriage as a meaningful one, despite its intention. It is not such an unreasonable request as you would like to consider it if you think about it. In reality, for this marriage to pass as authentic in the public eyes, you two need to live together and be together as husband and wife. In some ways, you could not avoid the traditional aspects of this marriage, even though it's a contract. You need to get rid of this thinking that she is forcing herself on you because it is not the case." Celia patted her hair, readjusting her posture to calm herself. Keaton stood fixed in the doorway and focused on the space in the air between them. He did not want to make further eye contact as he knew what she said was the truth.

"As for what I'm doing...." Celia continued, organizing some cushions on the steel blue chesterfield sofa at the foot of the bed, "I am putting the finishing touches on the bedroom. I want her to feel warm and welcomed when she arrives. Based on her color selections for the wedding, I figured these colors might be some of her favorites, so I had placed an order for these decorative cushions and pillows, that thankfully, just arrived today. A little personal touch, that's all it is, to make her feel at home." She smiled with contentment, stepping two paces back to get a full view of the whole room. "Now, you need to go get dressed and head to the airport; her plane will be arriving soon, and don't even think about letting Jaxen pick her up without you. You need to be there when she arrives. Your presence will give her some confidence that you are committed to upholding her terms. We do not want this starting off on a sour note—OK?" Her eyes brightened, relaxing the vertical wrinkle between her eyebrows. Her lips smiled slightly. She tapped him on the shoulder as she walked by.

Keaton did not respond and stood still for a moment after she had left. He took a deep breath and walked across the floor to his bedroom to get dressed. Some moments later, he got downstairs, where Celia was sitting in the sitting area having a glass of wine.

"Is that what you are wearing?" She asked, scrutinizing Keaton's outfit as he walked by.

He looked at her in consternation, "Is there something wrong with what I'm wearing, mom? I am going to the airport for a pick-up. I'm not traveling."

Celia snickered a bit and took a sip of wine, "Don't forget I know you very well, and I know that you have intentionally dressed this way to appear unappealing to Lia. It's going to take a lot more than dressing uncoordinated to look unattractive. You would also need to get rid of that striking face and that incredibly perfect body." She chuckled mockingly, finishing the wine in her glass in another sip. Keaton shook his head and walked away with a muffled laugh.

Two hours later, he arrived at the airport alone. Celia had intentionally sent Jaxen on an errand so that he would not be available to chauffer Keaton. He stared at the name card on the passenger's seat that Celia had printed with Lia's full name. "Mom is just impossible," he grumbled under his breath as he grabbed the card and exited the car.

Lia's plane had already landed, so he knew she would be in the arrival terminal in another 30 minutes or so. He leaned against the car, watching the bustling bystanders from the edge of his vision, momentarily checking his watch to gauge the time to enter the arrival terminal.

Twenty minutes in, he walked into the terminal and reluctantly held up the name card, all the while muttering in his head how ridiculous he looked when suddenly his eyes flickered towards a familiar face. It was the face from the video she had sent. He was surprised he still remembered her green eyes.

The slender figure, about six feet in height, walked towards him, a blooming smile formed across her face as she recognized her name on the card. He could not have guessed she was this tall from the video with her sitting behind a desk or was it the heels? He continued to stare in her direction, in an analyzing gaze. She had that Scandinavian elegance about her; you could immediately tell from a distance that she was a foreigner. She could easily be mistaken for a Victoria's Secret model, strikingly attractive, an in-your-face kind of beauty with a great body. Her make-up kept natural; she was quite feminine and took clear pride in her appearance. She appeared poised in a sophisticated and fashionable way. She wore a delicately black silk-satin cowl-neck camisole under a perfectly fitted blush-pink, open front blazer. Matching ultra-slim tuxedo trousers hung slightly above her ankle, accentuated by classy, pointy-toed, red bottom, leopard print pumps. Her accessories were small and discrete but of high-quality gold, a Cartier bracelet, and diamond earrings that highlighted her fair complexion.

He lowered the name card as she got within arm's length. "You must be Keaton?" She asked with an outstretched hand. Her green eyes radiated urbanity and uncompromising intelligence. Adjusting his posture to seem unfazed by her beauty, he extends his hand to meet hers in a casual handshake, trying hard to conceal the involuntary admiration in his eyes.

"And you must be Lia?" He responded, strengthening his voice to a fruity tone, intense in a pleasant way. She nodded in response as her beaming smile transitioned to her eyes.

They stood there for a moment in an awkward silence that Lia broke.

"Now that we know each other, shall we go?" She asked.

He shook his head as if to snap himself out of a daze. His hands were gesturing to her the direction to go as he led the way. She pulled along a beige carry-on roller with a gold handle while a black chic tote bag hung effortlessly on her left arm.

"Is that all the luggage you brought?" Keaton asked as he took the carry-on roller from her at the car.

"I shipped my things ahead," she responded, "They are already here in paid storage. I will see to them later; for now, all I need for a few days is in my carry-on." She helped herself to the passenger side at the front of the car, not waiting on him to open the door for her. He shook his head at her action with a cynical look.

"How long is the drive back to your place?" She asked as he entered the car.

"Roughly two hours," he responded, securing his seat belt.

"Promise you won't make this an awkward two hours. I can already see that you are quite uncomfortable, but there's no need. I don't bite." She glanced over at him from the corner of her eyes. She was a Norwegian woman, straightforward, and didn't hold back her thoughts.

"Why do you think I'm uncomfortable?" Keaton questioned in denial.

"Because it's written all over your face," she giggled, "If you're any more uncomfortable, your face is going to explode. How about this, you tell me what your favorite genre of music is, and I'll find a playlist of songs in that genre on my phone. We can listen to it on the ride to your home and make conversation by telling me which songs are your favorite from the playlist and why. That way, you will be comfortable listening to your favorite music, and I will learn something about you along the way. How about that?"

"Mu—, Mu — Music I like?" He stuttered, scratching the side of his head as if he were genuinely thinking about it. His idea was to really stay mute the entire way. He had a plan to give her the cold shoulder and not let her in. He wanted no misunderstanding about their relationship, kill any false hope of them having any form of realness in the approaching fake marriage.

Keaton glanced over at her and met her awaiting bright eyes, the eyes of an optimist, the kind of eyes that are almost spellbinding, that makes you act before you think, and just like that, he forgot about the plan.

"I—, I'm not partial when it comes to music. I generally listen to whatever goes with my mood. But for argument's sake, let's say R&B since that genre is kind of popular now. I can vibe to some good R&B". His face bore a meaningless smirk as he pulled out of the parking lot.

"R&B it is; I'll find a playlist." She reached into her tote bag and pulled out her phone and tapped through it for a few seconds.

"Ah, here is a good one," she said with glee, moving forward to pair her phone with the car's Bluetooth. Instantaneously Bruno Mars and Cardi B's song, *Finesse*, came blasting through the speakers. Keaton scrambled to adjust the volume on the car's control while Lia lowered the volume on her phone. The short-lived fright made them both chuckle. They were both apologizing excessively and giggling sheepishly. Who knew unsuspectingly loud music blasting through the speakers could be such a good icebreaker?

"How about this one?" She asked, expressively happy. Keaton kept his gaze straight ahead on the road. The residue from his hilarity at the situation lingered on his face into a relaxed smile.

"I wouldn't say *Finesse* is one of my favorites, but I don't have anything against it. It's a great song. I can feel it."

"I think I love this song."

"Why, because you are always 'dripping' in *finesse*?" he teased, quoting the lyrics.

"You said it, not me. Does that mean you've noticed my *finesse* but refused to compliment me?" Her voice got lighter, almost flirtatious.

She caught him off guard; not only did he notice her conspicuous perfection and intricate details, but he had also made a conscious decision at the airport terminal not to acknowledge it.

"I—I, I mean, you're...." He floundered, not knowing quite what to say.

"I was just kidding," she quipped, noticing his awkwardness by her remark. "I wasn't trying to put you on the spot. I was only having some fun with you. How about this song?" she asked, politely changing the subject, and referring to *Pray for Me* by Kendrick Lamar and The Weekend.

He felt a bit out of sorts as his mind tried to switch from its floundering, redirecting his attention to her question.

"I don't know. I think I have a love-hate relationship with this song."

"Why so?" She asked.

"Well—, the moody and broodiness is a little off-putting for me. But on the other hand, the message behind it is interesting. It's quite intense, with themes of loss, loyalty, sacrifice, and redemption; these resonate with me, especially as of late as it relates to being willing to make difficult sacrifices for the greater good."

She glanced over at him in brief silence; his words ran deep, she could relate, making difficult sacrifices for the greater good was not unfamiliar in her life. She had been making sacrifices ever since her mom died. She had sacrificed her adolescent years to take care of her grieving father, never having the opportunity to enjoy her youth nor to have a social life. She had to take on laden responsibilities in SANCORP from a young age to honor her mother's dying wish. And now that her father was no more, there was no one left to shoulder the burdens with her.

Looking back in the moment, she thought about all the sacrifices she has made for the greater good, for SANCORP. Sacrificed love, self, and now even the chance of a real first marriage. It was not so easy being the only heir to an empire. When her father told her about the contract marriage, he termed it a "short-term sacrifice for long-term projects." Accepting the marital contract on her terms was a rear privilege. Whether or not she agreed to it was irrelevant; as long as she made a choice beneficial to the greater good of SANCORP, that was the only valid option in her father's eyes. Now here she was, sitting across from someone in the same situation, who shared the same thoughts as her; it made her feel safe, understood, and in a weird way, validated and appreciated. She thought it was pitying that he was directing his resentment on the wrong person. If only he understood that we were pawns in the same chess game.

In her mind, she thought over their predicament. *Our fathers played this chess game of business, creating generational wealth long before we understood what legacy preservation meant. For years, they have been forming strategies and establishing processes to sustain both wealth and values for many generations. We are their legacies; the future of SANCORP and TrueTek rests with us. We are the pawns left to carry on the mantle, to complete what they failed against the hands of time.*

Individually a pawn may be weak, but together they create a force that is near equal in strength to the queen. That is what you and I are, a force to reckon with, for SANCORP and TrueTek. A force coined by our fathers for the greater good.

Undeniably, you and I have sacrificed a lot, but there is so much to gain in the end. I hope you can see it that way. I hope you can understand that I am not the enemy. I hope you can let go of the antipathy I am sensing you want to have towards me. I hope you can give this a fair chance. She glanced at him, wishing she had spoken her thoughts. But it wasn't the right time.

CHAPTER 17

"Are you okay?" Keaton asked Lia. "Yes, I'm fine." She replied, shifting her gaze to look outside the window.

"Are you sure," Keaton pressed, "you zoned out on me there for a moment? Was it something that I said?"

"What you said just had me thinking, that's all. It's nothing serious; are we almost there?"

"Yeah, we're pulling onto the estate now." He glanced over at her, still staring out the window, and he knew that whatever he had said had affected her more than she would admit. At that moment, he felt apologetic and worried about her, what was happening inside that head of hers. He was curious. In his thoughts, he had realized an even bigger problem. His plan to be cold towards her was slowly falling apart. There was something about her that was warm, inviting, an aura that naturally attracted positive energy. Was he in over his head thinking he was in control? He questioned himself as he pulled into the driveway of the estate. *I need to reconsider this,* he thought. *I cannot let her get to me.*

"Were here," Keaton announced, stopping the car in front of the houses' main entrance. He exited and walked around to open her door. Although they had connected briefly on the journey, she seemed to have regressed. As she got out of the car, she kept her face straight ahead, avoiding eye contact as if he were not there. *Maybe it is for the best,* he thought. *That is what*

I wanted anyway; the less communication we share, the better for everyone.

Jared, the butler, returned to the door with an enthused Celia following closely behind. With arms open to give a hug, Celia walked briskly over to meet Lia and embraced her warmly. She hugged her like she had known her for ages.

"Good heavens, you are stunning?" She exclaimed, her voice high pitched, gradually pulling herself from the embrace to better examine Lia.

Lia's green eyes lit up once more, and a fragment of her earlier joyous mood had returned. "Thank you, Mrs. Dawson," she politely giggled. "You flatter me."

"No flattery at all, you look amazing. By the way, call me Celia. Come on, let me take you inside, you must be exhausted, and jet-lagged. You've been on a plane for eight hours; you must need rest and something proper to eat."

Celia took Lia's hand, gently tugging Lia along by her side. Keaton shook his head. He was not surprised; that was how his mom was with everyone, cheerful and warm. He took Lia's pulley from the boot of the car and followed behind.

Inside, Celia had Lia seated in the sitting room while she returned with a glass of juice in hand. "Here, have something to drink."

Lia smiled and courteously took the glass of juice.

"Can I get you anything to eat?"

"No, Mrs. Dawson, I had something on the plane. I am not quite hungry now. But thank you."

"Okay, I have prepared a lovely room for you; I hope you'll be comfortable here."

"You have a lovely home, Mrs. Dawson, I already feel welcomed and comfortable just sitting here. Thank you."

"Aren't you a darling?" Celia giggled, sitting on the couch across from her. "I am happy you feel welcomed. I wouldn't have it any other way, and remember, you can call me Celia. Mrs. Dawson sounds a bit too formal; don't you think?"

"Sure," Lia replied with a genuine smile, taking a sip from the glass.

Keaton stood at the doorway of the sitting area, ping-ponging his gaze between his mom and Lia.

"I've put your bag in the bedroom upstairs," he interjected. "When you are ready, mom will show you to your room." He tapped his fingers on the side of the doorjamb before walking away.

"Did he say bag?" Celia asked, facing Lia, "Did you only travel with one bag?"

"I shipped my items ahead of my travel date. They are already here in paid storage. I'll make arrangements later to have them delivered here."

"Oh, oh, that makes sense. So why did you travel commercial? I thought you would have flown private."

Lia tittered a bit before responding. "It's just something I wanted to do, a decision I made on my own; in a sense, it felt liberating."

"You young people," Celia laughed. "I can never understand you all. Oh well, let me not keep you here too long. I want you to freshen up and get some rest so that you can join us for dinner this evening."

She got up from the couch, and Lia followed suit. "This way," Celia said, leading the way.

Upstairs, Celia showed Lia to the bedroom. "Keaton is right across the hall; you can let him or me know if you need anything. And I hope you'll find everything to your liking."

"It is perfect, Mrs. Dawson." Lia replied, "I—I mean Celia. Thanks again for doing all this; I do feel at home."

"I'm happy you do," Celia beamed, crossing her palms at the center of her chest. I'll leave you to it then. Make sure to get some rest." She exited the room, closing the door quietly behind her.

Lia rested her tote bag on the couch at the foot of the bed and strode across the bedroom, admiring the décor. She was impressed, subtle, yet chic; someone certainly tried to make an impression, one she very much appreciated. She took a deep breath with a smile on her face. A lovely calming Lia-smile, at ease with where she would be spending the next year of her life. It was a good start.

Downstairs, Celia met Keaton in the kitchen, seated around the island eating a sandwich.

"I thought you had left?" Celia asked, walking towards him.

"Why would I leave? I'm starving. I haven't had anything to eat since breakfast."

Celia walked around to the other side of the island, where she was directly facing Keaton. She rested her elbows on the countertop of the island, both palms cupping the sides of her face. Her eyes could barely contain her excitement, which made Keaton give her a 'you-are-crazy gaze'.

"So," she spoke in hushed tones, "Isn't she gorgeous? I mean, I knew Scandinavian women are generally attractive, but she is definitely on top of the list of most beautiful women I've met in my life. I'm surprised she's not already married."

"Mom," Keaton sighed, resting the half-eaten sandwich on the plate.

"What? You can't deny that she is beautiful".

"No one is denying that mom; I'm just not making it a big deal like you are. Do you remember that this is supposed to be a contract? I want to keep it that way? Discussing my business partner's appearance in my kitchen is not my idea of proper business etiquette."

"Oh, cut the crap Keaton," Celia rebuked. "You need to stop being so uptight about this and live in the moment."

"Mom, I just want to have this sandwich in peace. I'm already doing what everyone else wants; just let me be, ***please.***"

"Oh, alright, eat your sandwich. But do not forget to check on Lia when you get back upstairs. Just to make sure she's finding everything alright".

"Mom, she's an adult; I'm sure she'll be fine. Besides, if she needs anything, I am sure she will ask. She's pretty outspoken as far as I can see." Keaton took the plate with his sandwich and walked to exit the kitchen.

"And loosen up!" Celia yelled as he walked away. "You are going to pop a blood vessel if you continue walking around with all that tension in your face."

Keaton held his head straight, not acknowledging what she had yelled. At his bedroom door, he paused and glanced across the hall to where Lia was staying. He contemplated for a while whether he should check on her or not. He went inside his room, put the sandwich down, and walked across the hall. At her door, he attempted to knock, then hesitated.

What am I doing? He whispered, *Am I yielding to mom's advice? Why do I need to check on her? It's not like she is a child. Or am I the one acting like a child?* He swung his head back with a sigh. Forget it; *why am I overthinking? I am just courteous*, he thought. He then lightly knocked on the door.

"Just a second!" Lia yelled from inside. She sounded far away. A few seconds later, the door opened. Lia appeared in a bath robe; her hair was dripping wet, clutching a bath towel in her hand.

Keaton was immediately flushed and slightly embarrassed that he had disturbed her at such a time. He pressed his right hand at the back of his neck and slightly turned his head away from her. "I'm sorry, I didn't mean to disturb you; it's just that mom wanted me to check on you."

"It's okay, I have finished anyway. And I am wearing a robe; you don't need to turn away from me as if I'm naked." She asserted with a teasing smile.

He turned his head to face her, almost in slow motion. "I'm sorry, it's just that I—"

He could not find the words; maybe because he did not know why he had looked away, he was aware she was wearing a robe when she opened the door. But somehow, his brain screamed, *look away, she is wet and naked*! And he had obliged without a second thought. Now he was mortified.

Lia tittered at his awkward pause. "It is alright; you said you are here to check on me? I am fine. As you can see, I just got out of the shower, and I am about to get dressed and take a nap. I never realized how jet-lagged I was until I got into the shower." She smiled, and her eyes twinkled.

"Oh, good, well…I'll leave you to it then. If you need anything, I'm across the hall."

"Thanks," Lia smiled, slowly closing the door as he turned to walk away.

He slipped inside his room and closed the door, self-loathing. "Why the hell am I so awkward around her," he muttered. Jamming both hands into his pockets, he stared at himself in the mirror. He glanced over at the half-eaten sandwich for which he no longer had an appetite.

Great, he thought to himself; *this day just keeps getting better.*

CHAPTER 18

He undressed, tossing his clothes on the bed, and walked into the bathroom. The warm water was soothing, yet he did not feel better. And he wondered why he was losing his usually level-headed and in-control demeanor these last few times he spoke to her. He stood under the water, face-up and eyes closed, just letting the warm shower cascade down his body while the voice inside his head reprimanded him, *get it together*.

There was a knock at the door. *God, what does mom want now,* he grumbled inaudibly.

"The door is open; come in. I'm taking a shower," he yelled. Turning off the faucet. He grabbed a towel and wrapped it around his waist. Using another to dry his hair. He heard his room door open.

"Mom, if you are here to badger me some more about checking on Lia, I already did, and she's fine. It wasn't even necessary, all I did was disturb her. Sometimes, I don't know why I even listen to you." He said in a complaining tone while walking from the bathroom to the bedroom. He met startling green eyes peering back at him. Lia stood with arms folded, an amused grin on her face.

"So, you were badgered to check on me before?" She giggled, playing into the oh-God- its-her surprised look on his face. His brain said *Lia*, but his mouth said, "Oh Fuck!"

"I...I mean, Lia?" he said, stumbling over his words. His face near fell to the floor, as his brain now realized that his mouth just blurted the word 'Fuck'.

Lia chuckled at his expense then went into placation mode. "Don't worry about it. I completely understand; you thought it was your mom who knocked—well surprise!" He stood there, afraid to say anything else.

"I'm sorry if I startled you," she continued, "but I knocked, and you said, "come in."

"Yes..., I did. How can I help?" His response was restless, his eye scanning the room for the closest location to grab a shirt, hands gripping onto the towel around his waist as if it were going to fall any minute.

Never once did Lia's eyes stare at his bare chest, though she was tempted. "Well, a moment ago, you said if I needed help with anything, I should let you know. Well, I remembered something that I will need your help with."

"Sure, what is it?" he asked, walking briskly over to the closet.

Lia turned her head away from him, noticing his uneasiness. "I will need some help arranging the delivery of my personal effects from the storage facility. I have their card," she said, stretching a business card to his direction.

He quickly pulled on a black tank and sports shorts before walking back to her. He took the card from her hand, and she turned to face him.

"Comfortable now?" She asked smilingly.

He looked at her, flashing an I-just-made-a-fool-of-myself-again smile. Then gazed at the card in his hands. "I know these guys," he said, flipping the card to look at the backside. "So, you want me to give them a call…?"

"Yes, if you don't mind. It would be best to make the arrangements since you can provide them with the address and proper directions and the day(s) best convenient for them to deliver the items. Since this is your home, I don't want to overstep."

"Yeah, I can do that. I'll contact the office tomorrow to make the arrangements, and I'll let you know afterward when they'll deliver."

"Great," Lia beamed, "well that settles that. And sorry again if I startled you, that was not my intention. I'm leaving now; you can get back to what you were doing."

Keaton faintly pursed his lips and gestured a swift bye-motion with his hand as she turned to exit the room. Walking over to the bed, he rested the business card on the nightstand and did a dead-drop on the bed. Clothes were strewn all over but he was too drained to walk them over to the laundry basket. It was not that he was physically exhausted, but was experiencing a malaise, a general feeling of discomfort and uneasiness.

He checked the time on his phone and it was almost 5:00 p.m. Then it hit him; he had not texted Katie all day. He told her he would so he wrote her a quick message.

Hey baby, I hope you are not mad at me; I have had a crazy day. I know you are doing great and that you are moving forward to the finals. I have been watching the live streams of the championships every chance I get. Let me know if you are awake so that I can give you a call. If not, text me when you get this, and we'll talk when we can. Love you—my Forever.

Some time had passed, and there was no response from Katie. He naturally fell asleep, lying on the bed in the quiet, with cool circulating air and dimmed lighting.

Keaton woke up a little after an hour later to hunger pangs gnawing at his gut. He grabbed his phone and headed out. When he got to the staircase, Celia was coming up to meet him.

"Mom...."

"Keaton, I was just coming to get you and Lia. Dinner is ready".

"I was just heading down."

"What about Lia?" Celia asked, with kind concern, "Is she still asleep? Chef Bourdine has prepared an exquisite meal for us. I've also had him prepare a few Norwegian dishes for Lia; she's going to love it.... Well, don't just stand there; go get Lia!"

"Mom, didn't you say you were coming to get us? Do not let me stop you; you should get her. I'll meet you both downstairs."

Celia gave him a critical look as he walked past her. "So, you're joining us for dinner wearing sports shorts and a tank?" She asked before he got far. "Please go change into something proper before you sit at that table." Keaton stopped in his tracks, turned humbly like a chided child, and headed back up the stairs behind Celia.

Later at the dining room, Celia happily walked in holding Lia's hand, seating her in the chair next to Keaton, then sat on the opposite side facing them.

"You look beautiful, Lia; I adore that dress," Celia complimented, setting her wine glass for a pour.

With her usual candid smile, Lia replied, "Thanks, Mrs. Daw...Celia. You look beautiful yourself."

"Do I? Thank you," Celia smiled, glancing over at Keaton, flashing her gaze back and forth between him and Lia, an unspoken request for Keaton to compliment Lia.

Keaton read her eyes and released a slightly noticeable sigh.

"You both look beautiful," he chimed in respectfully, obliging his mother's silent request. "Shall we eat?"

Celia sent him a gratified glance and signaled the staff to plate the dishes.

"Lia," Celia said, "I requested a few Norwegian dishes for you this evening. Chef Bourdine has made a delectable Sodd. I believe he has paired it with Norwegian flatbread on the side..." She looked over at Chef Bourdine for validation, who endorsed her statement with a polite nod.

"And Pinnekjøtt...," she continued, "to be served with pureed Swedish turnip."

"That is very thoughtful of you Celia, I have not had Sodd for quite a while, but it used to be a favorite back home when mom was alive. I am looking forward to tasting it again."

"Great, so let's get to it then," Celia responded cheerfully, picking up her salad fork. They flashed polite smiles at each other across the table as they delved into the appetizers.

Celia was overjoyed when the Sodd dish was served, intently watching as Lia took the first bite. "How is it?" She asked in a mirthful tone before Lia even had time to swallow.

"It is quite tasty," Lia replied with a satiated grin. "It sure brings back memories. Her eyes then got reminiscent. "There's a funny story surrounding this dish in my home.... Two days after my 16th birthday, my mom hosted a confirmation ceremony for my uncle, my mom's only brother. He had just turned fifteen, and for Norwegians, confirmation is an important event, marking the transition from childhood to adulthood. So, it was a big deal for my uncle, as he wanted to be an adult ***so*** bad. He was never my favorite, mainly because we were in the same age group, so I refused to call him uncle then, and we would typically butt heads a lot. He would always find an opportunity to tattle on me to my mom over the simplest of things. You could say that we were sworn enemies when we were younger.

That day he was so full of himself, I could not stand it. We had a tiff, and the little brat accidentally broke the new phone I had just gotten for my birthday. Mom had me help her in the kitchen. I was in charge of preparing the carrots and potatoes for the Sodd. When it was time to serve, mom brought out the first few bowls of Sodd for grandpa and dad. I dished the bowl of Sodd for my uncle. I wanted to teach that little bugger a lesson...." She cackled as she continued to speak. "I sliced over a dozen Bulgarian carrot peppers into his bowl of Sodd, perfectly disguised as carrots."

"When he took the first bite...." She busted out laughing before she could finish the story..."about 30 seconds after he swallowed the first mouthful of peppers he thought were carrots, he was running around the room, freaking out—bouncing off the walls. He was sweating; tears were coming from his eyes. He was bawling, "it's too pepper, it's too hot!—Hot!—Hot!—Hot!" He had his hands fanning his hanging tongue like a crazy person. And what made it so hilarious is that no one else in the room knew what he was talking about because their Sodds were perfectly fine. He was red-eyed, leering at me. He alone suspected that I was the culprit...."

Everyone at the table broke out in a fit of laughter, including Keaton and even the staff. The recollected visuals had Lia laughing profusely. She was gasping for breath. Her laughter was even more contagious, mixed with her animation of the story. They were all howling in hysterics. Keaton was now in stitches, and Celia was chortling so hard she could not catch a breath.

"That's hilarious," Celia snorted, gobbling down her glass of water, her eyes teary from laughter.

"Remind me never to mess with you," Keaton joked, wiping the tears from his eyes. Their cackling gradually mellowed, creating a relaxed mood in the dining room. They conversed and cracked jokes all through dinner. Even Keaton had loosened up.

Celia glanced at both of them, pleased at how effortlessly they were starting to get along, and secretly hoped it would continue past the night, not only for Keaton but for her too. It was a breath of fresh air, being able to laugh so hard since Keegan died. At that moment, she honestly believed that Lia's presence in their lives was so much more than a contract. Instead, she told herself, maybe it was predestined, ordained by God.

CHAPTER 19

In the following days, things seemed to be going a lot smoother. Keaton felt less tense around Lia and graduated from his usual ambivalent and apprehensive behavior to a more composed diplomatic approach. He agreed with Celia that he could be civilized about the situation. And not see Lia as a villain. For now, she was a friend, a business partner, and they got along perfectly as such.

Now that Lia had received all her personal effects and had settled in at the estate. It was time to focus on the impending wedding, which was approaching fast. December 16th was literally in ten days. The wedding was to be held in the garden of the backyard.

With the press on the guest list, Celia was meticulous in every detail of the planning, adamant in her decision for a comprehensive wedding rehearsal to avoid any possibility for catastrophe on the big day.

A wedding rehearsal was not a priority for Keaton, but he was willing to play his part. He was inclined to cooperate with anything to get things moving along to get back to his life with Katie. On the other hand, Lia was with Celia every step of the preparation; she was living in the moment and enjoying the experience of a soon-to-be bride, pre-wedding jitters and all, no matter how short-lived it was meant to be.

As the final preparations came together, Celia's worries subsided gradually in the week before the wedding. The decorations were in order; she was less nervous Keaton would stumble over his words during the ceremony or make a fool out of himself during the kiss. A series of carefully organized rehearsals had quelled those fears. Vows were ready; the kiss practiced, everything down to the first dance had to appear seemingly natural for the press.

Keaton did not have a specific worry at this stage, just a general feeling of anxiety and nerves. Not the general stress and nerves one experiences before nuptials. Rather, his angst and nervousness resulted from him wanting to have the day come and go like a distant memory. He just wanted to 'get it over with.'

Lia's anxiety level also rose as the date drew closer, genuine angst and nerves, as is natural, in the days leading up to her big day, which had her questioning the decision to wed.

The two had been cordial leading up to the date, but Lia wanted a bit more than pleasantry from Keaton, especially at this point. She wanted to share how she felt and explain her emotions to her 'soon-to-be husband' as real partners would. But she knew Keaton's stance and did not want to spoil the genial relationship they now had. Keeping her thoughts bottled up inside was not doing her any good. She needed someone to talk to, someone she could trust.

Her terms to maintain traditional aspects of the wedding and marriage were agreed to by Keaton. Up to this point, he has kept to the agreement. He was giving her the wedding day she desired, written vows, and even bought a ring. He was prepared to wait for her at the end of the aisle before God and man. The rest was left for fate to decide if they could spend their lives together as husband and wife beyond the contract. His ability to like or love her had to happen naturally. It did not matter that she was starting to develop feelings for him. What mattered was, did he have any feelings for her? Those were the things she wanted to be honest about, to discuss. But until she was sure he had feelings for her, she had no grounds to push her agenda, no basis to discuss how she was starting to feel towards him if he did not feel the same.

For months she has been waiting to marry this man, and though the reasons for the marriage were by no means romantic and lacked the promise of a happily-ever-after, she was still hopeful. Now that she was face-to-face with him, and he had checked all the boxes of someone she could spend the rest of her life with, it was only natural that her emotions would start to reflect what was brewing inside her heart. And then there was the kiss …the kisses. Three, to be exact.

For all three rehearsals, they had engaged in a passionate traditional kiss. Though Keaton seemed nonchalant after the fact, those kisses have been the turning point for Lia. He had kissed her three times, and each time she realized that she will never have enough. His kisses spoke to the passion deep within her soul. They evoked visions of a beautiful forever, and in those moments, she precisely knew how fitting they were for each other.

But she seemed the only one who was feeling this way; she could not see that *I've-fallen-for-you* spark in Keaton's eyes. This whole time he had been like an exceptional actor playing his role from a script. It made her question; how he could have kissed her like that and felt nothing. Was he that cold inside? Were the kisses all for show? In the back of her mind, she kept reminding herself that it was not real, at least for him.

She sat under the pergola in the pre-decorated garden, lost deep in thought. Two days had passed since the last rehearsal, and she was still hung up on the way he had kissed her. It felt so real. *Was he playing with my emotions?* She thought. *Does he already know that I have fallen for him? Was this his way of punishing me for wanting to change a prearranged contract marriage into a traditional one? Was he giving me a taste of what he was prepared for me never to have? Was he kissing me this way on purpose, to make me fall for him only to break my heart in the end? Was it payback?*

She was so deep in thought that Keaton had called her twice without her hearing. It was not until he gently tapped her on the shoulder, did she realize that he had been standing there.

"What's going on with you?" He asked, handing her a glass of juice. "When I came back, I did not see you in the house, and I know mom is not around, so I went looking for you. I have been standing here for almost a minute, calling your name. You were so dazed that you could not hear me. What exactly is going on? And please do not say it is nothing, because clearly, you are worried about something. You have been like this since the rehearsals."

He sat across from her, waiting for her explanation. His eyes had a genuine concern.

She thought about what she would say at the moment. Here he was, the one person she wanted to discuss how she was feeling, but at the same time, she did not want to risk pushing him away with a love confession that might be too soon. *Am I overthinking?* she thought, glancing at his waiting eyes. *If I ask about the kiss now, he could always say that it was not real. He could also deny having any feelings for me. What should I do if I confess my emotions only to receive unrequited love? It was too soon to tell him;* She thought, taking a sip of the juice. She pondered quickly for something else to say.

"Am …, Its just work…" she said, looking down at the glass of juice in her hand, afraid her eyes would unveil the truth. "Since dad passed away six months ago, I have taken a lot on my plate. Between managing the ongoing projects he left, and being the CEO, it has been a handful. Now that I am attempting to work remotely, I am feeling a bit out of my element. But I am sorting it out. I will be fine. EVERYTHING SHOULD BE FINE once I get my office space sorted and my tech team works out the communication logistics.

"What do you mean?" Keaton asked, seeking more information. "Office space…?"

"I am in charge of all of SANCORP's operations. I need an office space here in New York to coordinate and manage these projects daily.

My tech team has been working on a virtual presence technology software that will enable seamless communication channels with my team just as if I were there. Virtually, through holographic technology, I will be able to walk through all the departments and the manufacturing plants, inspect the production lines, and interact with my colleagues in real-time in their individual spaces as I would typically do. This holographic option would be better than having a traditional fragmented virtual meeting where everyone has to be stationed around a computer." She took another sip of the juice, raising her head slightly to read the follow-up question on his face.

"Oh, I'm familiar with that technology. So how is it going? Do you need help finding an office space?"

"No, actually, SANCORP has several subsidiary companies in the US, including here in New York. I have already organized an office space within one of the larger subsidiaries in Lower Manhattan. Once the tech team here and back in Norway finalizes the communication set up and the wedding is complete, I'll be going into the office regularly to keep up with the operations."

"I'm glad we had this little chat," Keaton said with a weirdly satisfied grin. "I've been wanting to ask how you had planned on managing your company remotely for a year; now I know the answer. And now that I know what has been worrying you, it is perfectly understandable. It is a lot to handle; I get it. If you need any help at all, just let me know."

He got up from his chair and gave her a reassuring tap on the shoulder. She looked up at him with a deflecting smile. "Don't stay out here too long," he said as he left. "—It tends to get pretty cold out this time of year."

"I'll be in shortly," she replied, finishing the rest of her drink. Deep inside, she wished the conversation was about what was genuinely worrying her. But it was not all bad. She was happy to talk to Keaton about anything, more pleased that he showed concern and cared enough to notice her worry. The thought triggered a tender smile across her face. She picked up the closed book beside her, *Emily Post's Wedding Etiquette*, that she was supposed to be reading and made her way back to the house.

Inside, she entered the kitchen to clean the empty drinking glass, where she met Keaton again sitting at the kitchen island on his phone. She smiled at him and walked over to the sink to rinse the glass.

He looked over at her, resting his phone down. "By the way, where is your uncle, wasn't he supposed to be here by now. He's the one walking you down the aisle, right?"

She dried the glass, shutting it away in the cupboard above her, then turned to face him.

"He arrived two hours ago; he's out with your mom. I thought you knew…."

"I should have known, typical of mom, to do something like that. Isn't your uncle exhausted from his trip, he's barely arrived, and mom has him out already…"

"Actually, he's the one who couldn't wait to go into the city." Lia corrected with a smile, "He's returning to Norway the day after the wedding, so he's making the best of his short trip. As far as I know, he's only been to New York once before, with dad and me, and it was a business trip, so we didn't get to do or see much on the leisure side of things. I guess this time he's making the best out of it."

"Why is he returning to Norway so soon?" Keaton asked.

"Because he is the one overseeing things in the company for me, at least for now until I get things set up here. Primarily he is now the chief operating officer (COO) for SANCORP. Responsible for overseeing the marketing and sales, human resources, research and development, and other operations. Until I settle in, he's also my eyes and ears in SANCORP as the acting CEO. With my physical absence, his presence in the company is paramount at this time. It is not convenient for him to stay away for too long." She walked around the island to sit on the stool next to Keaton.

He shuffled a bit on his stool as she sat. "So, you guys aren't sworn enemies anymore? I mean since that Bulgarian carrot pepper incident." He chuckled at the memory of the joke she told during dinner.

She giggled. "We were kids back then; our childish differences are no longer relevant. We grew up together, more like brother and sister due to our closeness in age. He is the only close family I have left. When my maternal grandparents passed away, mom took him in and raised him, as he is her only sibling. He and I went to the same schools, the same universities, we were both groomed to take our respective positions in the company. My father has two sisters, but I have never been close to those aunts. They got married in their twenties and moved to their husband's countries. I believe one lives in London and the other in Australia. They have their own families and married wealthy husbands. I have never seen them much throughout my childhood. In a sense, my uncle, mom's brother, is the only close relative I have left since my parents passed away. Now we are as thick as thieves. He is very protective of me like an older brother, even though I'm a year older."

"That's amazing…." Keaton commended, with sheer admiration in his eye. "It's remarkable how young you both are; and are successfully running a billion-dollar manufacturing company across Europe like seasoned veterans. I mean, you are twenty-five years old, and CEO, and he is what…twenty-four and COO. Hats off to you both; it's fascinating".

She glanced at him sideways with an appreciative look in her eyes. "But you know, we never had a choice. Ever since we were young, our schooling, mentorships, internships were all preparation for what we are today. My parents made sure that we ate, slept, breathed, and lived SANCORP. My parents founded SANCORP together, and my mom worked side by side with my dad until the day she died. She was the COO, and my father was the CEO. My uncle and I have been groomed to replace them. Who we are today is exactly how my parents intended it to be. I'm sure they are happy wherever they are."

"And what about you?" she continued. "You are no different from us; you are also incredibly young, only twenty-seven, and the sole heir, the president of a multi-national conglomerate. I am sure that everything you have done along the way, your education, accolades, and training, have prepared you for this day. Even what we are doing now, this marriage, it's all for our companies. Our legacies. Our families. Admittedly, we are the same. We shoulder great responsibilities, we have a legacy to preserve, and we will do whatever it takes, whether we like it or not, to preserve what our parents built for us, to preserve it for the next generation."

He looked at her with agreeing eyes and a settling smile. What she said could not be more accurate. They were the same, bounded by responsibility; they had little to no choices in the things they had to do. It was a bittersweet life. Bitter, because they have never really had complete freedom to live the way they wanted. For the rest of their lives, they would have to shoulder the responsibility for the success or failure of their companies. But at the same time, there was some sweetness in the mix; financial security, stability, and after all the sacrifices, there would be a silver lining at the end of the tunnel. The day would come when they could genuinely be happy in the lives they intended for themselves—all in due time.

CHAPTER 20

December 16th, 2018: Wedding Day

It was the morning of the wedding, and everyone was up from the crack of dawn as if they had not slept the entire night. Celia, especially, was up from 4:00 a.m., running around as busy as a bee. Keaton and Lia stayed in their rooms for the most part after breakfast. At the same time, Celia supervised the finishing touches for the noon ceremony. Leif, Lia's uncle, could not get enough of the property and was out and about as soon as the sun came up.

At 10:00 a.m., Leif went up to Lia's room and knocked at the door. "Come in," she called from inside. Lia was sitting in front of the mirror in the middle of hair and make-up, her stylist applying the finishing touches to her hair. She was already glowing, with a smile shining bright as the north star.

"I came to check on you," Leif said. His voice echoed heartfelt delight.

"I'm almost done," Lia replied, looking at herself in the mirror.

"You look beautiful," Leif added, admiring her hair and makeup. "No matter what, today is still your wedding day, and you should enjoy every moment of it. Do not think about the formalities. Just be you and make this one of the best memories to keep with you for the rest of your life. "He stood behind the chair where she sat, pecked her on the cheek. Together they looked at her reflection in the mirror.

"Thank you," she said, affectionately patting his hand that rested on her shoulder.

Leif took a deep breath and smiled back at her. "Well, I'm going to get dressed, and I'll see you downstairs. Remember to keep that smile on your face; everything will be fine. I will be right beside you, walking down that aisle." They shared a parting smile as he left the room. In the garden, the guests were starting to gather. The press had arrived before all other guests for hours. The day was perfect for an outdoor wedding—warm, but not terribly so. And as noon drew closer, the sun got cooler, peeking out occasionally.

The day breeze swirled in the surrounding rose bushes and ornamental shrubs of the garden. A soothing strain of classical music serenaded the atmosphere. A well-dressed Celia adorned in a dusty rose embellished lace and satin floor-length gown, with draped bodice and an elegant neckline welcomed the guests. She was the epitome of timeless elegance, wearing her hair in a sleek updo showing off her willowy shoulders.

It was an intimate gathering, a handpicked selection of close friends and family of the Dawson's and Lia's closest friends. Public relations and legal representatives from TrueTek were also in attendance. They took their seats on either side of the aisle leading to the pergola covered in a picturesque mixture of flowering vines and *Innocent Blush Clematis*. The smell of fresh-cut flowers and wild lavender filled the air. Silver-grey Chiavari chairs were carefully organized on both sides of the aisles, thoughtfully accented with delicate, blush-pink sashes forming a crisscross design at the backs.

At 11:30 a.m. Keaton joined the ceremony kissing his mom on the cheek as he walked down the aisle to take his place next to the officiator at the pergola entrance.

Minutes later, the music stopped, and all heads turned to face the far end of the walk. The instrumental opening to the bridal chorus swayed through the air as Lia glided down the aisle like a white swan with beauty and grace. She wore a regal ball gown with a fitted bodice and full skirt; crimson, white with intricate crystal jewels that shimmered in the sunlight. Her long embellished cathedral veil cascaded behind her as she made her way down the aisle. She carried a white rose bouquet with silver-grey and blush-pink hand-tied detailing at the base. Leif held her left arm and smiled at her as they reached the pergola.

There were no bridesmaids, no groomsmen, just a polished Keaton, dressed in a tailored single-breasted, black tuxedo, with a classic white tuxedo shirt, waiting for her by the entrance of the pergola, where they saw each other for the first time since the night before. Keaton received Lia from Leif, exchanging a gentle smile. Lia was a bundle of nerves; the moment she caught a view of everyone waiting for her to walk down the aisle, everything she rehearsed went out the door.

When he took her hand and looked into her eyes, she became incredibly emotional, he looked at her with a comforting smile, and she suddenly became calm, taking in a deep breath in an indistinct way only they could see.

The music faded, and the officiator stepped up to the microphone. Bible in hand, he smiled at the intimate gathering of guests and proceeded with the ceremony. Hand in hand, face-to-face, with little space between them, they stood in front of the officiator, just as they had rehearsed. The ceremony was traditional and personal with a bit of humor, just as intended. During the reading of the vows, Lia had butterflies in her stomach. Even with the knowledge that Keaton's vows were scripted, insincere to say the least, they were still heartfelt and beautiful.

He placed the ring on her finger, and her heart fluttered, something she could not control. It felt like a beautiful dream, one from which she did not want to waken. It was nothing short of a real wedding. Within thirty minutes, they were pronounced husband and wife. The ceremony was sealed with an award-winning kiss, made perfect with emotional body language and intimate hand placements, precisely as rehearsed. Everyone rose to their feet, in resounding applause, some even in tears. The romantic feeling in the atmosphere was so intense it was almost tangible, palpable, and infectious.

He took her hand and walked her down the aisle, through the flashing camera lights from the press, cheers of congratulations, hugs, and kisses from close family and friends.

It was undeniably more than she expected it to be. And at that moment, she forgot that it was not all real.

The excitement on Keaton's face, however, was honest. He was beyond elated that the wedding chapter of his nightmare had ended, and now he could not wait for the year to come and go. A little secret he kept to himself all this while, he thought about Katie, every time he had kissed Lia. At the altar in all her glory, all he could see was his Katie. Visions of Katie standing before him as he exchanged his vows and slipped the ring on her finger were the reason his performance was so heartfelt. Keaton's desire for Katie unwittingly electrified his kisses with Lia, igniting a relentless passion inside her heart.

To the world and everyone present at the ceremony, Keaton Dawson married Lia Paton on December 16, 2018. But inside Keaton's heart, he got married to Katie Crozet on that very day. He surrendered his heart, mind, body, and soul to the woman he loved, though someone else stood in her place.

CHAPTER 21

Things were beginning to settle in the Dawson's household two days post-wedding. The wedding highlights were splashed across some of New York's most noteworthy business tabloids and newspapers. The business insider headlined: *'Eligible Bachelor and Sole Heir of Billion-Dollar Tech Conglomerate-True-Tek, has tied the Knot!' The New York Times* featured their romantic wedding smooch on the front cover. *Wall Street Journal, NY Daily News*, and *Metro New York* had the new couple splashed across their front and main page features. As intended, it was no longer a secret. The tongues were wagging, and everyone who needed to know was now aware.

The Dawson's attorneys had the ball rolling; a day after the wedding, the paperwork giving Keaton joint access to the TrueTek voting shares held by Lia, was well underway. The process would be finalized in a matter of days, and Keaton would be the majority shareholder in TrueTek. He was prepared to assume his role of president with the element of surprise.

In his home office, he sat content revising paperwork dropped off earlier in the day by his father's assistant, Lucas Hill, who was now his assistant. Though he hadn't physically appeared in TrueTek's headquarters since his dad's passing, he received daily updates on all operations as a primary shareholder and legal owner of the company. Secretly, with the help of his assistant, he kept a keen eye on decisions made by the board in his absence. As advised by his legal team, he had notified the board of directors after his father's funeral that he would take some time to mourn before assuming his rightful place.

As he got further into the reports, a sneer of contempt flashed across his face. His lips curled, one side rose upward, and the other side remained in place. His right eyebrow slightly raised, exposing more of the white part of his eye. An outward display of the disgust and anger he felt inside. It was now clear what Stefon and his father tried to warn him about; their efforts had merit. The majority of his father's projects were halted by the Vice President, now acting president, pending final review at the forthcoming AGM. The company politics was worse than he thought. They were indeed against his late father, and it was evident that they were actively trying to sabotage all the hard work Keegan had initiated before his passing.

Keaton scanned through the final pages of the report and flipped it close in a fit of rage. He tried to control his temper, rolling his hands into fists until his nails dug into the flesh of his palms. Not only were they halting his late father's projects, but it was apparent that they had plans to vote him out at the AGM. There were numerous attempts to contact the 'anonymous' shareholder of the thirty percent shares they needed to secure majority votes.

His assistant's report revealed that someone would try to fabricate a proxy for the 'anonymous' shareholder to achieve their despicable plans.

The conspiracy made Keaton's blood boil, knowing the lengths they were willing to go to push him out of his own company unjustly. Much like what they wanted to do to his father. He couldn't wait for the AGM; he was ready to weed them out like the thistles they were. Unknown to the board, the anonymous shareholder was now his wife, and within the next few days, he would legally have access to those shares.

He picked up his phone and dialed Katie; hearing her voice would put him in a better mood. He paced around the study while her phone rang on the other end.

"Hey, *Bébé*!" she answered in delight. "I thought you'd never call."

"I've missed you," he replied, breathing out as though the pressure was relieved from his tightening lungs.

"I've missed you more. I haven't heard from you in four days. You told me to wait for your call. I thought you had forgotten about me."

"Katie, how can you say that? I can never forget about you. I didn't call you because I couldn't. Those days leading up to the wedding were all about rehearsals and press coaching; there was no privacy. It wasn't convenient. But it's over now; the wedding has passed; my lawyers are working on joint ownership of the shares. Everything is going as planned."

"I'm just happy to hear your voice; being back home in our apartment these past couple of days has been hard for me. Your clothes are all here, your smell—everything here reminds me of you and keeps reminding me that for a whole year I won't be able to call you as I like, see you as I like...." She started to sniffle.

"Katie, baby, I know how you feel. Don't think about it like that, ok?. I am here, and I am yours. This situation is temporary. Remember, we decided that we are going to get through this together, and we will. I don't want you to keep going down a rabbit hole of troubling thoughts over things we can't control. Keep focused on the end goal, me and you, our forever..." His voice was calming and reassuring, but her sniffles didn't subside immediately.

"Let's change the subject…." He pleaded. "I'm extremely proud of you for securing your spot in next years' Olympics. You kicked ass in Canada. I followed all the live feeds of the qualifiers, and I am over the moon at how well you did. You are an amazing woman; you know that, right?"

There was a pause before her response. "I'm happy you were able to watch the championships. With everything going on, you still found a way to support me, and I'm grateful. Now that I'm back home, I am taking a well-deserved sabbatical before the hardcore training begins for the Olympics. Coach has already rolled out a grueling training schedule for next year; six to eight hours of training every day up until the month of the Olympics. That means I'll be training every day from January to June next year. It is going to be crazy."

"Baby, you've got this…this is what you've been working for; you are finally going to the Olympics, this is your dream, and I know you're going to be a force to reckon with. I know it, and you know it."

She giggled, "Thank you, *Bébé*. By the way, how are you

doing? I take it you are alone now since you managed to call me. Where are you now, and where is she...?"

"I am at home, in the office." He replied, "Lia is out with mom. I don't know exactly where they went or what they went out to do. I didn't ask."

"Does your mom like her?" she asked, her tone a tad contentious.

"Mom is just polite. He replied in an assuaging tone. "Like me, mom is doing what she needs to do to make Lia comfortable until the end of this contract. Don't overthink about it".

"Is she beautiful…you have refused to describe her to me or send me a photo like I asked. Why?"

"Because it's not important. Whether she's beautiful is not what I am focused on right now. In my eyes, she's just a business partner; nothing else matters—I thought we decided to change the subject; why are you going there again?"

"Keaton, you decided to change the subject; I didn't. It should be ok for you to tell me these things if there's nothing to hide. You told me the wedding would be featured in the press for legal publicity. Soon, if not already, her image will be public knowledge, so why do you refuse to send me a photo of her before I see her in the news?" Her tone had evident frustration, which got Keaton a bit agitated.

"Katie, baby…listen to me. Her physical appearance is not relevant. It's not important to me, and it should not be to you either. What is the point of seeing her picture? You'll only get yourself worked up over something that means absolutely nothing to me."

"I just need to know," She sobbed. "You might not understand why, but it's relevant to me. I need to know who I'm up against?"

"Who you are up against -baby, this is crazy." Keaton sounded baffled. "It sounds like you are saying this relationship is real. You've got to keep in mind that this marriage is business and temporary. If you start thinking like that now, it will only worsen, and before you know it, we are having meaningless fights or tiffs like this, which can potentially ruin our relationship. Is that what you want?"

"I don't want to fight." Katie sobbed. "I just don't want you to withhold things from me. I was hoping you could tell me everything, no matter how uncomfortable or irrelevant you think it is. I want you to trust that I'm secure enough to handle every information concerning this marriage. When you withhold things like this, it makes me think that you are trying to protect my feelings. Like you don't believe that I can see her photo and not be upset. It's like you are saying that I am insecure. Are you?"

Keaton scratched his head, exasperated, baffled at her question. He thought about what he might have said to make her believe he was in any way questioning her self-confidence. At that point, he gave up; he didn't want to keep going back and forth with her on the subject. It was clear she had made up her mind. His only option was to give her what she asked for, to appease her.

“Katie—baby, don’t be like that, please. If it means this much to you, I will send it to you. I have a few that the wedding photographer emailed; I’ll send all of them. Is that ok? Will you promise not to be mad at me anymore?”

There was a pause, followed by a few sniffles. “And you too, promise me that you won’t keep anything from me, no matter how uncomfortable you think it might make me. You need to trust that I can handle my emotions. Promise me.”

“I promise,” Keaton replied, switching the phone from his right hand to his left.

“I hate it when we fight,” she sniffled.

“It’s my fault. I won’t keep anything else from you. I promise.”

“I love you.”

“I love you too,” he replied with a relieved smile. Before you go, as I mentioned in our last conversation, I will initiate our contacts. Now that the wedding ceremony has concluded, the contract is in effect and is binding until completion. If I breach any of Lia’s terms, she will have grounds to terminate the agreement. Since one of her terms requires no contact with partner(s) of previous relationships, I must be cautious about how we communicate henceforth. But trust that I will make use of every opportunity I get to contact you. In a few weeks, I’ll be assuming my position in the company. I’ll have more freedom and flexibility in the office, which I’ll use to my advantage. I suspect that I’ll have a lot to handle for the first couple of months in the company, so we might not get to speak to each other as much as we want to. But I promise to make it work. Is that still ok with you?"

"I understand; we are in this together. I'll focus on training after my short break. With both of us being distracted, me with training and you with work. We won't overthink about the distance or the limited communication. It will be fine...." The admission in her voice put his mind at ease.

"Yes, we'll be fine. Now take care of yourself. I know how much the Olympics mean to you, but you need to pace yourself in training. Don't overdo it—promise? I love you...."

"I love you too...." She replied with a yearning smile.

"Forever...?"

"Forever." She consented.

They hung up simultaneously, both taking solace in their love for each other. That it would be enough to get them through, —It had to be.

CHAPTER 22

Minutes after the phone call, Keaton sends Katie a few photos of Lia from the wedding day. He deliberately omitted the ones of him and Lia together, especially the images of them kissing. For Keaton, the kiss was just for show, it meant nothing, and to be honest, it looked genuine only because he had imagined he was kissing Katie the entire time. But as the saying goes, "a picture is worth a thousand words," and those photos of him and Lia entangled in what seemed like a heart-throbbing, mind-blowing, happiest-day-of-our-lives kiss spoke words of love, passion, and soulmate. The type of kiss only true love could conjure, the best deepfake detector wouldn't be able to detect a hint of deception from those pictures. Hell, even while scrolling through the photos, Keaton had to remind himself, they weren't real. He had serious doubts about sending any of them to Katie but hoped to God that the ones he carefully selected would not cause a stir. He had to trust that she understood his position and that she could handle her emotions.

An hour later, he heard a commotion downstairs, laughing and rustling.

"Keaton! Keaton! Are you here?" the call bellowed from downstairs.

He didn't answer right away but knew it was his mom's voice. He headed downstairs.

Celia was halfway up the staircase. "There you are," she said with a broad smile. "Come help us with the bags." She turned to go back down the stairs.

"What bags, and where's Jared? Why didn't you call him for help?" Keaton had a confused look on his face.

"Oh hush, I'm asking you for help; if I wanted Jared, I would have asked him. Now come along and wipe that perplexed look from your face."

Keaton followed behind her from the staircase to the front door, where Lia struggled with both arms full of shopping bags. In a glance, Keaton counted at least five oversized bags on each arm. He rushed to assist her. "Where did you guys go?" He asked, taking the bags from her.

Lia had an abashed look, mixed with a sheepish smile on her face, flickering her gaze to Celia standing next to Keaton.

"If you must know…." Celia replied in a cheeky, cheerful tone, walking past Keaton towards the boot of the car. "We went into the city for brunch, which coincidentally was on Fifth Avenue. It was fate. You know us girls, we had to shop. I mean, who goes into the city and does not shop? After all, no one does luxury quite like New York City." She giggled, removing more shopping bags from the boot.

"So, that is what you both have been doing all day… shopping?" He looked at Celia, then at Lia, with an I-can't-believe-you-two chiding look.

"Oh, don't look at us like that," Celia hissed, walking towards him with the same number of bags he had just taken from Lia.

“I haven’t had this much fun in a long while,” she continued in glee. “Lia is such a peach; she is the daughter I never had. Full of life, endearing, and might I add, she has quite the eye for fashion. Which is not surprising; her taste is beyond sophistication.” She flashed Lia a glance laced with humor. “I thought I was the one taking her out for a treat in the city, but it was the other way around. We had such an amazing time, not only shopping, but we also went to a spa and Gagosian Art Gallery. After such a long time, I finally have someone with the acumen for fine art to accompany me back there. With Lia’s help, I was able to select a few contemporary pieces. I can’t wait for you to see them.”

Celia stopped in the living room and unloaded the bags. Keaton followed suit. Lia, who had returned to the car for more bags, joined them, setting down about six additional bags next to the others.

“Lia is congenial company; I finally understand what I have been missing all these years not having a daughter.” Celia turned to look at Lia with a wholehearted smile.

“Mom, do I deserve all these praises…?” Lia asked, smiling blushingly. “I am the one who should be thanking you. Back home, it seems I could never find time for relaxation, let alone go shopping. Being with you today was more therapeutic than leisure. It reminds me of when mom was alive; I consider your company a blessing in disguise.”

Celia held her hands up to her heart, brandishing a broad smile of unfeigned delight. “Oh, honey….” Celia beamed, taking Lia into a hug. Keaton stood there looking at the two, puzzled. *When did Lia start calling my mother, mom…? Is this really happening? One outing and they are all sentimental, practically best friends. Now, mom thinks she's the daughter she never had. How? When did they even get to this point?* The confusion was written all over his face.

"You see what I mean," Celia said, breaking from the hug and turning to Keaton, "She is such a darling."

"Where's Jaxen?" Keaton responded, changing the subject. "He drove you into the city today, so why is he not back."

"Of course, he's back," Celia said. "He and Jared are supervising the art delivery by the storeroom at the west wing. The delivery truck followed us here. They are ensuring everything is unloaded safely. They'll let us know once it's complete."

"So, is this everything from the car?" He asked, glancing at the assemblage of shopping bags, then at Lia and his mom consecutively. "There are a few more bags in the car," Lia replied, a hint of shyness flickered across her face.

"OK, I'll go grab those." He said, taking the opportunity to leave the room.

Lia followed behind him. At the car, Keaton grabbed the rest of the bags he saw in the boot. At the same time, Lia took two Chloe bags from the back seat.

"That's everything," Lia said, smiling as she closed the car door. He flashed her a genteel smile and closed the boot of the car. She walked ahead of him back through the main entrance, but slowly so he'd catch up.

“I hope I didn’t offend you when I called Celia mom. You had a perplexed look on your face when I did, I wasn’t trying to overstep; it’s just that we bonded today, and I do consider her a mother figure. It has been so long since I’ve had that maternal bond; it happened so naturally --I couldn’t help saying what I felt....”

She didn’t make eye contact as he was walking closely behind her. He opened his mouth to speak, then hesitated, not wanting to say what was really on his mind. Like the fact that he thought their ‘mother-daughter, so-called bond’ was happening way too fast. And that he thought she was trying to mosey up to Celia by calling her mom. He wondered if she had a genuine interest in things his mom liked, or she was just pretending to get mom’s approval. Was there an ulterior motive? These were the thoughts that were racing across his mind the moment he had witnessed their maudlin display in the living room.

He swallowed the words on the tip of his tongue, forcing the thought to the back of his mind, giving her a diplomatic response. “No, not at all. I am not offended. If anything, it kind of caught me off guard. However, I think I understand the connection between you both. Plus, my mom tends to have that effect on people. Her genial personality sucks you in; It’s hard not to love her.”

Lia snickered, “Yes, she is a breath of fresh air; she makes you feel safe with just a smile. I feel like I have known her all my life. You are quite lucky; still having your mom, and such a great one at that, I envy you.” Her tone suddenly got emotional, and she looked away as her face turned red.

Keaton quickly realized what was happening. The time Lia spent with Celia reminded her of her relationship with her mother. The memories turned poignant as reality made clear that her mother was no longer in this world. He could feel the sadness radiate from her. Her pain tugged at his heart, call it affective empathy, but the sensation of loss also overcame him, and he mirrored her emotions.

He took her bags and escorted her to the sitting area, left, and returned with a glass of water. "Here, have some water…."

"Thank you," she replied, swiping at her eyes, sniffling quietly. To provide the comfort she needed, he sat next to her, a little awkward at first, but he wanted to be frank with her. He was still grieving his dad, but he had found ways to deal with it. He tried to help her to do the same.

"I'm conscious of your feelings. I feel the same way every time I think of my dad. It's more difficult for you, having lost both parents. But you know what has helped me to cope? Acknowledging my pain. Trying to ignore your pain or keep it from surfacing will only worsen it in the long run. If you genuinely want to heal, you need to face your grief and actively deal with it. "You once mentioned that you had to take care of your grieving father when your mom passed. Have you realized that you haven't adequately grieved her?"

Her grip tightened around the glass as she tried to suppress the tears threatening to spill from her eyes. She avoided responding as it would only lead to her crying, and she wasn't ready for Keaton to see her that way.

"When you should have been grieving the passing of your mother, you were helping your father to cope. Then he passed away, and before you know it, you are hurling headfirst into the responsibility of carrying on the legacy. You haven't had time to grieve either of them. There is unresolved grief that you need to handle. You may not have realized it, but I have noticed that you are overtaken by profound sadness since you've been here each time you mention your mother. I am not qualified to give you advice on how you grieve, but I can say this from my personal experience. Don't keep suppressing it. Go up to your room, get in the bath, and just let it out if you need to cry."

She looked at him with a grateful expression and a few more heartfelt sniffles.

"Sometimes that's all it takes. And I'm not talking about those pretty sobs you ladies call crying. I mean bawling, bleeding the salt of your soul, and let the grief pour from your eyes in torrents and snots until your face is no longer this beautiful. That's when you know you have meaningfully cried." He smiled at her, and she tittered through her sniffles at his successful attempt to humor her.

She nodded in agreement, wiping her eyes. "Yes, I'll do what you say." He gave her a comforting tap on her shoulder and got up to leave the room. When he was almost at the entrance of the kitchen, his peripheral view caught Lia heading upstairs. He felt somewhat relieved that he was able to give her some solace. As he entered the kitchen where he had earlier told his mom to wait, he thought that he too was all too familiar with suppressing grief, pain, and hurt. Celia's eyes widened as he entered the room, eager to know what was going on.

Before she could ask a question, Keaton spoke ahead of her. "Mom, what exactly are you doing?" She looked at him, bewildered by his question, baffled by the concerned look on his face.

"What do you mean?" She asked.

"Mom, I know the person you are; good-willed by nature. So, I am not oblivious to why Lia has taken a liking to you. But mom, don't you think you are going too far by referring to her as the daughter you never had?"

"Keaton, but it's the truth, she is a wonderful young lady, and I have taken a liking to her, I…."

"Mom, it's barely a month since she's been here. Do you honestly believe you know her that well? I know you mean well, but based on the nature of our relationship, it is best to keep things professional. I am just saying, please be cautious, don't go building an unbreakable bond with her that will only complicate things in the future. Please…."

"Keaton, please don't give me a didactic lecture. Don't get me wrong. I understand what you are saying, but it is not in my nature to be uncaring. She is a great girl, and I like her. If it makes you uncomfortable that I said she's like the daughter I never had. I won't say that again. But as for being detached and apathetic in my feelings towards her. I cannot promise you that.

—For heaven's sake, Keaton, Lia will be living with us for an entire year. How do you plan on getting through that year? By being indifferent or ambivalent? Listen to me. Take things in strides, don't close yourself off, or change who you are because of your situation. From the moment you accepted this marriage, you have decided to be indifferent towards her. But have you noticed that it hasn't been working out as you have planned? Why do you think that is? I'll tell you why. It's not in your nature to be uncaring towards those around you, just as it is not in mine."

Keaton folded his arms across his chest as he stared her down.

Noticing his body language with a half-eye roll, she said, "I know you want to be this way towards Lia because of your relationship with Katie. I get it. But I have told you before that sometimes our circumstances change, and we often have to change our perspectives. I am not saying you should let go of your values. But you need to open your arms to change, plunge in it, move with it, and see where it takes you. Sometimes that's the only way to make sense of it all. I have had a long day. I'm going up to rest. Think about what I have said...." She smiled as she walked past him.

He took a seat at the kitchen island, contemplating. The last thing he wanted was to drop his guard. What was he to do? His mother was right; he couldn't hinder her from getting closer to Lia. A small part of him wanted to loosen up a little, but the other part feared what could happen if he did. He made a promise to Katie, she was his forever, no matter what his mom thought. It was impossible for him to "plunge into this relationship and see where it goes."

He pursed his lips and turned his head towards the large kitchen window. His thoughts were decisive. *If mom wants to get closer to Lia, then fine, I won't stop her. But I will maintain my stance. There will be no riding the waves in this relationship, no matter what Lia wants or what mom wants.*

CHAPTER 23

A week later, Keaton received the documentations from his legal team. He was now the joint holder of the shares Lia held and legally recognized as the majority shareholder of TrueTek. Keaton would join TrueTek's board of directors and shareholders at the annual general meeting in three days. His mind was at ease; he was more ready than he could ever be.

He took Lia to select a car for her daily commute to the now-ready lower Manhattan office in the days before. Everything was falling into place. After she had chosen the car she wanted, he assigned her a personal driver. With him taking on the presidency role in TrueTek and Lia managing her company remotely, he thought they both would have busy schedules daily, which meant less time for personal communication. Being at peace with his mother's and Lia's fast-growing fondness was also working to his advantage. Celia kept Lia occupied with every chance she got, and he was starting to appreciate it. Keaton had the space he wanted, and he only had to be cordial. Some days it seemed he didn't even exist. He was optimistic that if things continued to go on the way, they were going in the past week, the year would be a breeze. He would be back to his everyday life in no time.

January 1st, 2019

9:30 a.m., not a minute more nor a minute less. Keaton walked into the board room of TrueTek's headquarters, accompanied by Lucas, his assistant.

"Keaton!" said Marquise Watler in a curt greeting. He was TrueTek's acting president, who was seated at the head of the table where his father once sat. Watler peered at Keaton with crow's feet draped eyes over the wide-framed glass that sat crookedly on his nose. He was in his sixties, had salt and pepper hair, with a full-silken beard. His face was seasoned with age and creased like vellum.

Keaton accepted his reception with a respectful glance and nod, then sat at the foot of the table in the empty chair they had left for him. His eyes scanned the room; everyone seemed to be present, as all the seats at the table were filled. Some faces he quickly recognized others not so much. Since he walked into the room, other than Watler's shallow greeting, everyone else kept quiet, so Keaton said nothing.

"Right on time." Watler blurted, breaking the silence in the room. He got up and walked to the end of the table towards Keaton.

"Welcome back, Keaton. I haven't seen you—since you left for studies in France some years ago. You are the spitting image of your father in his younger years. How have you been?"

Watler looked at Keaton with a half-crack smile, with one hand resting on Keaton's shoulder.

"I've been well," Keaton replied. It was not easy losing my father so suddenly, but I am doing better now."

Everyone else at the table who was not familiar with Keaton now knew who he was, and with that, the silence tumbled into a choir of condolences and greetings.

"I sympathize with you, Keaton," Watler continued, "We have all lost one of the world's finest business moguls. Keegan Dawson was the pillar of this conglomerate and will forever be. I am sorry I could not make it to his funeral. I was out of the country at the time. However, I am thrilled that he has you as his successor; undoubtedly, one day, you will be the pillar of TrueTek just as he would have wanted."

To Keaton, His words were derisive and insulting. *One day? Why not now? He thinks me a fool, Keaton thought, smiling in my face with empty words of sympathy while plotting to vote me out.* Keaton mirrored Watler's smile, looking straight into his face without a blink.

"Thank you for your words of sympathy," Keaton responded. "I am sure dad is watching over this meeting today; soon enough, he will be proud that all he has done for me to carry on his mantle will not be in vain." Watler tapped Keaton's shoulder, flashing a critical glance, before walking back to his seat.

"On a lighter note," Watler exclaimed. His focus turned to Keaton. "Congratulations are in order. I learned you got married some weeks ago. Your father would have been proud. I remember he got married to your mother around your age. You are truly your father's son. Birds of a feather...." He muffled a casual chuckle.

"Yes, I got married recently. As fate would have it, I received the news that my father had passed when I was about to return home with the woman I had chosen to spend the rest of my life with; with dad's untimely death, I have realized that life is too short, no one knows what the future holds. So, I decided to go ahead with the marriage as planned."

"Spoken like a wise man..." Watler said, shuffling through the folders in front of him. "Well, I wish you and your wife a happy marriage and everlasting love. A tip from an old man who has been married a few times; a happy wife is not always equal to a happy life. Because even happy couples argue. The key is to listen and always see her as your equal. Make decisions together, appreciate her. Most importantly, expect, and accept change. I am certain your father would give you the same advice if he were here."

"Thank you; I will remember that" Keaton replied.

"Hmm." Watler grunted, "Now let's get down to business, shall we...?"

Everyone at the table flipped open the folders in front of them. The agenda was read, followed by the minutes, and the meeting went straight into the matters on hand. After a lengthy review of the financials and discussion on pending and completed projects, it was time to elect and reelect the president and board members for the new business year.

Watler cleared his throat, straightening the glasses on his face. His gaze ping-ponged across the table at all the key stakeholders in a sort of conspiratorial agreement.

"Now...," Watler emphasized, twiddling a pen in his hand, "the board had discussed this at length, months ago when we learned of Keegan's passing, and more recently in preparation for today's meeting. There is no disputing the fact that you...."

He focused his stare on Keaton "...are the legal heir to this conglomerate. And as the heir, you will continue to enjoy the perks of a major stakeholder related to your involvement in the company's strategic vision and key operations. However, we, the executive board members, have decided that it is not the best business decision for you to assume the role of president at this time. At least not until you have worked your way up in the company for some time...."

His eyes squinched almost in a squint as he focused on Keaton. Keaton kept quiet practically the entire meeting, waiting for this moment. His face formed a half-smirk; he removed his gaze from the documents in front of him to look up at Watler.

"And why does the board believe it's not in the best interest of the company for me to be president at this time? Please, elaborate..."

"Well, for one..." Watler said, taking off his glasses to inspect the lenses. "You have not been a part of TrueTek long enough to have what it takes to carry the burden of this conglomerate. We are talking about a multi-national operation that takes years of experience, grit, and guile to manage. You are too young and frankly too inexperienced to take on such a responsibility. Especially so soon after your father's passing, and not to mention, you practically just got married. Running this company requires long hours and a lifetime commitment. —Something we the board members believe you are not yet ready for."

"And what if I say that you and the board members are wrong? What if I say I do have what it takes to be TrueTek's president? What if I tell you that this is what my father has been preparing me for all these years? Academically I am overqualified, and when it comes to experience, I know the functions of this company as much or even more than any of you sitting at this table. I was involved in the business operation of this company from the age of sixteen...." Keaton stood up from his seat and walked to the head of the table; he looked out on everyone in the room before he spoke again.

"I have been analyzing TrueTek's performance indicators and financial statements ever since I was in high school. More than fifty percent of the services and products created by TrueTek over the last ten years have been worked on by my father and me."

He looked over at Lucas, who immediately started handing out files to everyone.

"The proof is in the pudding...." Keaton continued. "In front of you, these folders detail all the projects, products, and services that I was a crucial influence as well as being instrumental in their development and execution." Keaton took up one of the folders and paced confidently, looking each person in the eye before he began his presentation:

"Seven years ago, the FreeZone project began. This project turned out to be one of the world's most significant subsea ventures, delivering improved internet boost to over forty countries in Southeast Asia, Africa, and the Caribbean. This project made TrueTek investors billions on completion and practically raised the bar for all the other tech companies in our sector. I was the brains behind this groundbreaking idea. The FreeZone project was my father's first charge to me when I completed my undergraduate degree. He wanted to see if I had what it takes to lead this company into a revolutionary era. I spent months submitting idea after idea to my father; he turned them all down until I went to him with this one.

This idea was so innovative that he had no problem getting the funding, and you..." he pointed to each stakeholder at the table. "All of you sitting here made billions from this project —my idea."

Short, furtive glances shot across the conference table at each other like daggers, A widening of the eyes, pursed lips, steepled hands, and furrowed brows all silently revealed their consternation at Keaton's stance.

"And let me continue —SPORTFIC- 2013, Digital response launch- 2015, and more recently, the biotech manufacturing project dad launched in Europe before his passing. I was the originator of all these ideas. And my father made sure they were executed, and undoubtedly, all of these projects have and will continue to make TrueTek's investors billions. Gentlemen, it's all there in front of you—the legal documents showing my involvement in all the projects I have mentioned. Back then, my father did not disclose my contribution at the launch of these projects for reasons he and I knew. He wanted to be the only one held accountable if the projects failed. So, publicly he withheld my identity. However, the legal documents filed on completion of each of those projects clearly state my contribution. So, gentlemen, to say I am "young and inexperienced, not ready to run this company" is farfetched and an ill-informed opinion." He flashed an accusatory glance at Watler. "I have been making this company billions of dollars with my father for years now. I am the creative mind this company needs to champion it into the new technology age. My competence is not to be questioned, for I have proved my ability, and it's only the beginning. You are yet to see what I am capable of."

Everyone nervously scanned through their folders as Keaton spoke, and a stream of debating prattle ensued amongst them. Keaton walked back to his seat, bearing an exultant and powerful expression on his face.

Watler took a moment to go through the rest of the folder's contents; his eyes narrowed to slits. He flipped the folder close and looked around, observing the disarray of thoughts, and muttering across the table.

"Be that as it may..." he glowered at Keaton. "I think I speak for everyone here when I say that a seasoned executive should handle the operations of this conglomerate. Your father founded TrueTek, but the investors are the backbone of the company. And they need someone who will lobby, and make wise, frugal business decisions on their behalf...."

"And let me guess...." Keaton interjected, "You are that person that the investors need?"

"The executive board has made its decision...." Watler sneered, "and they have agreed that I should resume the role of president, henceforth. I am willing to take you under my wing to give you the additional training you will need. And maybe in a couple of years, you will be ready to champion this company in the future. But until then, I believe the decision is final."

Watler glanced at each stakeholder for a confirming response; the majority rose their hands to vote in his favor. A satisfying grin flickered across his face.

"Well, Keaton, I believe the board has spoken. And I hope you will be accepting of this decision. Together we can do great things for this company; with your innovative ideas and my direction, we can be unstoppable...." His mouth formed a smirk.

Keaton released a barely audible tut-tut sound before looking straight at Watler. "And that's where you are wrong, Watler. The board hasn't spoken; you have. As far as I see it, this is a one-person show with a bunch of cowards and minions at your mercy. I am not one to underestimate. I am my father's son, and I am not to contend with—This company belongs to the Dawson's, and I am its sole heir. It was my father's wish and mine to be his immediate successor in TrueTek—and that, I will be"

"And how do you plan on doing that?" Watler asked, peering at him. "You do not own majority voting shares. You need to have over fifty percent to outvote or contend any decision of the executive board. We all know Keegan left you his shares, but that's only forty percent. Enlighten me, dear boy, how do you plan to overthrow this decision? All of us here, including the anonymous shareholder, have submitted our votes and proxies in favor of me, as TrueTek's president, for the new operational year. That is sixty percent voting shares against you—just accept what it is—the decision has been made."

Keaton scoffed at his conclusive blabbering. "You know—I wanted to hear it from your mouth. When I learned of your conniving plans; it was shocking enough. But to know you have the guile to execute fraud in front of the rest of the stakeholders and me is appalling."

"What are you insinuating?" Watler asked, removing his glasses again with a challenging look on his face.

Keaton sighed and rose from his seat. "You just said you have the votes of all the stakeholders here, including that of the anonymous shareholder—sixty percent to be exact? But I don't recall giving you my vote, so how did you come by it?"

"Make yourself clear!" Watler spat; infuriation shaped his raised eyebrows.

Keaton chuckled, bold and patronizing. "Next time you wish to forge a proxy for an anonymous stakeholder. Make sure you find out the identity of that person before you execute your plans."

"What impudence!" Watler shouted, "...are you accusing me of forgery? Here! Look at it yourself." He slid the folder with the proxies down the table towards Keaton.

"There's no need to look at that document Watler. Because I know, and you know, that it's falsified. I know because I am the holder of those anonymously held shares."

Watler's eyes popped open wide in shock and disbelief. His bottom lip seemed to have fallen off his face. "What...What do you mean?" Watler stuttered. "Those shares belong to an anonymous stakeholder—when traced, I discovered they are owned by a company listed as SAN Holdings LLC. I have investigated thoroughly, and you nor your father have no affiliation with that company. So, what exactly are you talking about?" His face grew red and rigid, irate, and he was pissed.

Keaton looked at Lucas again, who issued another set of documents. Keaton went back to his seat, giving everyone a moment to review the paperwork.

"What does this mean?" Watler asked, slightly daunted.

"SAN Holdings LLC is a subsidiary of SANCORP. SANCORP is the European company my father partnered with in the biotech manufacturing project. The anonymous holder of those shares happens to be Lia Paton, daughter of the late Bill Paton, founder of SANCORP. And it gets better...." Keaton asserted with a jabbing tone pausing for emphasis. "Lia Paton happens to be my wife. Legally, I am the joint holder of those stakes, making me the majority shareholder of TrueTek's voting shares. Seventy percent to be exact!"

Keaton stared across the table at Watler with brash eyes. Watler nervously scanned through the document a second time, glancing over the rim of his glasses, the color draining from his face. His expression gave away his inability to accept what he saw in black and white. His eyes refused to believe it was real.

The other stakeholders flashed Watler disapproving and condemning looks. They had all been deceived into believing that Watler had obtained the proxy of the anonymous shareholder legitimately. One of the other executives of the board stood up with a diffident look on his face. He cleared his throat before acquiescing to the solid proof in front of them. His gaze flickered before giving a sincere apology on behalf of the rest of the stakeholders, excluding themselves from having any knowledge of the fraudulent scheme.

Their votes were recanted and recast, making Keaton TrueTek's president, as he was rightfully meant to be. Watler was escorted out of the board room by awaiting law enforcement officers. He gave Keaton a cold, vile gaze as he passed by.

The room settled; Keaton breathed a sigh of relief. *I hope you are seeing this, dad, he thought to himself. I know you are proud of the outcome; I am too.*

He returned his focus to the members in the room and addressed them as the newly appointed president of TrueTek. His speech was brief, yet he connected with everyone in the room. They were convinced and confident in his vision and his proposed democratic approach for the way forward.

Keaton left the board room in a buoyant mood. He was right where he needed to be, where he and his father envisioned he would be. He felt accomplished, identifying and eliminating those in TrueTek with ill intent. He realized right there and then that his father was justified in everything that he did. Without his efforts, it was evident he would have lost his position in the company. But now, he was determined to make it all worthwhile, fueled to lead TrueTek into the progressive future on the horizon.

CHAPTER 24

In the following months, things at home and TrueTek were going exactly as planned. He was doing exceptionally well for the youngest president of a multi-national conglomerate, balancing home, and work-life responsibilities. Communication with Katie couldn't be better. Being at TrueTek practically all day, seven days a week till the wee hours of the night, created perfect opportunities to keep in touch with his beloved.

Long-distance was no longer a severe issue; the phone sex was mind-blowing. Besides, they were professionals at it. He knew just what to say and the perfect tone to use to send shivers up her spine halfway across the world. Their orgasms were explosive, and the narratives were riveting. They were each other's drug, unique how they could get each other high in erotism with a simple text message saying, '*I need you.*'

Katie had kept her word and never asked much about Lia; he was pleasantly surprised that she never brought up anything about the photos he had sent. Or the ones she might have seen in the news. Katie was certainly capable of controlling her emotions. Maybe it was because he was able to give her all the attention she needed. Perhaps the distance and the fake marriage weren't driving a wedge between them because he made sure she was a priority.

He never once forgot to send her a good morning text message if he couldn't call or check up on her training and health. And before he left the office each night, he would speak to her every opportunity he got. Not to mention, he was skilled in the art of seduction. At a whim, he could pull her mind away from her everyday concerns of life, training, and the distance between them. To bring her into a world of eroticism and sensuality, heightening her desire and arousal, making their phone sex experiences even more intense and pleasurable. It certainly kept them both sane, not being able to get some for practically four months.

When it came to Lia, he tried as much as possible to avoid her on all personal levels. He knew her work schedule and made sure he left the house before her every morning and returned at night when he knew she would have fallen asleep.

Lia hadn't revealed her feelings towards him, but he had figured it out by the third month into the marriage. The way she smiled at him, the way she always wanted to touch him whenever they spoke. Lia was sincerely playing the 'wife role.' She made efforts to prepare his meals, tried to select what he would wear to work, supervised his laundry and ironing, and tried ineffectually to spend alone time with him.

There were countless dinner reservations that he never made. Movie date nights that he had to cancel. Nature trails that Celia had to fill in. But there was always a good excuse. His role as president in TrueTek was indeed highly demanding. Lia knew it all too well, and so she was more than understanding.

She, too, had those days, early mornings, late nights, stressful projects, that had her pulling out her hair or crying alone in the bathtub some nights. Nevertheless, Keaton supported her whenever she had a work-related breakdown or experienced emotional distress, accepting that she was now an orphan. These were things he could relate to, personally and emotionally, so his conscience wouldn't allow him to watch her suffer alone. But that's as far as his care towards her extended. He evaded every other personal attempt of her to get close to him. He had a working formula, and to him, it was infallible.

At the end of the first quarter in TrueTek, he had successfully realigned his and his father's vision for the company, surrounding himself with a superlative team of executives. It was time to relaunch the most important of the projects that Watler halted—Project Globo. For this project, TrueTek's patented design of helium-filled stratospheric balloons would provide a reliable and cost-effective way to beam Internet service from the sky to some places in the world that lack it. This project was one he had hoped to work on with his father, and for that reason, it was dearer to his heart.

The FreeZone project was a significant eye-opener to the possibilities of digital services that access to reliable internet could bring to the parts of the world in dire need. Before his father's passing, their goal was to expand internet connectivity across sub-Saharan Africa to the other countries the FreeZone project did not cover. Though the FreeZone project was groundbreaking, the cost of infrastructure alone was exorbitant.

This time around, Project Globo would not only be an economical option, but it would open up a world of digital services to areas where connectivity to communities is under-resourced or where the communications infrastructure is non-existent. Instead of extending the Internet from the ground from cell towers, Globo takes to the sky via a complex system of stratospheric balloons. These balloons would travel along the perimeter of outer space to boost and expand internet connectivity to remote bucolic areas within sub-Saharan Africa, fill coverage gaps, and overall improve network resilience in the world of internet provision. With the success of this project, the possibilities of TrueTek's reach would be endless.

When mid-May rolled around, Keaton was at a crossroad with the funding of the Globo project. Sure, the balloons were ready, but some of the initial investors had withdrawn months ago when the project was halted. It was a hefty task convincing the majority of them to get back on board. The previous shut-down of the project by Watler, without proper explanation to the investors of the reason behind the halt, made them skeptical.

Among the challenges, he had to examine every aspect of the project before finalizing his decisions. Undoubtedly it was an innovative development, bound to benefit TrueTek and all its stakeholders. But it was also a new venture, and so, he had to look at the downside; what if it failed, putting TrueTek in another position where it may subsequently face losses. There was so much riding on the success of this project that it gave him sleepless nights. The success of this project was imperative because there were so many who wanted to see him fail.

He analyzed the company's financial resources and found that proper use of the reserves available, together with exceptional project management, could achieve the results he needed, even with the loss of a few investors.

He knew what to do, was shrewd enough to manage the financials, and had a clear vision for completing the project. What was lacking was an ingenious project manager he could trust. Though he had kept on the project manager hired by Watler, he was nowhere ready to trust him with a project so dear to his heart. With everything else that was riding on its successful launch. He had no plans entrusting it to anyone remotely close to the likes of Watler.

CHAPTER 25

May 25th, 2019

It's Saturday morning. Keaton sits in the pergola in the backyard garden. He had decided that Lia would be the best person to trust with the management of project Globo. She had an excellent rapport with some of the affluent international investors on board with the project. Her years of experience as the Project Management Director for SANCORP and her successful track record with the projects she handles between SANCORP and TrueTek in the European Market were all too impressive to overlook.

There was only one problem; he had evaded her so much that he felt outright embarrassed to approach her now for help. So, he sat there in the garden contemplating the best approach. He had to ask himself, what would he do if she turned him down? His ego would bruise beyond repair; the thought of it swelled his pride and clouded his judgment.

"You are home on a Saturday; that's quite strange. Any particular reason?" Celia asked, joining him under the pergola with a pitcher of lemonade.

"Morning, Mom." He responded, turning his attention to her.

"When I didn't see you at breakfast, I thought you had left for the office. When Lucas came to drop off some documents for you a while ago, I realized you were here. What is going on?"

"Oh good, he came, so where are the documents?"

"I told him to leave them in your study; what are they for?"

"It's the documents on project Globo. I had him put together a proposal to present to Lia. I need her expertise on the project."

"Hmm—so that's why you are home today, you need her help. Funny how that works, when you—need her, you can 'magically' become available, and when you don't, you are inexplicably busy every day."

"Mom, please don't rub it in. I already feel bad about asking her for help; I've been considering how to approach her all week. Please don't rub salt into my wound."

"Ask her, be a man. If there is anything I've learned about her, it's that she's not petty, and she is very professional, unlike someone I know."

"Mom, I am not petty, and I am professional; I have my reasons, you know it—by the way, where is she? I don't remember seeing her car or her driver this morning. Did she leave for the office?"

Celia cracked a cheeky smile, "She has gone out alright, but not to the office."

"What do you mean, has she gone out for leisure? If she has, then there's nothing wrong with that, so why do you have that mischievous smile on your face?"

"She has left with a rather dashing young fellow. I particularly think he's a handsome young man. Remarkably smart, he joined us for breakfast this morning, made quite the impression."

Celia's eyes lit up as if she was excited about this mystery man; the way she praised him made Keaton a bit angsty.

"What man? Did she leave with a man, or are you kidding…?" His face contorted in contempt, the expression on his face was pinched, and without realizing it, his cheeks went flushed.

Celia burst out laughing. "So, you are jealous?" She giggled in amusement; her chest was visibly contracting, and her eyes got watery; she laughed almost to the point of breathlessness. Every effort to suppress it only increased its strength.

Keaton's flushed cheeks went from blush to mad red, his eyebrows arched in taunted fury, he found nothing funny. "I am glad you find this amusing?" He growled. "How could you let her leave home with a stranger? What if something happens to her? How would I explain it?"

"And who says he's a stranger?" Celia gibed between giggles, fueling the fire.

"Well, isn't he? I, for one, have never met him, so he is a stranger to me; this is unacceptable! I can't believe you are OK with this. Mom! Did Lia really leave home with a man?" The muscles in his neck got tight; he was visibly bothered.

"This is hilarious…." Celia continued to giggle, "You need to see your face, why are you getting so worked up? She is an adult, is she not? If she wishes to leave home with a charming male counterpart, who am I to object?" Her eyes were now red from laughter.

Self-consciously he tried to compose himself, realizing he was indeed getting worked up.

"I am just worried, that's all…" he desperately tried to save face. "As long as Lia is in New York living under my roof, she's my responsibility. It's only natural that I get concerned over things like this. It's not that I am jealous or getting worked up over nothing. I just need to be sure she'll be safe."

Celia took a deep breath, calming her amused self. "OK, stop your blabbering. Who are you trying to convince, yourself or me? I can see that you are jealous; you practically turned red the minute I said she left with a man. It makes me think that there's more to you avoiding her than meets the eye. Are you afraid you won't be able to control yourself if you got too close…?"

"Mom, don't read more into this than there is. I was only concerned, that is all. Obviously, you are not bothered by her entertaining and going out with random strangers, so be my guest."

"Don't get your boxers in a bunch. I was only pulling your legs. Lia did leave with a young man, but it's not what you think. On the contrary, she's only doing me a favor. The fellow happens to be Rhett, the broker from Gagosian Art Gallery. They got some new pieces in, so he came personally to deliver the catalogs. I have entrusted Lia to make a few selections on my behalf; she has left with Rhett to inspect the pieces in person. Though…" She cast Keaton a puckish stare. "Rhett has taken a liking to her, so if I were you, I wouldn't get so comfortable with him around." She tittered impishly, pouring herself a glass of lemonade.

"So, you deliberately misrepresented Lia's outing just to get a reaction out of me?"

"But, of course, and I got exactly the reaction I expected. Keep lying to yourself. Let us see how long you'll last."

"Whatever, mom." Keaton rolled his eyes childishly. "So, when will she be back?"

"Oh, soon, she did leave right after breakfast, and I don't know of her having any other engagements in the city, so she should be back by lunch."

"OK, I'll try giving her the proposal then."

"You should and stop hesitating; project Globo is a brilliant development. The savvy businesswoman she is, she will be ecstatic to be a part of it."

"We'll see," he said.

CHAPTER 26

Lia did not make it home for lunch; instead, she returned around 2:00 p.m. and went straight to Celia's room. And Celia did not hesitate to direct her to Keaton shortly afterward. Lia knocked on Keaton's bedroom door, only with the knowledge that he wanted to see her. After a few knocks, it was evident he was not there. She returned to Celia, who told her he might be in his study.

At the study, she knocked at the door.

"It's open," Keaton answered from inside.

Lia opened the door and poked her head in before entering.

"Oh Lia, it's you? come on in." He was mildly surprised to see her there as he was the one planning to go to her. He got up from behind his desk with an inviting arm gesture.

"Your mom told me you wanted to see me." She wore an expectant look on her face.

"Yes, yes I do…I was waiting for you to return. I would have come to you myself; It seems mom beat me to it. Here, have a seat…." She walked towards the oversized armchair to the corner of the office; he smiled back at her, an aberrant smile, like someone trying to smile, forcing himself to look natural or less nervous.

She sat down; her green eyes peered up at him, waiting for the reason he wanted to see her. Noticing the silence, he fumbled back to his desk to get the proposal files.

“There is a pioneering project my dad and I have been working on while I was away. He had tried to execute it before my return. Unfortunately, with his passing, it got halted by the then-acting president. I want to revive that project and see it to completion. I need an exceptional team to execute the plans to guarantee its success. That’s why I wanted to see you….”

He handed her the file. “I can’t think of anyone else more fitting than you to lead the project management team and work with me on this venture. Have a look. Let me know what you think….” Lia widened her smile as she took the file.

He walked back to the desk and sat on the edge of it, fiddling his fingers as she read through the proposal. Almost to the few last pages of the file, she looks up at him with a twinkle in her eyes.

“This is brilliant,” she exclaimed. “I mean, I have heard about plans of this nature, and I believe I have seen a few prototypes, but nothing as comprehensive as this.” She scanned through the pages again. Her smile was more prominent.

“So,” he paused for a beat. “Are you saying that you are interested…?” Shifting his weight off the desk. His tone had a hum of anticipation.

“Well, of course, these are the projects I love, the ones that make a remarkable difference across the world. I still can’t believe you have actual patented stratospheric balloons….” Her voice shrieked with excitement.

“We were the first to have our design patented.” He responded. “Inevitable, other major tech companies will eventually take on this venture, but I want TrueTek to be the first. The major groundwork is complete. The longevity testing of the design in the stratospheric conditions is comprehensive. What we need now is a team to champion the project to the finish line. We need to finalize the designs of the auto launchers, wrap up the stratosphere navigating blueprints and finally launch."

"I can see that," Lia responded. The excitement had spread from her eyes to the rest of her body. "It's all here; I am looking at it...with everything in place, if we execute the project now, we can launch the first prescribe set of balloons within four months."

Keaton's eyes popped; she was saying exactly what was on his mind. It confirmed he had chosen the right person. She's knowledgeable and was equally as excited about the project as he was.

"So that settles it?" Keaton affirmed with a beaming smile. "You are on board?"

"Most definitely," she said with a beaming smile. "I mean, we can go through the formalities on Monday. I guess you'll want me to meet with the team I'll be working with and the investors. I recognized some familiar names in the proposal. It should be a breeze getting the others on board if you want. I know a way...."

"That's fantastic," Keaton replied, moving closer to her. She handed him the proposal and sprang on him in a hug. "We'll make a great team," she whispered in his ear, her head tucked between his neck and shoulder.

His eyes widened, a little awkward for him, but he agreed in response. Lia left the study after looking at him once more with enthused eyes and an I'm too excited-I-can't-wait smile.

Immediately after she left, Keaton made arrangements with Lucas for the meeting on Monday. Lia was right; he had to get the ball rolling right away; only then could he be closer to seeing project Globo launch within four months.

On Monday, Keaton brought her into TrueTek for the initial meetings. Lia interviewed the project management team she would be leading, then it was off to meet with the investors in Keaton's office at 1:00 p.m. The investors were worried about the auto launchers for the balloons. Were they capable of filling and launching the balloons into the stratosphere, above airplanes, birds, and the weather as proposed? Testing was pending, and they were skeptical about the impact on their pockets if it failed. The meeting was brief, Keaton and Lia were able to pacify their concerns. They had an unerring plan designed to be effective, and with so much of the project underway, the chances of it failing were significantly less. Lia had her work cut out for her. She now needed to assemble the team that would complete the customization of the auto launchers piloting a successful launch test to appease the investors' concerns before moving forward.

But this was her niche; she headed one of the largest technology manufacturing conglomerates in Europe. Assembling a team to complete the manufacturing of auto launchers was 'a walk in the park'. It all came down to the monies the stakeholders invested; they wanted to ensure their returns. Here was where Keaton stepped in, he was also a genius with numbers, and by the end of the meeting, they had received the green light, pending the auto launcher test.

"You were brilliant in there…." Keaton praised Lia, walking her from his office to the elevator.

"And so were you…it's refreshing to get to see you in your element. I am impressed." Lia glanced at him to the left of her shoulder.

He pushed the call button for the elevator, and they stood side by side in awkward stillness, waiting. He opened his mouth now and then to say something else but hesitated.

"Well, I'll make some calls to get that team together…" she said, breaking the silence. "Once I return to my office, I'll get on it."

"Great, you'll let me know how it goes...?"

"Yes, I should have an update by evening; I'll let you know when I get home."

The elevator doors opened, Lia smiled at him and stepped in. He attempted to give a clumsy wave as the elevator doors closed.

He walked back to his office, entering through the behemoth glass doors of the open floor space that sat on the top level of TrueTek's headquarters. It was the only office on the 10th floor. The entire area was a diagonal layout with the front view and entrance doors made entirely of glass. The glass in front was a one-way view. While he could see everything happening outside of his office, no one outside could see what was happening on the inside.

On the interior, his office had a modern feel, emphasizing light-filled openness that created no barriers to interaction and no impediments to mobility. The layout was proportionately organized, with an extensive carbon steel executive desk positioned where his back would be towards an oversized window that provided a natural flow of light from the outside. His desk is organized with a silver-grey Apple desktop in the center. A white ceramic vase of miniature succulents to the far left and a silver antique pen holder with a built-in clock to the far right. All his files and paperwork were neatly stacked in the desk draws below.

A large well-framed portrait of his father hung to the back wall left of his desk.

The rest of the space had comfortable seating in understated neutrals that kept the room calm. At the same time, they were inviting and comfortable for long or casual meetings, tying in with the rest of the furniture, projecting a quiet elegance fitting seamlessly with the architectural simplicity of the modern office—an overall pleasing sense of order and clarity.

He sat at his desk, leaning backward in the chair with his hands in a clasp, a content smile on his face. All the investors were back on board. The project management team had an exceptional leader; the funds were readily available. Project Globo's successful launch was in clear view. He could feel it. Once Lia prepared for the auto launchers testing. There were no foreseeable hurdles to D-day.

CHAPTER 27

Lia was a Godsend for project Globo, at least in Keaton's eyes. Her connections, level of professionalism, and expertise were just what he needed. Within days she had selected an elite team to complete the Auto Launchers, and within four weeks, the manufacturing process concluded.

With a few minor bumps in the process, the auto launcher's testing was a success, and project Globo commenced mid-June.

Throughout the next three weeks, Keaton and Lia worked tirelessly. As the lead for the project management team, her involvement every step of the way was crucial, from procurement of the vital resources to partnering with significant telecommunication partners within the sub-Saharan region to the executions of the final launch. They worked day and night to see project Globo to completion within the allotted four months.

Meanwhile, in July, Katie had left for Saitama, Japan, for the Olympics. He had to balance his commitment to project Globo, his work relationship with Lia, and communication with Katie to support her through the competition. Competing at the Olympics was a life-goal achievement for Katie; her commitment and dedication in preparation for it were unparalleled. He knew just how important it was for her and made every effort to tell her that he was still there for her, though not physically available.

Early August, Lia, and Keaton traveled to the Central African Republic to inspect the initial launch site. They were thrilled to find that the site's infrastructure was conducive to the launch. They returned to New York a week later to organize transporting the balloons and preparing the team for the final launch in September.

By the end of August, Keaton returned to the Central African Republic with the launch team, equipped with all the resources to support the launch. Lia could not go with him this time as the schedule clashed with other projects she was working on, but that didn't stop her enthusiasm. For this trip, Keaton would have to remain in the Central African Republic for the entire month of September. Not only to facilitate the initial launch but also for post-launch investigations, ensuring that project Globo achieved what they had set out to do.

Two weeks in the Central African Republic and Keaton was through the roof with the outcome. Project Globo had successfully launched. He spent the next few days tracking the algorithms developed by his team to ensure that small groups of the balloons would cluster over specific regions within San-Saharan Africa. Their target was to cover half of the Forty-six countries of the San-Saharan in the first launch. In the third week, the balloons had already clustered over twenty of the targeted countries. Within the next few days, the rest of the clusters had arrived at their destinations. Project Globo had officially proclaimed a complete success five days before the end of September.

An overjoyed Keaton video called Lia the next day. He was practically nerved racked at the success rate; he couldn't wait to update her.

"Keaton? Is everything alright? I tried calling…." Lia answered bright-eyed on his phone screen.

"Lia! Lia! Listen…. You are not going to believe where I am calling you from right now". He moved his phone around, giving her a view of a remote village outside Bangui Luxembourg. "Do you see this?" He exclaimed, his left hand covering his mouth, and his eyes widened.

"Are you in a village…" Lia asked in glee; her face glowed as her eyes scanned the view.

"Yes! Yes, just outside of Bangui Luxembourg. Before Globo, there was no accessible internet connection in this part of Luxembourg. But now, I'm standing here using my phone, connected to internet signals only made possible with Globo. Can you believe this? We did it!" He sprung into the air in a celebratory leap, warping Lia's view.

"When will you return?" She asked with a big smile on her face and dilated pupils. "I need to see the stats. I need to watch the footage from the launch. There is so much I have missed. I'm so mad that I couldn't make it on this trip. This project is evolutionary. I am beyond pleased. I want to scream!"

"I'll be back in four days. I should be home by October 1st. I can't wait for you to see all that we have accomplished. It is mind-blowing. I can't believe it, and I'm the one experiencing it." His mouth formed a broad grin.

"Hurry and get back here; you are making me anxious." Lia giggled.

"I'll call you from a few of the other sites that now have internet. I will give you a tour of the country while I am here...."

"I'd love that." She replied with a sincere smile.

"OK, I'm off to a few more locations. We'll talk soon. If not, I'll be home within a few days. I spoke to mom yesterday. Let her know when I'll return. See you soon." He lifted his hand to the phone's camera view, waving goodbye.

When he hung up, a wholehearted smile lingered on Lia's face. It wasn't just about the thrill of their accomplishment. But how well they worked together and how much their relationship had grown over the months of the project. Seemingly he was no longer indifferent like before. And the communication was no longer for cordiality. At least that's how she felt. In her mind, it took a project for him to notice how good they were together. And it couldn't have happened at a better time, with just a few months leading towards the end of their marriage contract. She was thrilled that things were starting to turn around.

She considered that fate had a hand in initiating project Globo, just when she was about to lose hope. Now she couldn't wait for him to return. Indeed, there was so much that she was missing. But it wasn't all related to statistics and footage from the launch. He was the source of her yearning.

Keaton left the Central Africa Republic a day earlier than planned. He couldn't wait to show Lia what all their efforts had accomplished. And yes, there was the call of duty back at

TrueTek to report to the investors and handle the publicity for project Globo.

He landed in New York on September 30th and got home minutes before midnight. In an exhilarated rush, he dashed through the main door and headed to the staircase. The entire drive from the airport, he prayed Lia wasn't asleep. He was bursting with everything he wanted to share but kept his early return a surprise for added delight.

Almost to the foot of the staircase, he noticed a light in the sitting room and doubled back to take a look. Celia was sitting with an open photo album in her lap and a coffee mug in her hand.

"Mom?" He called, stepping into the sitting room.

She looked up hesitantly as if her ears had deceived her.

"Keaton…?" She rested the mug on the coffee table. "You are home…I wasn't expecting you—Lia said…."

"I know, mom," he grinned, walking over to hug her. "I am a day early, change of plans. It's almost midnight anyway, so still on schedule." He joked. They hugged, and Celia sat back down. "I'm so proud of you, and he would too…." She looked down at the photo album that was now next to her on the couch.

Keaton's eyes followed her gaze to the album, opened to a photo of her and his dad. "Mom…" His tone filled with compassion. "Why are you up so late looking at photos of dad?"

"Did you forget…" She asked in a low teary voice. Keaton cleared his head for a second; then, it dawned on him. October 1st was his father's birthday.

"It's Dad's birthday?" He sat beside her, leaning her head to rest on his shoulder. "I'm sorry, mom. With all the excitement from the project, it skipped my mind. I forgot that you would always stay up the night before dad's birthday, baking his birthday cake. You would be in the kitchen until midnight, waiting for the new day to start. So that you could wish him happy birthday before anyone else did—How could I forget?" His tone went somber.

Celia sniffled. She shifted her head from his shoulder to look at him. "Don't get it wrong.," she said, looking into his eyes. "...I'm not moping because he's no longer with us or because I can't celebrate his birthday with him. Rather, I'm overjoyed that this year on his birthday is the day you would return from Africa having accomplished another of his and your life-long dream. I know that this should be one of the best birthday presents he would have ever received wherever he is. Since I couldn't make him a cake this time, I thought I'd sit here and tell him about all the wonderful things you have accomplished. It is the best way to wish him a happy birthday this year...." She gave him an unconditional 'we-are-extremely-proud-of-you-smile', raising her hand to pat his cheek.

He held his palm against her hand on his cheek, smiling back at her. Unspoken thankfulness, joy, and wistfulness. "Dad would be so happy if he was here...." He sighed.

"It's already midnight; let us wish him happy birthday together, shall we?" Celia said, forcing a broad smile.

They looked at each other, then turned to look at Keegan's photo in the album and wished him a happy birthday. Keaton hugged her again in a comforting embrace. He breathed a quiet sigh as they pulled from the hug.

"Go see Lia," Celia said, tapping Keaton's hand. "She kept me company and only went up because I advised her to; she should still be awake. I'm sure she'll be happy to know that you are back. She couldn't stop talking about the project. It's amazing what this project has done for both of you...."

Keaton rendered a pursed smile. "I do have a lot to tell her. I was rushing home, hoping that she'd be awake—I'll go see her now." He said, getting up from the couch. "You should go to bed now." He pecked her on her cheek and left the room.

CHAPTER 28

Upstairs, Keaton knocked on Lia's door. "Mom is that you…?" She answered from inside. Keaton didn't respond, hoping to surprise her. Just by hearing her voice, the thrill of the project he had traveled with suddenly returned. Within seconds she opened the door. Her eyes bulged in surprise. "Oh my God, what are you doing here!" she screamed, covering her mouth. "I thought you said you'd be back tomorrow…."

"Technically, it is October 1st; it is already past midnight," he teased.

"You know what I mean…." She giggled. "I didn't expect you'd be back at this hour…."

"I have so much to share with you; I just couldn't…."

"Come in!" She shrieked, "You don't know how anxious I've been waiting for you to return. Let me see! Let me see!" She hopped up and down, making him chuckle.

"Snap!" he said, slapping his hand to his forehead. "I left my bag downstairs; let me grab it and a bottle of wine. We have much to celebrate. I'll be right back." He left the room in a hurry.

Lia hurried to the mirror, checking her face and hair, and quickly fixed her top to sit perfectly over her boobs. He returned juggling a bag in one hand and a bottle of wine and two glasses in the other. Lia cheerfully took the glasses and the bottle of wine, resting them on the side table. Keaton sat his bag down on the couch at the foot of her bed and opened it, removing his tablet. Lia ran over and sat beside him.

“So, the footage…? She asked, gleefully rubbing both hands together. He chuckled as he powered up his tablet, which he later handed to her with the video footage of the launch. As she watched, he left the couch to open the bottle, pouring into both glasses.

“Oh my God, Keaton!” She exclaimed, “This is surreal. I wish I were there. I can’t believe we did this.”

“When dad and I came up with this idea years ago, never could I have fathomed what an incredible experience it would turn out to be.” He sat back down beside her, holding both glasses. Her eyes welled up as she watched on.

“I mean, when we came up with the idea, primarily we had considered that a satellite-based solution would be ideal for a country like the Central African Republic. After much research, it was evident that the tricky terrain and lack of terrestrial infrastructure were barriers resulting in low internet penetration.

Project Globo was the solution that would offer instant reach and better speed, and the cost wouldn’t be as astronomical as previous projects of its kind. Lia, what we have done is revolutionary. We have provided access to the very best enterprise applications to parts of the world lacking internet coverage not only to the Central African Republic but to twenty-three other countries within Sub-Saharan Africa. And I could not have done it without you.”

She looked up at him with an appreciative smile, resting the tablet on the bed. He mirrored her smile and handed her the glass of wine.

He raised his glass in a cheers-giving gesture, and Lia followed suit. "Here's to the successful completion of project Globo. Here's to the beginning of a revolutionary movement. Here's to a lifetime partnership between TrueTek and SANCORP, and here's to you, Miss Lia Paton, for everything you have done to facilitate the project's success. I am forever grateful."

They clinked their glasses and took the first sip, which led to two other refills. By the time they had finished watching the rest of the footage, they were on the second bottle of wine. By the revision of the statistics, Keaton had opened the third bottle, and by 3:00 a.m., they had finished four bottles of wine, a tub of butterscotch ice cream, and were laughing hysterically. A raw display of happiness, accomplishment, and sheer awe of what they had achieved in such a short time.

Keaton stumbled to get up from the couch to grab the bottle of wine from the side table. He poured, but only a little came out. "It's empty," he declared, looking at the bottle. Lia giggled with the empty glass in her hand.

"Isn't this our fourth bottle? I think we have had enough. If we drink anymore, we are sure to get drunk."

"You are right," he replied, resting the empty bottle back on the side table. "I think I am already a bit tipsy."

He walked back to the couch and sat beside her. He took the empty glass from her and held both of her hands, looking directly into her eyes. She swallowed a bit, holding onto his stare.

"I know I might sound like a broken record, but I can't thank you enough. I am finally starting to understand why dad partnered with SANCORP; you bring so much to the table. We work well together, and I look forward to working on many other projects with you." He gave her an appreciative smile and a gentle squeeze on her hands.

Her green eyes looked deeper into his, filled with longing, bursting with emotions she could no longer conceal.

"Is there only a work relationship between us? Do you feel anything else towards me?" Her eyes moved around, scanning his face for the answer she desired, searching his heart through his eyes.

Within himself, he searched for the appropriate answer—a million voices shouting inside his head. Her face was close to his; he felt the warmth of her breath. There was no denying that working on project Globo brought them closer. He found it harder to resist being this close. Harder to be indifferent. Before he could gather his thoughts, his body reacted, and he was kissing her like a reunited lover. The concealed passion was bursting from within them both like hot lava from a freshly erupted volcano.

She flung both arms around his neck, climbing onto his lap. She kissed back twice as hard as he did, in earnest, urgent need. She was gripping his body as if in fear he would disappear.

His hands were under her blouse; he lifted it over her head, revealing her diminutively succulent breasts. She leaned into him, and they were in his face, ripe and white. An extraordinary feeling overcame him, like a toddler unboxing a new toy. The sight of her breasts sent electrifying bolts of lust and erotism from his brain to his shaft. It rose in rebellion, pushing against her thighs.

He picked her up, rising from the couch. Her legs locked around his waist and her hands held tightly over his shoulders. He laid her down on the bed, pulling off her shorts and delicate lace thongs. The more of her nakedness he saw, the more aroused he got. His mind was blank to reason; the only thing he could see was what he had been missing for months; his body craved the intimacy; it had been so long.

His breathing intensified, his heart thumped rapidly and irregularly, wanting to burst through the cavity of his chest.

He ran his fingers along her inner thigh; her chest arched, forward and upright. Her legs spread as his hand made its way to her perfectly manicured pubic mound. She gasped as his fingertip brushed across her labia, skimming the edge of her pink flushed clitoris.

Her hips swayed in a circular dance; she groped her breasts, panting as his fingers slid into her, exploring her burning, wet fleshiness like an explorer on a new expedition. An intense desire stirred inside him; he observed her response to his every touch. Without words, her body told him what to do—controlling the movement of his fingers meticulously while the base of his palm rubbed tenderly against her clitoris.

Her moans got louder, the movement of her legs and waist went into overdrive. She pulled Keaton up onto her. "I need you," she moaned, passionately removing his shirt, kissing his neck and chest. Her hands rushed to unbuckle his belt, pulling at his pants.

She flipped position, mounting him so she could pull off his pants, taking his stirred shaft into her hand. The feel of it hardening against her palm was luxuriating, surreal. His stomach convulsed as the friction on his dick against her hot, moist palm intensified the sensation. His eyes closed, and he pushed his head back into the bed, his chin upright. Completely submerged in the feeling he had been missing, needing for so long, he could think of nothing else.

He felt his member emerge into a pool of burning goodness. Lia inserted its entirety into her. Her clasp tightened around his erection as she sank lower onto him.

His eyes popped open; she was on top of him, her green eyes rolled back as her head swung backward. At that moment, it was real; this was happening, his consciousness slowly returned. The person on top of him was not Katie.

With urgency, he lifted her off of him and sprung from the bed. The shocking realization had hit him like a deer in headlights. He fumbled to put his clothes back on.

"What—what are you doing?" Lia asked, her voice croaked and breathy. Her expression, riddled with confusion and disbelief.

"Lia, I am sorry, I can't do this.... I should never have let it get this far. I—I'm...."

"What do you mean....?" Her eyes welled up with tears, her face flushed; she felt exposed, rejected, and vulnerable.

"We were both caught up in the heat of the moment. I am to blame; I never intended for this…this to happen. I'm so sorry".

He pressed one hand to his temple, leaning against the door. He was in a state of confusion while her heart was breaking. She knelt in the bed, pulling the sheets up to cover her nakedness. Her eyes wandered in emptiness, and her body went numb. Her hands trembled as she clutched the sheets up to her chest, tightening her grasp around it, wanting to be rescued from the humiliation. Tears raced down her cheeks, and the sight of her tears pierced his heart. He knew how she felt; he was feeling it too.

"Why?" she sobbed, her green eyes cloudy with tears. "Why are you doing this? Why are you rejecting me?" She cried in a sniffling whimper.

"Lia, please, it's not like that. I never meant for this to happen. I tried my best to avoid a situation like this. Because I knew it wouldn't lead to anything good. The truth is, I am in love with my girlfriend, Katie. From the very beginning, it has been her—the reason for my indifference was not to be mean to you but to be loyal to her.

"Now, I don't know how to feel or what to believe anymore. My head is a complete mess. My heart feels like it's dissecting inside my chest. I feel like I am betraying her and hurting you, and I don't know what to do. Please—forgive me…." Tears rolled down his face as he stood against the door—pants on and shirt in his hand. He looked at her with sincerity. But that didn't stop the hurt; he felt her pain, watched her heart break as tears cascaded down her cheeks.

He wanted to go to her, hold her, and comfort her, but he couldn't. His pain, disorientation, and bewilderment were paralyzing.

"You never really planned on giving us a chance, did you?" She swiped at her eyes, trying to stop the tears. Her lips trembled as he spoke. "I gave up my personal life to be here, but you, what have you given up? I gave you my terms to have a fair shot in this marriage, yet you disregarded everything and kept in touch with your girlfriend.

"I have been nothing but loyal and patient, waiting for you to see me the way I see you. I have fallen for you from the very first day you kissed me at the wedding rehearsal. And I've only fallen deeper ever since. Do you know how hard it is to be in love with someone under the same roof and not be able to express that love? I have suppressed my love for you for months now, waiting for you to feel the same. It's like a ticking time bomb, and tonight mine has exploded. I can no longer contain it. Keaton, I am in love with you!" Her butt fell back onto her heels as she clutched the sheets tighter. A flood of tears gushed down her cheeks, blurring her vision.

His heart became heavy and sore; he did not know how to respond. He sniffed quietly, tears rolling down his eyes. The more Lia cried, the more he ached inside until he couldn't physically bear it any longer. If he remained in the room, he was bound to tell her how he truly felt.

"I'm truly sorry…." He sniffled, turning to open the door.

"Stop!" She yelled, her face wet with her tears. "I only need to know one thing, and please be honest. Am I the only one who feels this way? Do you honestly feel nothing for me?"

Keaton turned back around to face her; he dared not speak the truth. He hadn't had time to make sense of his feelings; how was he supposed to make sense of it to her? His silence impaled her, and she whimpered in hurt and rage.

"You dare deny it!" she screamed, tears rolling down her face. "You do have feelings for me, and you know it! How you looked at me—touched me; your feelings have changed towards me these past four months. And what about now? You were ready to make love to me and in the middle of it you...." She pulled the sheets up to her face with shaking hands; a great sob escaped her to the point of choking.

Compelled to comfort her, he moved closer, but a part of him wouldn't let him and kept him frozen a few meters from the bed. She brought the sheets down from her face; life seemed to have drained from her eyes. Her face was red as if bruised and eyes swollen from constant wiping.

She saw pity in his eyes; it infuriated her and injured her dignity. "It's alright," she sniffled, "you don't need to answer me. Keep lying to yourself if that will make you happy or feel less guilty. Just do me a favor; for the three months left in this marriage, please stay away from me, and I will stay away from you. Keaton, I am not like you; I can't hide my feelings anymore; my heart won't let me. It's better this way; let us keep our distance. At the end of the contract, I'll leave here, and we can go back to our lives like this year never happened. I wish you both well...." She paused in a tremor of sniffles. "...I truly do, now, please leave; I want to be alone."

"Lia, please, I-- I...." He stuttered, trying to find the appropriate words to say.

"Just leave!" she screamed, tossing a pillow at him.

He backed away from the bed, hesitantly towards the door. "Lia, I'm truly sorry...."

He turned to open the door and left the room.

At the closing of the door, the build-up of ache in her heart exploded; she fell to the bed in a disheveled heap as her pain poured out in loud cries. Keaton stood outside the door, broken by the sound of her screams. It was torture, not knowing what to do. God knows he only wanted to do the right thing. And that meant being loyal to Katie, the one who has been waiting for him through it all. He made her a promise, one he intended to keep. His love for her had never wavered. But at the same time, he couldn't deny something else was brewing in his heart for Lia.

He walked away from her door across the hall to his bedroom. He fell face down on the bed, pulled a pillow over his head, letting out a gut-wrenching grunt. There was a tightening in his chest; that made breathing feel like razor blades moving through him. Trying to make sense of what was happening to him absorbed all his energy. He was mentally drowning, reminding himself to breathe, convincing himself that the pain would go away. Was he being callow, believing he could contain his feelings for Lia?

CHAPTER 29

When the sun came up, Keaton rolled over on his back; he had spent the entire night in one position and hardly got any sleep. He walked into the bathroom and took a shower then got dressed for work. It was already 7:00 a.m., and he wanted to be in the office by 8:00, with a two-hour drive into the city that wasn't at all possible. The sore ache in his heart was still fresh, and he wondered how Lia was at that moment.

He grabbed his bag and headed out the door. In the hallway, he met Lia just as she exited her bedroom. She was dressed for work, wearing a pair of shades that he imagined was to conceal evidence of the night's teary episode. He stopped in his tracks, and she looked over at him, then hurriedly closed her door and headed towards the staircase.

"Lia, please, can we talk?"

She continued to walk away, not answering.

"Lia." He rushed behind her and grabbed her hand. "Please, just..."

"Let go of my hand!" with a stifled scream, she yanked her hand away from his grip. He felt her hand trembling as she pulled.

"Are you going to avoid me? Is that how you want to handle this?" He asked in hush tones, trying not to alert his mother.

"You are such a hypocrite!" Lia yelled, her voice bore anger, her expression inflamed. "Hasn't that been the way you handled everything in the first five months of this marriage? It was alright for you to ignore and avoid me then, but now I can't do the same? What do you want from me!"

"Lia, I know you are mad at me, and you have every right to be. I know I have been a complete jerk initially, but you also have to understand where I am coming from; I have been in a relationship with Katie for three years, I couldn't just end it at a whim. I can't dismiss the love I have for her so easily. I—I."

Lia made a cynical giggle, "And so, you believe you are the only one who was in a relationship before this arranged union? It speaks to how arrogant you are. You have no idea what I gave up agreeing to this marriage, and all I asked for in return is a chance at a fair experience. Have you ever once asked yourself the question—between both of us, who is benefiting the most? I have moved halfway across the world, gave up my relationship, my life, moved to your country to get married to you and live under your roof for reasons more beneficial to you. All because my father demanded it. I have no one here. I had to grieve the loss of both parents being away from the only family I have. I have practically adjusted my entire life, work, and everything I hold dear. I thought I'd at least have a meaningful marriage experience in all this, but it seems I was only naïve. In your eyes, I am just a tool to accomplish your goals. You use me only when it benefits you, and as soon as you get what you want, you'll discard me with absolutely no concern for my feelings."

Everything Lia suppressed was spilling from within her, and it came with temper and tears streaming down her cheeks beneath her shades.

"For five solid months, I felt avoided; you treated me like an insignificant housemate. My attempts to get close to you were thrown back in my face. You stood me up every date night, even on my birthday. You never once tasted the meals I made for you or even acknowledged my efforts out of common courtesy. How do you think that made me feel? Even then, knowing you were disregarding the terms of the contract. I never voiced it or made it an issue in hopes that you'd eventually appreciate me, lying to myself that you were genuinely busy with work every day of the week for five months.

Keaton couldn't believe what he was hearing as he listened to the torment he caused her. Guilt hung over his head like the *Sword of Damocles*, waiting to slice him through at any minute as she continued her rant:

"In these last four months, things started to change; you were better towards me. You treated me as your equal; we had late work nights that turned into date nights. How many times did I wake up in your arms having fallen asleep at your office working on project Globo? How many times did we almost kiss if we were not interrupted? In the last four months, the feelings I initially had for you grew stronger, and I stupidly believed that you were starting to feel the same. And last night happened...." She paused as the memory ripped wider the raw wound his rejection had made in her heart. She held onto the wall for support as her legs became weak; the recollection drained all that was left of her to the point where it became unbearable to continue standing or speaking. She became light-headed, her heart rate raised, and her vision got patchy. She barely had time to raise her hand to her head when her body collapsed to the floor in front of him. It happened so fast. Keaton's brain took a minute to process what was happening before he dropped to her aid.

"Lia! Lia!" He sat on the floor, bringing her upper body into his arms, her head on his chest. He removed her shades and frantically tapped her cheeks, trying to revive her, but she was unresponsive.

"Mom! Mom!" He screamed, holding Lia tighter. "Mom, call the ambulance!

Celia rushed upstairs with a frightened look on her face. "Oh my God, Keaton, what happened, why—why is Lia…?" Her hands over her mouth, she was stuttering in panic.

"Mom, please call the ambulance!" He screamed! As he hyperventilated. Celia rushed to her bedroom and returned on her cell phone, feverishly giving their address to the emergency dispatcher on the line.

"Lia, please don't do this! Please, please, please wake up." He had her in a rocking motion, his heart racing, chanting the exact phrase repeatedly.

It wasn't long before they heard the sound of the ambulance in the distance. Keaton picked up Lia's limp body and ran with her downstairs to meet the ambulance by the front door.

He climbed into the ambulance after the paramedics had put Lia in. Celia wanted to do the same, but the paramedics insisted only one family member was allowed.

“I’m her husband,” Keaton cried. “I have to be with her.” He held onto one of Lia’s hands while the paramedics placed an oxygen mask over her face.

“I’ll meet you at the hospital,” Celia yelled as the ambulance doors closed. The ambulance pulled away from the estate, and Celia and her driver rushed to her car. The entire staff assembled at the driveway, curious and alarmed.

In the ambulance, one of the paramedics questioned Keaton.

“Can you talk me through what happened before she fainted?”

Keaton stammered to piece his words together. He was visibly flustered.

“It was an argument, she was yelling at me, and then—then she just collapsed.... It’s—; it’s all my fault.” His voice was breathy, croaking with remorse.

“Will she be alright...?” He asked, desperation in his eyes.

“Well, she’s breathing, the paramedic replied. “that’s always a good sign. We’ll know more once we get to the hospital. Does she have any health-related issues we should know about?”

“No—no, not that I know of....” Keaton replied, clasping his hand up to his mouth, rocking back and forth in a panicky wreck.

Soon they arrived at the hospital, rushing Lia off to the emergency ward. Keaton was asked to wait while the doctors examined Lia. He paced the hallway of the emergency ward, praying incoherently—his hands on top of his head.

Some minutes later, the doctor came out of the room to find him. Keaton rushed towards him.

“Doctor is she ok?” he asked, sounding out of breath.

“Yes, she’s stable now…and you are Keaton, her husband, right?” The doctor asked, looking down on the paramedics’ report chart in his hand.

“Yes, yes I am—what happened to her? Why did she…?”

“You want to know why your wife fainted? —well, first, why don’t we have a seat. You seemed a bit worked up; let’s get you settled. The doctor walked Keaton to the seating area, where he explained the reason Lia fainted.

“From my examination, it seems your wife had a temporary drop in blood flow to her brain in response to a trigger. The trigger could be anything from standing too long, fear, pain, or intense emotional stress. In your wife’s case, we’ve concluded that emotional stress is more likely the trigger since the paramedics’ report states that she fainted during an argument. The stress may have caused a drop in her blood pressure, and I believe that’s why she fainted.”

Keaton pressed his face into his palms in despair with confirmed knowledge that Lia had fainted because of him. *How do I always end up making things worse?* He thought, *I only wanted to talk to her, to make sure she was ok; instead, I caused her to be in the hospital.* He shook his head despairingly at the latter thought.

“However,” the doctor continued. “I’d like to keep her overnight for observation; there is still a bit of blood pooled up in her legs which should clear soon, but I’d prefer to have her here to make sure it does. Other than that, she's in excellent condition, and if you wish, you can go see her."

"Tha—Thank you," Keaton stammered, shaking the doctor's hand. He then rushed off to Lia's room.

He walked into her room, not knowing what to say. Lia looked up at him with pain-riddled green eyes.

"Please leave," she sobbed, turning her head away from him.

"Lia...."

"Please, that's all I am asking. I want to be alone. Each time I see you now, my heart pains. It hurts, and I don't want to feel like that anymore. So, please—go."

A knot moved to his throat; he despondently picked at his fingernails.

"If that's what you want, I'll leave the room. But I'll be waiting outside. I will not leave you here by yourself. The doctor said you'll be staying overnight for observation. I'll get you something to eat and some fresh clothes. I'll be back later...." He released a pained sigh and turned to leave. He could hear her stifling her cry as he left the room.

Just outside the door, he bumped into his mother, rushing in.

"Oh, Keaton, where's Lia? Why is your face like this? Is she ok?" Keaton nodded in response. Before saying:

"She's ok; she's in the room. It would be best if you went to see her now."

Celia's expression had a mixture of panic and confusion, she needed answers from Keaton, but she needed to see Lia more.

She entered Lia's room while Keaton stood outside the door. He moved towards the window of her room, where he could scarcely see their images through the openings of the window blinds.

He could see Lia breakdown in Celia's arms, and it made him feel worse than he already felt. He turned away, mad at himself, wanting her to go back to her chirpy self, not wanting to see her cry. As much as she thought he was emotionless and oblivious to her feelings, that was far from the truth. There was a battle going on inside him; he was navigating a complex minefield between her, his, and Katie's feelings to avoid detonation, to avoid hurting anyone. The thing was, he was miserably failing, realizing he had stepped on Lia's landmine, and now he didn't know how to remove himself without causing severe damage.

He pulled his phone from his pocket. It was almost midday. More than twenty missed calls were in the notifications: from Katie, his assistant Lucas, and Trent, one of his childhood friends and college buddies.

He texted Lucas: *I can't make it to the office today. Clear my schedule for the rest of the week.* And put the phone back into his pocket.

Moments later, Celia came out of Lia's hospital room. She looked at him madly and at the same time like she was sorry for him.

"Let's take a walk," she said, striding past him. He walked alongside her. They got outside to the seating area on the hospital grounds, where she sat on a bench looking into the distance.

"Come sit," she commanded, tapping the bench space next to her. Keaton sat, also looking into the distance.

"What exactly happened between you two?" Celia asked, turning to look at him.

"Last night, you returned home excited to see her, and in less than twenty-four hours, she's in the hospital, hurt, distraught, begging to return to Norway. What is going on?"

Keaton looked at his mom, his face pale.

"She wants to leave?"

"Yes, that's all she's been crying about since I've been in her room. I begged her to sleep on it until after she is discharged; hopefully, she will."

Keaton took in a deep breath; he instantly had a headache.

"What I don't get is why?" Celia continued. "Neither of you is saying anything when it is obvious you both are hurting. From what I can see, it is clear you did something to upset her, so tell me, what did you do?"

I have no reason to keep what happened from mom, he thought. *Besides, she already figured I am the reason Lia is in the hospital, so what is there to hide?*

"Last night in all the celebration, we got a bit tipsy and carried away. One thing led to another, and we got intimate. When I realized what was happening, though, it had gone too far—way, way too far. I stopped it. Lia confessed her love for me, and I couldn't reciprocate. Now she feels like I have rejected her, and believes I am only using her and…."

Speaking about it made his heart bleed. Talking about it to his mom gave him more clarity as to why Lia was hurting so badly.

"So that's what the argument was about this morning? I could hear Lia yelling from downstairs, but I couldn't clearly hear what she was saying. So that's why she passed out; your rejection emotionally stressed her?"

His silence was confirmation enough; he had no strength to explain why he had to do what he did; there was no point. He knew his mom would sympathize more with Lia. And he wouldn't blame her. He blamed himself for not controlling the situation better. Now it was too late.

CHAPTER 30

"Tell me something. Do you have feelings for Lia?" Celia asked, holding on to Keaton's hand.

"I don't know. I don't know how to categorize what I feel for Lia. And that's why it's so hard to give her the answer she needs. Yes, I'll admit that working on Project Globo brought us closer. There is a definite attraction; however, I don't know if it's love or infatuation. Before last night we had never been so intimate; it happened so fast I couldn't think straight, and I failed to control the situation before it got out of hand. Now everything is a mess, and I don't know where or how to start fixing it. Lia hates me and wants nothing to do with me. She won't even allow me to explain. And Katie..., I haven't been able to speak to Katie since it happened, she's been calling me, and I can't answer because I feel like I have betrayed her trust."

"Why is Katie calling, wasn't there an arrangement that you'd be the one to call her?"

"Yes, but she must think I'm still in Africa. I told her she could call me anytime when I was there since Lia wouldn't be around. Initially, my return to New York would be today. Knowing Katie, she must be calling to wish me a safe flight. I see her missed calls, but I cannot find the courage to call back or text her. I'm so confused."

"I know you love Katie, but now it seems you feel the same way for Lia. You are confused because you never thought you could feel the way you do for Katie towards anyone else. Now that that has changed, your heart and mind don't know how to handle it. I know because I have been there."

"What you need to do now is to think of what's best for you and your heart with consideration on your new status and responsibilities. You may or may not take my advice; nonetheless, I believe you are more compatible with Lia. Marriage works best for like-minded people who share similar perspectives, visions, and goals. I don't know much about Katie, but I know she is a competitive figure skater at the peak of her career. Is she ready to give all that up to move to New York and settle down with you? She's young and independent, which is excellent; however, she is nowhere close to Lia's level of maturity. She is in a different country at least six times for the year for one competition after the other. How do you plan to build a life with someone like that—raise children?"

Keaton, looking bewildered just hung his head in despair as she talked: "As president of TrueTek, your partner needs to be exceptional, someone who is your equal, who understands the line of work and can support you when things get tough, and trust me, it will. You met Katie when you were studying and had little or no obligations when you were not responsible for the future of a billion-dollar multinational company. At that time, your relationship might have made sense. You could travel with her all over the world to support her dreams. But what about now? Have you thought about how your relationship would work now that you are president? You won't be able to support her in the same ways you did before. Katie is used to the relaxed, wild, and free life you showed her at the beginning of your relationship. Where you were carefree and could travel the world or do anything for her to support her, now that you are no longer living carefree, will she be able to adjust? Katie is still chasing her dream; she is still making her name in the world of figure skating. You and Lia, on the other hand, are already living your dreams. You have already made your names and are at that stage of maturity to start a family, be husband and wife, raise children and build on the empires you both inherited."

Keaton's face drained with the enormity of Celia's diatribe. Much of what she said hit onto key points that he never took the time to entertain in thought much less closely examine. *My personal life is a wreck*, his inner child wailed.

Celia leaned into him and massaged the back of his hand. "You once told me that you fell for Katie because she wasn't shallow and didn't care much for material things. Well, how about Lia? Lia is your equal; she is not superficial; she doesn't care about what you have or how affluent you are because she can match it. Yet she fell head over heels for you. What does that tell you? Her love for you is genuine.... And before you get upset, know that I am by no means underrating Katie. I am simply showing you both sides of the coin, opening your eyes to the bigger picture. Katie is a great girl in her element; however, she wouldn't last a day in your current world from where I'm sitting.

Think about what I have said. I hope it gives you some clarity on the confusion you are experiencing. I have to leave now. I have the annual Dawson Wellness charity auction to attend. Please take care of Lia. I'll be back as soon as it is over."

Celia pecked Keaton on the cheek and got up from the bench. He said nothing but looked bereft as she left. He had a lot to consider, and it didn't seem to be getting any easier.

Later that day, Keaton returned to the hospital after he had left to get fresh clothing and food for Lia. Lia still didn't want to see him, so he gave the items to her attending nurse. He sat in the waiting room outside her room until night came.

Around 8:00 p.m., his phone dinged, another text message came in from Katie:

Hey Bébé, *I hope you had a safe flight, and you are home now? Call me as soon as you get this. I've been trying to reach you all morning. I am worried. Love you.*

In his worried and confused state, he forgot to return her call. He still felt guilty, but he couldn't make her worry about him. He walked further down the hall, a reasonable distance from Lia's room, and dialed Katie.

"Hey *Bébé*, I'm so glad you are okay. I tried to reach you before your flight. I thought...."

"I know, I was careless. I forgot to charge my phone overnight, and it died. But I'm good; I'm home." He cringed at his lie. His eyes closed, using two fingers to massage his left temple."

"Oh...," Katie replied, pausing for a beat. "Well, I'm relieved; I thought something terrible had happened."

"Everything is fine. How about you, how is it going back home now that you are France's Olympic silver medalist. Are they still praising and paving the streets with gold for you?"

Katie giggled at his humor. "The reception has been overwhelming. I wish you were here. The outpouring of love and admiration is so much more than I ever imagined. I am so grateful for the experience and the opportunities it has brought me."

"Yeah, I'm incredibly proud and happy for you. Not only did you surpass your dream of making it to the Olympics, but you also earned yourself a silver medal. You are among the top three best ice figure skaters in the world. That is a significant accomplishment, and you should be proud."

"I am. And this silver medal is even more motivation for me. I will train harder, compete harder. I won't stop until I'm a multi-gold medalist in the Olympics in the years to come.

But for now, I wish I could celebrate this win with you. Although it won't be long, only three more months and we'll be together again. I am so excited I can't wait." Katie yelped in anticipation.

Keaton sat at the next waiting area he came upon and went silent for a moment.

"*Bébé*, are you still there?" Katie asked.

"Yes, I'm here."

"Aren't you excited? It's only three more months until we can be together again. Why do I feel like I'm more thrilled than you are?"

“I am excited and anxious to be with you again. I’m just a bit tired, and jet-lagged that’s all?”

“Oh, I understand. So should I let you go?”

“No, I can talk. I might not be as upbeat, but I still enjoy your company.”

“I know you do.” Katie giggled.

“Katie, can I ask you something?”

“Of course.”

“You mentioned earlier that this medal is more motivation for you to train harder for the future Olympics to be a multi-gold medalist. How long do you plan on competing? I mean, where do you see yourself in five years?”

“Well, I’ll compete as long as it takes to achieve my goals. I have always envisioned myself being at least a five-time gold medalist in the Olympics. I didn’t win gold this time, but I hope to at the next Olympics. So, I guess I’ll be competing over the next five years, preparing myself to earn Olympic golds in the figure skating competitions to fulfill my dream. Why do you ask?”

“I just realized I never asked you about your long-term goals before. It’s nothing serious. We are going to build a life together; I want to know what plans you have for the future and how I can support you, that’s all.”

“You are the best,” Katie said in awe. “And it won’t always be about competing. In between, I want to travel the world with you too. We will have the best of both worlds. Live our lives the way we want to, fulfilling our dreams together; we will create our paradise."

"Yes...we will," Keaton replied, forcing a joyous tone.

"Anyways, as much as I know you enjoy my company. I would hate to keep you from getting a well-deserved rest. After all, the sleep you have lost to achieve a successful launch for Project Globo, you need some quality rest. But before I go. I wanted to tell you that my parents are planning a celebratory trip for me to Greece. As you know, that is where my mom's family is from; It will be kind of a family reunion plus a celebration of my Olympic win. They are planning to leave in a week, though it hasn't been finalized as yet. It will be a good pass time for me since you won't be around for a few more months. I'll use it as a distraction until I'm ready for training again. I'll keep you posted once the dates are confirmed.

"Love you and go get some rest—Muah!"

"Love you too. And again, I'm proud of you."

"Bye, *Bébé*..."

"Bye."

CHAPTER 31

Keaton hung up and walked back towards the waiting area closer to Lia's room. A replay of the conversation, particularly Katie's plans for the future, lingered in his thoughts and a recollection of his earlier discussion with his mom.

When he got back to the waiting area, he walked alongside Lia's room and peeked through the window. She was asleep. He sent a quick text message to Celia, letting her know Lia was already asleep and she shouldn't bother to stop by after the charity auction. Exhaustion and hunger pangs nagged him, but he refused to leave until Lia was ready for discharge.

He returned to the seating area and made himself comfortable. It was now minutes to 10:00 p.m., and he was the only one sitting there. He laid his head back on the couch, closed his eyes, and tried to clear his mind, and before he knew it, he fell asleep.

"Mr. Dawson…Mr. Dawson," in his sleep, he could hear someone calling his name, barely audible. Keaton was so fast asleep that he thought it was a dream until he felt a tap on his shoulder. When he opened his eyes, a nurse was standing over him. He ran his hand across his forehead and released a breathing sigh.

"Yes?" He answered, looking up at the nurse.

"Good morning Mr. Dawson. My name is Gianna; I am your wife's attending nurse. I just wanted to let you know that the doctor has signed off on her release. She is free to go. I will need you to sign off on these as well," She handed Keaton Lia's discharge documents.

Keaton took the documents; he looked disoriented, his eyes still adjusting to waking mode.

"What time is it?" He asked

"It is now 6:30 a.m.," the nurse replied, looking over at the large wall clock hung to his left.

I can't believe I slept all this time, he thought, releasing a faint sigh. He scanned through the documents on the clipboard and applied his signature.

"Here you go," he said, handing it back to the nurse.

She briefly double-checked them and confirmed his fulfillment with a smile.

"That will be all, Mr. Dawson. I have informed your wife that you have been waiting all night. She is preparing to leave as we speak. You may assist her if you wish."

"Thank you," he replied, and Gianna left.

He rubbed his eyes to refresh them further, checked his phone, and read Celia's response to his earlier text message:

Thanks for the update. Since she is being discharged tomorrow, I will see you both at home. Please take care of her.

Outside Lia's hospital room door, he knocked. "Lia, it's Keaton. Can I come in?"

"Yes." She answered with indifference.

He cautiously entered, closed, and stood behind the door. "Is there anything I can help you with, anything you need me to carry?"

“No, this is everything,” Lia replied, looking down on the overnight bag Keaton had brought for her.

“Let me get that,” Keaton said, picking up the bag. “I’ll be taking you home. My car is parked outside.”

Lia nodded; all the time, she avoided direct eye contact. “I’m ready, so let’s go.”

Keaton stepped aside, allowing her to exit before him, and followed closely behind. He opened his mouth a few times to speak but hesitated, not wanting to upset her again. When they exited the hospital, he walked ahead of her towards the parking lot and opened the front passenger car door.

“I would rather sit in the back,” Lia said, opening the left rear door. She entered and closed the door before he could. Keaton sighed, walking around to the driver’s side. He placed her bag on the passenger’s seat next to him and pulled out of the parking lot. On the route back to the Estate, Keaton rehearsed an entire conversation in his head. The conversation he wanted to have with her. It was seamless in thought, but he couldn’t get his mouth to open long enough to speak.

He glanced at her through the rearview mirror. She kept her body slanted towards the car door, her focus outside the window and a taut look on her face. He swallowed and took a deep breath, stimulating himself to say what was on his mind.

“Lia, it was never my intention for this to happen. I only wanted to….”

“Were any of the things that have happened between us ever your intention? Lia interjected, her English precise and meticulous. “You always seem to start your apologies, or whatever this is with 'it was never my intention.' "It was never your intention to be beguiling and emotionally misleading these past four months, knowing fully well how I felt about you? When you returned from Africa, it was never your intention to kiss me, practically took me to bed only to reject me once you were inside me? You never intended to ensue an argument after the fact, even though I asked you to stay away from me? A fight that got me hospitalized. It's always never your intention!

"You keep 'unintentionally' hurting me, and my heart can't take it. I thought I was strong enough to withstand anything, but apparently, I'm not strong enough to withstand your rejection and unrequited love. When I woke up in the hospital and learned that I fainted because of emotional stress, that's when I realized how badly your rejection had affected me. I have been handling high-stress business deals for years now, and I have never collapsed under pressure until you. Initially, I thought we could be incredible together, that you were what I was missing. But now, I realize I have been delusional. You are not good for me. Since the beginning of this marriage contract, I have been the only one compromising, losing myself, being embarrassed, stood up, and used. I am only noticed when it's convenient or when it benefits you."

Keaton cringed at her words. Every word a dagger to his heart. But she would not shut up. He was driving, he couldn't walk away. He was captive as she spilled all her angst.

"You blatantly disregarded the conditions of the contract and stayed in touch with your girlfriend when I foolishly honored the terms and stayed faithful and loyal to you. In the agreement, you signed to the provisions that I would experience this marriage as proper husband and wife, allowing a reasonable chance to determine whether we are compatible. Have you stayed true to any of it?" She didn't wait for his answer.

"You haven't—but I have. And I am done being naïve and hopeful. I have accepted that you do not feel the same way I feel about you. I have accepted that we are not compatible. I have accepted that there is nothing between us other than a business partnership. So, I do not need an apology, I do not need to hear that 'it was never your intention.' From today, let's go back to communicating only for business. Let's forget about what has happened. In three months, this will be over, and we can go our separate ways as you wish. Until the end of our agreement, I will remain here not to complicate things for SANCORP and TrueTek's partnership. That's all we are to each other, business partners, so promise me, you won't mislead me anymore or engage me with anything remotely outside of business. Promise me now; that's all I want to hear you say."

Keaton listened to everything she said and kept his gaze on her as much as he could through the rearview mirror. Her expression was impassive and detached; she meant every word she had said. He took a second before responding.

"I promise."

CHAPTER 32

Some weeks had passed, and it was harder for Keaton to keep his promise; however, Lia was unwavering in her decision to engage in communication for business only. She was classy and kept it professional; she did everything she had to ensure stability in the projects they collaborated on and entertained nothing more. No small talk, no breakfast or dinner together, no jokes, no casual salutations, it was driving Keaton up the wall.

Celia was irritated by the distance between them and blamed Keaton. She wanted Keaton to fix it, but there was nothing he could do. Lia would leave home early and return late nights, just as Keaton would in the beginning.

Keaton secretly waited up to see that she was home safe, but that's all he could do. He began to understand how she initially felt. What annoyed him the most was Lia's friendship with Rhett, the art broker from Gagosian Art Gallery. Rhett and Lia now hung out most weekends, and Rhett was at the estate almost every Sunday to have supper with Lia and Celia.

It was evident that their relationship was strictly friendship and casual business. However, from Keaton's perspective, Rhett was quite tactile, and Keaton was curious about what Rhett was telling Lia to make her giggle so much every time he was around. He was irritated by it but kept it to himself.

With Katie in Greece unwinding, he kept their conversations to a minimum, giving her space to be with her family and not burden her with his work-related disgruntlement. His restlessness wasn't so much about work; subconsciously, it was his excuse to mask the real reason behind his agitation; being blatantly ignored by Lia.

By the middle of October, the publicity for the success of project Globo had a global impact, boosting the success of TrueTek's established and new projects. And the biotechnology project between TrueTek and SANCORP started to manifest projected returns; everything was falling into place. Also, it was months to the end of the marriage contract, but he was not as enthusiastic about it as he should.

On the 18th of October, he was at TrueTek until 10:00 p.m. He had a full day that kept him outside the office going from one meeting to another. He returned to his office around 7:00 p.m. that evening and worked until 10:00 p.m., wrapping up the details of the day's consultations.

When he realized how late it was, he decided to check his emails before heading home. That's when he saw an email from the United States Technology Administration. The email rendered an invitation to the award ceremony as a finalist for the National Medal of Technology and Innovation. He knew Project Globo was nominated, but it was unbelievable that it was now a finalist for such a prestigious award.

He sprang from his chair with a rousing cheer, bursting with joy. He grabbed his bag and dashed out the door—passing Jaxen, who was waiting outside his office. Jaxen quickly followed and hurried past him to open the car door.

"Straight home, Jaxen!" He yelled with excitement, leaning forward to tap the back of Jaxen's seat.

"Yes, sir," Jaxen responded and drove off.

Keaton was grinning and anxious to get home to inform Lia. He thought of how excited she would be, knowing that her collaboration helped secure such an award for project Globo. Some hours later, when the car stopped at the front of the house, Keaton rushed out in the elation, leaving his briefcase behind.

He got into the house, yelling from downstairs. "Lia! Lia! You won't believe it!"

He ran upstairs and pounded at her door. He loosened his tie as he began to feel warm from the thrill.

"Lia, open up!"

"She's not here," Celia said, walking up behind him. "What is all the yelling about?"

Keaton turned to his mother, still ecstatic, ready to tell her the great news, then his brain processed what she had said.

"Wait—what do you mean Lia is not here? He looked at his watch. "It's almost midnight; where is she?"

"She is attending a vernissage with Rhett, a private exhibition for his gallery. He picked her up two hours ago. I was supposed to go with them, but I canceled at the last minute. I am not so young anymore; I don't think I can keep up at these late-night events."

"Wait, Mom, why wasn't I informed?"

"Why would she inform you? Last time I checked, you two were only 'business partners.' She's not obligated to inform you of her plans if it's not business-related."

"But you could have told me, mom…."

"I am telling you now, besides, Lia only agreed this evening. Rhett has been asking her all week, and she never gave him an answer. When she returned from the office, she told me she decided to take up the invitation and wanted me to tag along. I was all for it, but then I opted out due to the time of the event and the last-minute rush."

Keaton turned red in the face; he removed his tie and took off his jacket, pressing his hand to his forehead.

"Where is the event?" He asked, his tone irritated and bothered.

"I told you, Rhett is the host. The private viewing is at his gallery—the Gagosian Art Gallery in the city.

Keaton rushed downstairs and grabbed the car keys from Jaxen, who was making his way inside.

"Don't do anything stupid!" Celia shouted, watching him from the staircase atrium. She shook her head in a snicker and went back to her room.

What should have been a two-hour drive into the city only took Keaton a little over an hour —He was speeding and fuming the entire drive.

He stopped the car in a no-parking zone on the opposite side of the street in front of the gallery. He sprinted to the entrance and was quickly halted by security,

"Invitation only." The security rumbled, stopping Keaton with a hand to his chest.

"My wife is in there!" he yelled as his frustration grew,

"Sir, unless your name is on the list, I can't allow you to go in."

Keaton's jaw clenched; he was hot and flushed and his muscle tensed beneath his fitted navy-blue collared shirt, projecting his broad chest.

In a fit of rage, Keaton swung at the security, knocking him to the ground, and rushed inside. His eyes scanned the room for Lia, but he saw Rhett first, standing next to someone with Lia's frame. Rhett's hand was at the bareback of the female standing next to him. Keaton's blood boiled. He navigated the throng of viewers, making his way to the far end of the gallery where Rhett stood.

When he got close enough, he pulled Rhett's hand from the female's back, grabbed her hand, and turned her around, as he suspected it was Lia.

"Keaton? what are you doing here?" Lia asked, genuinely shocked.

"We are leaving." He commanded, grabbing her hand, and pulling her towards the exit.

Everyone's attention turned to them, and people shuffled, giving him room as he stormed out with Lia.

Rhett hurried behind them, calling off security, who was heading back inside for Keaton. Lia remained silent until she was on the outside.

"Let go of me!" she screamed, pulling her hand from his grasp. "What the hell is wrong with you?"

"What are you doing here, this late with him!" yelled Keaton, flashing a despising glance at Rhett, who had just made it outside.

"Calm down Keaton," implored Rhett, walking closer towards them.

Rhett was around the same height as Keaton. Asian-American, Slim-built, smooth dark-brown hair with deep honey highlights, smoldering dark eyes, and attractive facial features like a K-Pop Idol.

"What gave you the guts to take my wife and keep her out this late without my permission? Who do you think you are!" Keaton bellowed , pointing into Rhett's face.

Rhett scoffed, looking over at Lia. "Your wife is an adult; she has the right to decide where she goes and how late she stays out. Are you really bothered that she's out late, or because she's out with me?" Rhett asked in a taunting tone with a satirical smirk.

"Keaton, why are you here?" Lia asked, pulling his attention from Rhett. "What is this? What are you doing? You storm in here. Embarrassed me in front of all those people, why? What do you want from me?" Lia began to tear up; her expression had an even mix of upset and humiliation.

Keaton took a deep breath, trying to control his anger and annoyance and the voices in his head telling him to stomp Rhett to the ground. "I came to take you home. I don't care if you hate me, but what you are doing is improper and does not represent my image. To the public, you are my wife, and I will not tolerate this behavior from you. Now let's go!"

His voice echoed a stern resound, and he retook Lia's arm, pulling her to the car.

"Let go of me!" Lia screamed, trying to tear away.

Rhett ran after them and pulled Lia from Keaton's grip. "She said to leave her alone. Why are you causing a scene here?"

Keaton's nostrils flared, his heart rate increased; the built-up aggression and disdain he had towards Rhett fueled his anger. In a split second, he punched Rhett in the face, knocking him to the ground, pinned him in the middle of the empty dark street, punching him repeatedly.

Lia released a ghastly scream, pulling Keaton off of Rhett.

"Stop it, Keaton! Stop! Please stop!" She was shaking, screaming, and crying

Keaton let up, releasing Rhett, his fist still clenched, breathing heavily in a temper. He turned away to calm himself. Lia rushed to Rhett's aid; he was coughing, his face bloody. She sat him up, wiping the blood from his face with the hem of her dress.

"Er du…er du ok?" she cried in her native Norwegian, her hands trembling as she cleaned his face. *"Jeg beklager så mye"*… so, so sorry," she whispered unintelligibly. Her screams had alerted the security guard, who was now making his way across the street. When he got close, Rhett stopped him.

"Paul, it's fine; I am fine."

Keaton looked back at Lia kneeling beside Rhett, sobbing, wiping his face with her dress. The sight alone was galling. He picked her up over his shoulder, kicking and screaming, and took her to the car.

"You'll be hearing from my lawyers!" Rhett shouted.

Keaton sat Lia on the front passengers' seat, buckled her seat belt, got into the vehicle, and manically sped away.

"You can't just leave him there!" Lia cried, looking back at Rhett's and the security's image disappearing into the distance.

"He'll be fine," Keaton fumed, pulling his phone from his pocket speed dialing his lawyer.

"Gagosian Art Gallery in the city, Rhett Xiong, take care of it for me. I'll explain more in the morning." He hung up and continued speeding, not responding to Lia yelling and bawling at him for what he did to Rhett.

When they got home, she exited the car, rushing to the house before him. He chased and caught up to her at the bottom of the staircase and held onto her hand.

"Lia, please let me explain."

She turned to look at him, her face wet from crying, her hair a mess, make-up running, and blood on her hands and the hem of her dress.

"Explain what!" she asked in a fuming tone. "What is wrong with you! Why do you keep patronizing me…? What do you want from me?" She dropped to the foot of the staircase, bawling.

Keaton swung his head back, his hands pressed against his forehead, realizing the ruckus he had caused and what it was doing to Lia.

He swallowed hard, chastising himself. *What am I doing?* He thought. *I no longer have control of my emotions. What is happening to me?*

Lia was mumbling incoherently between tears. Keaton pulled her up from the floor and held her tightly in his arms; She sniffled uncontrollably, pushing him away, beating at his chest.

"I'm sorry," he said brokenly, withstanding her flurried blows, keeping her in his embrace. He succumbed to the overwhelming feeling that had been distorting his emotions for months. He lifted Lia's chin and pressed his lips against hers; both eyes closed, cupping the sides of her face, his fingers in her hair, his tongue exploring the taste of hers. Suddenly, Lia jerked herself away and fired an open-handed slap to his left cheek. She bolted up the staircase crying.

He stood motionless and speechless, his heart pounding inside his chest, watching as Lia disappeared from his view, followed by the slamming sound of her bedroom door.

CHAPTER 33

The following day Lia locked herself inside her bedroom and wouldn't answer anyone. After learning what had happened at the art gallery, Celia got mad at Keaton for acting out of character. She didn't hesitate to jump on board with damage control, and by midday, they had received confirmation from their lawyers that there would be no charges against Keaton and the incident silenced.

"She must be furious at you. It's past midday, and she hasn't left her room. Not even for a bite." Celia complained to Keaton, staring him dead in the face as they sat at the kitchen island.

"I'm mad at myself," Keaton replied, looking at his bruised knuckles. "I have never been in a fight, never been easily riled, and yet seeing his hand on her exposed back at the gallery infuriated me beyond control. I just wanted to rip his head off."

"What I don't get is why you haven't told her how you feel instead of confusing her, creating more tension and unnecessary misunderstanding between you. You made her a promise not to mislead her anymore. Now you have broken that promise with that bitter brawl at the gallery and that kiss last night. You said you are unsure of your feelings for her, yet you get insanely jealous and overprotective whenever Rhett is around. I have noticed how uncomfortable and distressing you have been this month, restricted to communicate with her only on a professional basis. From my point of view, you are not confused about your feelings; you are scared of what it means, scared to admit you have fallen for her. Take my foolish advice and be honest with Lia before you cause irreversible damages to her heart and jeopardize the business relationship between TrueTek and SANCORP."

Celia left the kitchen, leaving Keaton with guilt tugging at his heart. He went upstairs and knocked on Lia's door again for the hundredth time.

"Lia, I won't leave until you open the door, even if I have to sleep here." He sat outside her door with hands around his knees and a poignant look on his face.

Two hours later, Lia opened the door, dressed to leave. Keaton sprang to his feet, a bit lightheaded from sitting uncomfortably for so long. Her attire caught him off guard, took him a minute to gather his thoughts, or even remember why he was waiting outside her door. He looked at her from head to toe, dressed in a form-fitting red dress that hung just below her knees. The red made her green eyes pop, the sleekness and length of the dress, and well-paired black stilettos highlighted her already leggy feature and her smell—breath-taking.

"Where—where are you going?" He stuttered, regaining control of his wondering eyes.

"Out, for a drink." She responded, not making eye contact.

"Alone?"

"Yes, I am capable of buying myself a drink."

"I didn't mean it like that, I…."

"I know what you meant. I will have a drink by myself, lest you beat up anyone else. And for the record, Rhett is my friend, the only friend I had since I've been here, and you just ruined everything. Now he won't even take my calls. I hope you are happy; you have succeeded in alienating me. So, I might as well go drinking by myself. God knows I need a drink."

"Can I take you to where you are going? I need to talk to you."

"About what? Unless it's business, I will not entertain it. I can't keep going in circles with you. I am the only one getting hurt in the process. So, is it business?"

"Well—, yes and no."

Lia took a deep breath and walked past him. He ran after her.

"Okay, Okay, it's about project Globo." He ceded, holding his hands up, positioning himself in front of her. "I received some exciting news yesterday; the main reason I came looking for you; I'll admit things got out of hand last night, but I can explain. Just let me grab my jacket, and I'll take you where you are going, please?"

Lia cast him a doubting eye, then nodded in agreement. "Thank you; I'll meet you downstairs." He rushed to his bedroom and changed into a deep-blue pair of jeans, a white button-down undershirt, and a navy-blue crest blazer and made a mad dash downstairs to meet Lia.

On the drive, Lia sat in the back to the left of him. He gazed at her through the rearview mirror a few times before asking, "Where should I take you?"

“I didn’t have a particular place in mind. I was going to ask my driver to take me someplace of choice.”

“I know a place in lower Manhattan; I can take you there if you like?”

“Sure, at this point, why not.”

They kept silent the rest of the journey; Lia kept her gaze outside the window while Keaton occasionally glanced at her from the rearview mirror. Sometime later, they arrived in an upscale area of Greenwich Village. He took her into a dimly lit cocktail lounge with just the right amount of sophistication to match her attire.

Keaton ordered the first round of cocktails suggesting one of his favorites for Lia, which she respectfully declined, placing her order with the waiter.

“So, what is it about project Globo that you wanted to tell me?”

“Can we at least wait for the drinks first?”

“Keaton, I am serious. I agreed you could accompany me not to have drinks but to discuss the ‘great’ news you received on project Globo. So please, what is the news?”

Her words stung him like a wasp, not deadly but painful. “I deserve that…” he conceded, “I’ll just get to the point.”

“Project Globo has been selected as a finalist for The National Medal of Technology and Innovation, the award ceremony is next Saturday, and I want you to accompany me?”

Lia’s eyes lit up; she waited until the waiter served her drink and left before gushing her excitement. “Are you serious?” She squealed, grabbing onto his hand, forgetting she was mad at him.

"I'm serious; we were nominated, but I never thought we would be this year's finalist. I mean, the list of nominees is all top tier; the competition was fierce. But we have been selected, so that means you were right. You said we would win the award, and we are now a finalist, so hats off to you for believing in the project—for believing in me."

Lia removed her grasp from his hand, noticing the enamored expression on his face and the ardent nature of his tone. She swallowed.

"Keaton, I am elated, extremely happy for you. Not only did you successfully launch project Globo, but you are chosen for one of the most prestigious awards in the field. This accomplishment is everything you told me you and your father envisioned for this project. You should be so proud of yourself."

"I am, and I couldn't have done it without you. When I got the news, you were the first person I wanted to tell. You have to accompany me; you deserve this award as much as I do."

"I will—for this, I definitely will." Lia smiled from her eyes, taking a sip of her cocktail.

Keaton also took a sip of his cocktail, contemplating whether to share his other thoughts with her. He wanted to clear the personal tension between them, but she already made it clear she wanted to discuss nothing outside of business, and he didn't want to risk upsetting the mood.

But then the moment was perfect and controlled; it seemed the best opportunity. He opened his mouth to speak; then, he heard someone calling his name.

"Keaton! Is that you?"

He looked in the direction to see Trent walking towards him with a broad grin.

"Keaton, you bastard." Trent jibed, slapping Keaton on the shoulder. "You haven't returned my calls. Are you avoiding me?"

"I've been busy running a company; you wouldn't know what that's like." Keaton retaliated. They looked at each other with a friendly smile, laughed, and engaged in a bro-hug.

"And this must be your—wife?" Trent asked, turning his eyes on Lia with a flirty gaze. "I would remember your beauty anywhere. I saw your wedding photos in the tabloids". Trent took Lia's hand and kissed it.

"Let me introduce myself; I am Trent. Keaton's best friend since childhood, high school, college, university, you name it. I am the fun friend."

Keaton pulled Trent's hand away from Lia's.

"Don't listen to anything he says." Keaton joked, looking at Lia; he then turned to Trent, "and aren't you overreaching saying we are best friends?" He and Trent chuckled.

Trent kept his flirty gaze on Lia, "Keaton, you lucky bastard. You outdid yourself this time. Damn! —Mrs. Dawson. No disrespect to you; you are gorgeous."

Lia blushed. "Her name is Lia," Keaton affirmed.

"I can't believe you got married and did not invite me; I thought we were friends—"

"It was a private affair," Keaton said promptly, cutting him off. "By the way, I thought you were in Paris; when did you return?"

"A month ago," Trent replied, "you would have known if you had answered or returned my calls. My dad pulled me back here for some award he'll be receiving next week. You know him, whenever he's publicly recognized, he wants the family by his side to play the 'picture-perfect' family. I am here to play my role." Keaton chuckled at Trent's expression.

"I have been calling you because the guys and I want to hang out for your birthday next weekend before I leave. We haven't seen you in what…a year? We have to hang out."

"I would love to, but I can't. I have an award ceremony to attend that weekend; it's the same day as my birthday. TrueTek is a finalist for The National Medal of Technology and Innovation. I have to be there."

"The Technology award? That's the same ceremony I will be attending with my dad. From what he told me; it will be over by 6:00 p.m. we can hang out after. Come on, Keaton, we have so much to catch up on, and I leave for London the following week. What do you say?"

"OK, fine, but only if Lia agrees because she will be attending the ceremony as well."

Keaton looked at Lia, his eyes willing her to object, but she was oblivious to his cue, or she pretended to be.

"Fine by me," she responded. "You should celebrate your birthday with your friends."

"Great," Trent said in glee. "See you next Saturday; I will inform the guys. And you, Lia...." he retook Lia's hand and kissed it. It was a pleasure meeting you; stay beautiful." He tapped Keaton on the shoulder and left.

"Well, he's something," Lia said when Trent was out of sight. Keaton sighed and took a sip of his drink.

"For someone who claims he is your 'best friend,' you seemed a bit apathetic seeing him?"

"Ha...." Keaton scoffed, "Trent is one of those friends brought into my life by an unavoidable family entanglement. Our fathers were childhood friends and operated in similar business fields; they encouraged us to be close. We went to the same schools from kindergarten to university. We have been around each other for more than half our lives."

"So, he is your best friend then...by default." She giggled.

"But Trent and I are day and night, total opposites, and if it were not for our fathers, I don't believe we would be friends otherwise. He's into the wild, wayward, carefree kind of life. Drink, party, and live lavishly at the expense of others. I bet he is only here because his dad froze his accounts, forcing him to return for this event. It has always been like this in the past. He is the only son of his family, and his father would give anything for him to take on his responsibilities in the company. However, he doesn't want to work; his sister runs the company alongside her father. I bet it is her efforts that placed them as a finalist for this award. Put it this way; his father wishes he was the daughter and his daughter the son."

Lia snickered, "I can see that; he does give off an obtrusive vibe."

Lia finished her drink and a second and a third while Keaton only had two. After Lia's sixth cocktail and a few jaunty outbursts, Keaton decided it was time to take her home.

Later that evening, he got back to the house around 10:00 p.m., Lia was fast asleep on the back seat. He parked and quietly opened the rear door, and carefully picked her up.

Upstairs in her bedroom, he laid her on the bed, removed her heels, covering her with a blanket. He sat by her side for a few minutes, watching her sleep. His face unknowingly relaxed in a pleasing smile.

What are you doing to me? He thought. For some time, he has been trying to decipher his feelings for her. He tried to convince himself that what he felt was more infatuation than love. More physical than emotional. But that was the biggest lie he had ever told himself. As he watched her sleep, he felt drawn to her; he felt a lasting and meaningful connection.

He was always physically attracted to her, but now it was so much more than that. Now it was her values, personality, and how much she cared about him personally and professionally and she hadn't failed to show it. Whenever he has a great day at work, she was the first person he wanted to share it with. It was undeniable that their values were totally in sync.

Now he found himself constantly drawing her to mind, remembering the way she made him feel. He sometimes gushed over her qualities and his emotionally compatible feelings, maybe because they share similar views on family, work, and underlying beliefs. Perhaps it was their shared emotional experiences that deepened their connection. He could not pinpoint what exactly was pulling him to her, love, or infatuation; one thing was for sure; the feeling wasn't going away; it was only getting stronger.

CHAPTER 34

The following Saturday night, Keaton, Lia, and Celia arrived in the trendy downtown neighborhood of Tribeca, New York City, at the Tribeca Rooftop for the award ceremony. Lia and Keaton traveled together chauffeured by Jaxen. While Celia traveled separately chauffeured by Paxton, accompanied by a security detail of six.

Lia was splendiferously stunning in an elegant floor-length midnight-black mermaid gown. The detailing included a fluted hem and fitted bodice that flawlessly accentuated her silhouette—accessorized by a statement necklace with ruby red gemstones. Under the night light against the strong color contrast of her dress, the emerald color of her iris was attention-grabbing. She wore her hair in a deliberately messy *bouffant up-do* with delicate loose curls effortlessly swept to the right of her face.

Keaton complimented her wearing a chic slim-cut black suit, box-fresh white shirt, and perfectly tied bow tie. Classic black patent shoes paired well with the suit's formality—embellished by subtle OMEGA Prestige cufflinks and a Jaeger-LeCoultre Hybris wristwatch, which only accentuated his striking masculine allure.

He escorted Lia and Celia on both his arms to their seats by the venue's large, windowed walls that gave them a magnificent view of Manhattan and the Hudson River.

The evening started with a cocktail hour with the reception layout, providing room for guests to mix and mingle. The room was crawling with high-profile finalists, some of the biggest names in the technology industry. It created the perfect networking opportunity, and Keaton was impressed at how well Lia worked the room, interacting flawlessly with everyone who approached them. Trent made his appearance alongside his father and sister. He and Keaton chatted a bit while Trent drooled over Lia before leaving for the bar.

Keaton received continual compliments for his 'marvelous wife,' as Lia stood out in the room both by appearance and intellect. After a presentation from a special keynote speaker recognized in the technology industry, the award ceremony commenced. When the first and second runners-up were announced and awarded, Lia gripped Keaton's hand in a shrouding squeeze.

"Certainly, Project Globo won," Lia whispered confidently with a sparkle in her eyes. Keaton smiled at her with a lingered stare. TrueTek's project Globo was announced as the National Medal of Technology winner, sending Lia and Celia in a rousing scream as the room broke out in applause.

Keaton walked to the stage with a dumbfounded look on his face and glinting eyes. He received the medal and stood speechless as the applause settled down. He looked out into the gathering at Lia and his mom and gave an accomplished smile.

"I didn't write a speech because I didn't think we would have won," Keaton joked, standing at the microphone. "However, my wife—" he looked at Lia again. "She knew it from the beginning and was more confident in my abilities than I was. First, let me say I am incredibly thrilled to be the recipient of this award. Thank you to the Technology Administration for recognizing the effort and ingenuity put forward in Project Globo. And to all my peers and other awardees tonight, I am honored to share this recognition with you." Thunderous applause followed and Keaton beamed with delight as he waited for the applause to die down.

"In any setting, receiving recognition for your hard work and contributions in a room full of your peers is not only emotional but genuinely gratifying, especially when you have the unwavering support of those dearest to you. Tonight, I am privileged to be accompanied by two extraordinary women in my life who have been significant in the achievement of this award. My mother, Celia Dawson—mom, you are the anchor of my life, for the dreams I never thought could come true. You and dad believed in and supported all my goals and efforts and today is a result of your resolute support and encouragement."

He looked at Lia, and without thinking about what to say, it seemed to have naturally spilled from his heart out his mouth.

"And to my beautiful wife, Lia Paton-Dawson." He continued, "You came into my life at such a crucial point; with the loss of my father and taking on the company's presidency, I was lost and burdened, yet your presence seemed to have made everything better. We worked on Project Globo side-by-side, and since then, you never cease to surprise me with all you can do and all that you can achieve. Thank you for being my equal, for believing in me and my capabilities, and for never doubting just what I could do. Thank you for never leaving my side when

I was doing everything to push you away. Today, I know how blessed I am to be with someone as beautiful, intelligent, kind, and loving as you. I couldn't have done this without you-— Thank you."

Resounding applause followed his speech, and he kept his eyes on Lia, who was tearing up, desperately blinking, fighting back the tears. She carefully got up from her table, not drawing too much attention to herself, and hurried towards the exit. Keaton realized what was happening and casually left the stage to chase after her.

He caught up with her on the rooftop's open terrace, vacant as all the guests were seated inside.

"Lia, please wait."

She rounded on him, her face taut in fury. "Was any of what you said in there true, or was it for the cameras? Tell me! *Vær så snill å fortell meg!* Tell me!"

Keaton was upended by her vehement reaction. He instinctively placed his right hand across his left breast. "I said what was burdening my heart, what has been responsible for the conflicting feelings I have been dealing with lately."

Lia wiped her eyes and walked to the rails of the terrace, looking over into the city.

"You praised me in there like you are a doting husband like we have been living a life of bliss. Is this all for a show, a game?"

She muffled her upset tone so as not to draw attention from the gathering inside, wiping the constant stream of tears away from her eyes.

Keaton tried to speak to respond to her question, but she cut him off. "This relationship has brought nothing but confusion and hurt to my life. One minute you are avoiding me like the plague, the next minute, we are working on a project together, baring emotions to each other, leading me to fall more in love with you. We act on those emotions, and in the middle of almost making love to me, you discard me, impale my heart, leaving me to lick my wounds. You told me you are in love with your girlfriend. I accept and ask you to stay away from me so that my wounds can heal. But before those wounds had a chance to heal, you burst them open again in a jealous scuffle at the gallery causing even more confusion and, to date, without explanation. You say you love her, but you kissed me that same night after the gallery with such passion and desire, and tonight in front of all these people, you dote on me like I am the best thing that has happened in your life—why?"

"Lia, there's a lot that has happened between us, and it's confusing and convoluted not only for you but for me too. I have been trying to make sense of it all. To understand what I feel for you, but it's more complicated than it seems...."

"Is it complicated? —or are you making it complicated?" Lia sobbed. "Just answer me this-—do you love me?"

Keaton paused; he looked at Lia, then out into the night, then back to her again. His brain was screaming, *yes! —I love you—I have fallen in love with you!* But his heart was conflicting, thinking of Katie, wondering if he felt this way for Lia because he longed for Katie. The battle between his heart and his mind kept him frozen and speechless to her question.

When he realized the torrent of tears flowing from Lia's eyes due to his silence, he tried to quell it, to explain.

"Lia, I am still trying to figure out what I feel for you. I need a little more time, please—I...."

"Nei! You are selfish, insensitive, and cruel." She snapped. "While you are trying to 'figure' out what you feel for me, do you think it is fine to keep toying with my emotions, to keep hurting me, confusing me? I am in love with you, Keaton! I am vulnerable and weak to you, and because of that, when you do these things, have these mixed feelings, mislead my emotions, I fall harder for you. Each time the hurt is devastating, it penetrates the deepest parts of my heart and rips it open, and the damage is becoming more and more irreversible. Ever since that night we almost made love, my body has helplessly yearned for you. I need all of you. I can't pretend that everything is alright like you are doing. I am not confused about my feelings; I know exactly how I feel. I love you...." Her sobs deepened with tremors of sniffles; her shaking hands covered her mouth to muffle the escaping wails.

He walked closer to hold her, and she backed away from his reach.

"Lia..." before he could say anything else, Trent came onto the terrace.

"Am I interrupting anything?" He asked, ping-ponging his gaze between Keaton and Lia.

"Keaton, I have been waiting for a while now; we need to go; the guys are expecting you."

"Not now, Trent," Keaton responded, in a visible foul mood, worsened by Trent's undesirable interruption.

"Don't ruin your plans on my account," Lia sniffled, swiping at her eyes, looking away from Trent.

"I am leaving with mom…." She hurried past both of them, leaving the Terrace.

"Lia…" Keaton yelled, trying to go after her.

"Let her go," Trent said, blocking his path. "Evidently, you both are upset. It is best to give each other some space and regroup when you have had time to think. From what I have overheard, you have much to consider, so let's go—the guys are waiting. Where we are going has the right atmosphere to recharge you and clear your mind."

Keaton was not in the mood for any of Trent's escapades, but admittingly he needed to clear his mind, and running back home after Lia would be the least helpful.

"Fine, let's go." He said, agreeing with Trent. Then they both left the Terrace.

CHAPTER 35

On the outside, Trent gave Keaton the address to meet and went ahead of him while Keaton waited for Jaxen to get the car. Later they arrive at The GentleMen Lounge on East Hudson, in New York City. Jaxen stopped at the entrance allowing Keaton to exit and proceeded to park.

Keaton meandered into the lounge removing his jacket, questioning his decision to meet with Trent; he couldn't recall one positive experience he had ever had hanging out with Trent. At least the other guys would be joining, he thought, settling his mind. Liam and Chad are pretty level-headed; things should not get out of hand while they were around.

A few meters into the lounge and he spotted Trent eagerly signaling him. He strode over to Trent at the bar, who was opening a tab.

"Where are the others?" Keaton asked, looking around.

"They are upstairs in the VIP Suite; follow me."

The deafening music from the club section of the lounge below the bar floor and the flashing neon lights in the lounge instantly sent a jolting vibration across Keaton's frontal lobe. They made their way upstairs, and as they got closer to the VIP suite; the sound of blaring music slowly dissipated.

"Leave it up to you to choose the brashest place in New York City to hang out," Keaton chastised, looking at Trent.

"It's your birthday; you need to loosen up a little," Trent responded with a wild grin on his face. "Besides, you just won one of the most prestigious awards in Tech history; you should be in celebration mode right now.

"Look who is here!" Trent yelled as they entered the VIP suite. Liam and Chad greeted Keaton one after the other with a bro-hug and hearty laughter, expressively happy to see him again after so long. The VIP suite was at the top of the building overlooking the city—sleek decor with a rooftop pool.

"Keaton, it has been what…a year almost since we've seen you. how the hell have you been?" Liam asked, retaking his seat.

"I've been well; you know how it is. I've got a company to run now; it has kept me busy; sorry if I'm not as available as before."

"We know how it is, Keaton," Chad empathized, "And I'm sorry about your dad. When I heard he had passed, I was sitting the Bar exam; I could not make it. My condolences."

"It's alright, Chad; I'm doing better now," Keaton said, taking a seat.

"Here come the drinks!" Trent yelled as three scantily dressed ladies entered the room with various champagne, shots, and cocktails on trays. The guys chatted among themselves as the ladies served the drinks. Keaton cringed at the sight of their attire, but he wasn't surprised—It had Trent written all over it.

Unlike Trent, who Keaton knew from childhood, he met Liam and Chad during his MBA studies at Oxford. They were New Yorkers from high-profile families and quickly became friends. Keaton thought highly of Chad and considered him the pragmatic one of the group. Chad was an intellectual property attorney from a family of distinguished lawyers. From university, he had been the one who cemented the group, the voice of reason. He was also a devilishly handsome, six-foot African American with an alluring voice, uniquely fascinating and powerful.

Liam, on the other hand, was the impressionable one. He was pretty sensible but tended to get easily influenced, especially by Trent. Liam, a British American, 5ft. 9inches, light caramel skin, and grey eyes that sometimes looked blue or green depending on his attire and lighting. His family made it big in wealth management, and now he works as a Director in his father's company. Liam's parents divorced when he was much younger; his mother returned to the UK. Since then, he has lived between New York and the UK for most of his life, accounting for his sophisticated accent.

Trent was the cocky one in the group and most likely to lead them astray; he lives for partying, traveling, women—an all-around lavish lifestyle. His wealth came from a generational technology and telecommunications conglomerate similar to Keaton. He's what you'd call a 'Pretty boy,' handsome facial features that were easy on the eyes—Caucasian with a tan complexion, strong jawline, high cheekbones, and thick stubble beard. He always wore his hair in a medium fade to the sides and back with longer brown-blonde hair on top, complementing his raging dark-blue eyes.

After the girls left the room, Trent and the guys raised a toast to Keaton, wishing him happy birthday with a round of shots, followed by cocktails and then champagne that Trent sprayed on Keaton in a celebratory jest.

Later they moved to the rooftop and sat around the pool to catch up. A rowdy Trent started howling at the moon following another round of shots, sporadically singing happy birthday to Keaton.

Trent clinked his glass to Keaton's and then sat down, looking directly at him.

"Liam and Chad are too chicken-shit to ask what we have all been thinking since we saw it in the papers last December. But I need to know. So, I am going to address the elephant in the room." Said Trent, taking another shot.

"How did you not get married to Katie? Instead, you end up having a shot-gun wedding with this new catch of yours—what's her name again? —Ah…Lia."

Keaton released an annoyed sigh followed by a drink. Somehow, he knew this was coming; it was never just black and white with Trent.

"Is this why you wanted to 'hang out on my birthday, to inquire about my life? Why am I not surprised?" Keaton replied, casting Trent a 'you-are-unbelievable' gaze.

"Come on, Keaton; we are all dying to know—right guys?" Said Trent, glancing at Liam and Chad for agreement. Chad and Liam remained silent, not agreeing nor opposing, as they too were curious but too considerate to pry.

Trent continued to probe to get Keaton to speak.

"What I don't understand—" Trent continued, "You were with Katie upon till the day you returned home when your dad died. And in less than three months, you get married to a completely different person that none of us knew you were dating. How can we not be curious? We are your friends; you need to come clean with us. Were you only with Katie for the ass and had Lia in the waiting all along? What is it?" Trent prodded, his hand gestures seemingly pulling a response out of Keaton.

"You don't know what you are talking about." Keaton snapped.

"And that's why I am asking you to make it clear." Trent persists, "I am dying to know. Don't get me wrong, Lia is a total upgrade from Katie; she's like a ten on the hot rating scale, and Katie is like a firm six or seven. But you chased Katie for like two years; we all know you were head over heels in love with her. We thought she was the one you would marry. So, what changed?"

"Nothing changed," Keaton responded in an aggravated tone, taking a sip from his cocktail glass. I am still in love with Katie. My marriage with Lia is transactional, strictly business." His mouth spoke the words, but his expression rejected the latter.

"What do you mean?" Trent questioned, pulling his body to the edge of the seat to look closely at Keaton.

"Exactly what I said it means. My dad arranged Lia and I's marriage before he passed to secure a business deal. The marriage is contractual and concludes at the end of the year;

then we go our separate ways?" Keaton's expression warped as the reality sunk in that Lia would be leaving in two months, and he was still at odds with his feelings.

Trent burst out in a cackling laugh. "You are not serious—and you kept this away from us? No wonder you have been so distant since your return. This explains it.

"But wait, you mentioned going your separate ways so casually as if it's that simple. From what I overheard of you and Lia's argument earlier this evening, you both have feelings for each other. She seems to be in love with you. So how can it be that simple?"

"Is Katie in on this—I mean, how did she take it when you got married to Lia?" Liam asked with a speck of confusion in his eyes.

"It took a lot of pleading to get Katie to accept that I had to marry Lia. In the end, she agreed to wait for me since the marriage would be temporary. In two months, I am free to go back to my life with her."

"So why don't you seem happy about it? Chad asked, genuinely concerned for Keaton. "Are you in love with Lia?" Chad being the reasonable one, Keaton was inclined to answer his question.

"I don't know if I am in love with Lia; I have strong feelings for her. But what if those feelings are only superficial as a result of my longing for Katie…?"

"I was at the award ceremony," Trent interjected. "I heard your thank you speech. You are definitely in love with Lia—not to mention the heated argument you both had afterward; she is crazy about you, she's obviously mad because you won't admit you feel the same.

"You have been married to Lia for almost a year, living under the same roof, not to mention she is smoking hot; of course, you would fall for her. Can you honestly say you haven't slept with her?" Trent asked with a speculating look on his face.

"I haven't slept with her," Keaton responded defensively. "Well, sort of—not really—I don't know."

"What do you mean by 'sort of,' 'not really,' it's either you slept with her, or you didn't?" Trent pressed.

"We almost did, in the middle of it, I realized I was making a mistake, and I stopped it…so essentially we didn't?" Keaton explained.

"When you say you stopped in the 'middle of it,' what exactly do you mean? In the middle of kissing? Once you were both naked…? What point was the middle?" Trent nudged for clarity.

Keaton hesitated, almost embarrassed to respond. All three guys were staring at him, zoned in as if at the climax of an intriguing movie.

"I mean…" Keaton paused, "we were past kissing, past being naked—we…."

"Don't tell me the 'middle' was at penetration?" Trent impatiently blurted. Keaton nodded with a discomfiting expression on his face, confirming Trent's speculation.

"Get the fuck out of here!" Trent yelled in disbelief, a broad grin on his face. "You are telling me you penetrated her—you were inside of her, and then you decided, 'oh this is a mistake' and left? Trent poked in a sarcastic tone. "Who the hell does that? Was it not good? I mean, it's either you have a ridiculous level of self-control, or you are just foolish, neither of which is good in that scenario. Guys, have you seen Lia? Who the hell passes up on that, especially during sex?"

"Shut up, Trent," Chad yelled with a peevish expression on his face. "Not everyone is like you; every situation doesn't have to be sexual and about the physical. What Keaton did is understandable; he's considering the feelings of both Katie and Lia plus handling his own conflicting emotions. At least appreciate that he is in a complex situation."

"There's nothing complex about it; maybe if he had slept with Lia instead of punking out, by now, he would be certain if he is in love with her or not. What he did only creates confusion and unnecessary hurt for himself and Lia, evident from their argument tonight." Trent rebutted.

"Trent has a point," Liam added.

Chad rolled his eyes, ignoring both Liam and Trent, and turned his attention to Keaton. "Look, I understand the complexity of the position you are in, but from what I hear from you and Trent, your feelings for Lia may not be superficial.

"You need to figure it out and fast because the contract ends soon. From what I hear tonight, Lia is in love with you, and if you can't reciprocate, she's going to leave feeling rejected and hurt. If by then you reunite with Katie and find out that you are no longer in love with her as before, then you risk losing both of them."

"You think I don't know this?" Keaton asserted, "That's the source of my confusion. I am torn; I know there is a risk of losing both of them if I can't make sense of my emotions before it's too late."

"I maintain my stance," Trent interjected, "you need to make love to Lia, and I guarantee after a night of passion, you will know if what you feel is superficial or not. Nevertheless, let's not end the night on a bleak note. I'll close the tab and bring us some parting shots; I'll be right back."

Trent left and returned a few minutes later with four shot glasses on a tray. He handed one to Keaton, took one, and passed the tray to Liam.

He raised his shot in a parting toast, "Keaton, Happy birthday! It was great catching up with you; keep in touch and stop ignoring my calls. I don't want to wait another year for your birthday to catch up. And I sincerely hope that after tonight you will figure out the affairs of your heart. Do consider what I said earlier; go home and bang Lia; she is your wife after all."

Trent guzzled his shot in a throwback, followed by Keaton, Liam, and Chad. In a few seconds, the scantily dressed ladies returned with a birthday cake lit with sparkler candles.

"Compliments of the house," one said, resting the cake on the table before Keaton. A few other ladies appeared dressed in bikinis, joining the guys with music and drinks.

“What is this?” Chad asked, looking at Trent. Keaton’s eyes bared the same question, also looking at Trent.

“Guys, I am changing the tone in the atmosphere,” Trent grinned. “Sending Keaton off in a happier mood, lighten up and enjoy the ladies.”

The ladies served more drinks and helped Keaton to cut the cake. Chad agreed to spend a bit more time to chat to Keaton about other things while Liam and Trent undressed down to their boxers and got into the pool with the girls.

An hour passed, and Keaton started to have hot flashes and became anxious.

“Are you ok?” Chad asked, noticing his sweating and change in behavior.

“I think I may have had too much to drink,” Keaton replied, opening a few more buttons on his shirt. “I think I should call it a night.”

“Yeah, I think you should,” said Chad; you don’t look so good.

“Let me call Jaxen,” Keaton said, reaching into his pocket for his phone, his face flushed and beads of sweat forming on his nose and forehead.

“Hey!” Chad yelled, getting the attention of Trent and Liam, who were partying with the girls in the pool. “Keaton is not feeling so well; we are going to call it a night.”

“That’s cool,” Trent yelled back; Keaton, “I’ll try to see you before I leave. Go home and get some and remember to thank me.” He grinned with a mischievous look on his face.

Keaton shook his head, confused at Trent's comment, but waved and left with Chad; he picked his jacket from where he had left it in the VIP Suite and made his way downstairs. Chad ensured that Keaton had made it to the car Jaxen had waiting in front and informed Jaxen to take him straight home.

When the car drove off, Chad had an unsettling feeling and went back upstairs to speak to Trent. He called Trent from the pool and pulled him aside.

"Did you put something in Keaton's shot? And don't even think of lying; it's no coincidence that you went and got the parting shot, personally served Keaton, and after that, he started sweating bullets. What did you give him?"

"Nothing gets past you, does it?" Trent grinned. "It's just a little liquid Ecstasy to get him in the mood to do what he failed to do before with Lia. Face it, I am right; if he sleeps with Lia, he will figure out what he really feels for her. It works every time; trust me, I know."

"Christ, Trent, you are impossible. What makes you think this is what Keaton wants, and what makes you feel it's right to drug him. What if it turns out badly? What then? Did you even think of that before pulling such a reckless stunt? Of all the stupid things you have done, this is by far the most absurd."

"Stop being all-righteous, Chad. I am doing Keaton a favor. You didn't hear the argument between him and Lia. They are miserable, Lia wants him bad, and he wants her too; he's being a coward. After tonight, all this confusion he's going through will be history. Trust me, the way he'll be feeling, he will definitely give her what she wants."

"I swear you have the reasoning capacity of a sex-craved teenager." Chad scolded. "I am calling Keaton; you are ridiculous."

Chad walked away, calling Keaton, whose phone rang several times, but no answer. Knowing how out of sorts Keaton was when he left, it wasn't surprising that he didn't answer the call. Chad left the lounge, praying Jaxen would take Keaton straight to bed; that's all he could do.

CHAPTER 36

Shortly after 2:00 a.m., Jaxen arrived at the Estate and walked Keaton inside the house. By this time, Keaton had removed his dress shirt and was sweating profusely. A torrid feeling overcame him, charging his emotions and sexual desires.

"I can handle myself." He muttered, pulling away from Jaxen's hold. "I am not drunk, just a bit tipsy. You may leave."

"Sure, sir," Jaxen responded, watching as Keaton zigzagged up the staircase. Once Keaton was no longer in view, Jaxen excused himself from the main hall. Upstairs, Keaton stood outside his door, peering across the floor at Lia's. Subconsciously he tries to fight the irresistible feeling to go to her. Still, a collective mood of sensuality and an overwhelming need to be sincere with Lia took precedence over his sense of reasoning.

Keaton dropped his jacket and dress shirt and wandered over to her room door, instinctively turning the doorknob; it opened; he entered, closing the door behind him.

He ogled Lia's silhouette in bed under the dimly lit night light, surmounted by a sweltering sensation below his belt. Walking over to the bed, he sat at the edge, having a closer look at her sleeping form. The earlier mildly increased thumping of his heart rose steadily to a pounding beat as he got increasingly aroused at the sight of her, barely dressed, in a sheer see-through negligee.

Keaton gently stroked her hair away from her face, looking down at her with wild passion in his eyes. Lia shifted at his touch, her eyelids slowly fluttered to fully open. Startled by the shadowy figure over her, she let out a terrified scream springing from her prone position and moving her body to the opposite side of the bed.

"Keaton?" She queried, squinting her eyes as his appearance became clearer. "What are you doing here?" She clutched a tuft of the bedsheets covering herself.

"Why are you acting surprised to see me?" He slurred in a randy tone. "You said you needed all of me, well here I am. I am all yours."

"Keaton, you are drunk; look at you—Why are you shirtless?" Keaton looked down at his bare chest and back at Lia with a lecherous gaze. Lia shifted a bit farther from him, clutching the sheets.

"You need to leave; clearly, you are drunk."

"I am not drunk," Keaton asserted, pressing his hand against his forehead, somewhat annoyed by her accusation.

"You want to know how I feel about you? Well, I am here to tell you." He got up from the bed in a wobble and teetered to the side of the bed closer to Lia.

Lia crawled to the other side as he came closer, shifting out of his reach. Her eyes were unsettled in a panic. Keaton stopped at the foot of the bed, turning to face her.

"Ever since Project Globo, I have existed in a constant state of confusion. I think about you in more ways than I should. I have feelings for you that I never thought I could have for anyone else. Your silence gives me anxiety. When you distance yourself, I am worried beyond control. I get recklessly jealous of you, and lately, I have had this immense need to protect you—possess you. I don't know what you have done to me; it's like you are a siren; I lose my shit whenever I'm close to you. Like I am under some spell. All I wanted was to marry the girl of my dreams, to build a life with Katie. Then this marriage happened—you came along, and now I am all kinds of fucked up in my emotions. I can't think straight. I can't make sense of my feelings anymore. Before, I knew Katie was the love of my life; but now," Keaton paused for a beat, "I don't know what to believe, what's real and what isn't. Do you see what you have done to me?" He spoke in a raised voice. He swung his head back, pressing both hands to his forehead as if he had a maddening headache.

"Keaton, you are not yourself; you need to leave."

This time Keaton ignored her comment, not on purpose, willed by the burning desire he was undergoing, his brain numb to reason.

"Maybe Trent was right." He muttered, moving closer to Lia, "Maybe I need to go all the way; perhaps then I can make sense of what I feel for you."

"Keaton, what are you talking about? Please don't come any closer." Lia screeched, backing up as Keaton climbed onto the bed.

"Isn't this what you want? You told me hours ago on the rooftop that you need all of me. I am here to give you what you want, to make you happy, so you can stop hating me."

He pulled Lia's legs, rendering her flat on her back, positioning himself over her.

"Keaton don't do this," she sobbed, terror in her eyes, realizing he was wildly acting out of character.

"Why is it you women never seem to know what you want?" He yelled, using one hand to pin Lia's arms over her head. "You have been aching for me all this while. Now that I am here, you don't want me anymore."

"Keaton, not like this; you are drunk. Please let me go."

"Stop saying I am drunk; I am not drunk!" He yelled, ripping open her negligee.

"Nei…no Keaton, please stop this," Lia screamed, wriggling under his weight, trying to free her hands from his hold. Keaton forcibly kisses her in heated frenzied passion; overwhelmed by the moment with no self-control, he was at the brink of no return.

Lia stopped squirming as he kissed her; Keaton paused and looked deep into her eyes with dilated pupils, opening and closing his eyes as if to clear the fogginess to comprehend why he was on top of Lia.

Lia's eyes were teary, but they had a particular desire that Keaton understood even while being drugged. "Look me in the eyes," Keaton said, still pinning Lia's hands. "Look, me in the eyes and tell me you don't want this."

Lia sniffled, her watery eyes starting to overflow in subtle streams down her cheeks slowly. "I do, but not like this, not while you are intoxicated." She cried, "Keaton if you do this, you will wake up regretting it and will push me further away. I can't spend the next two months under this roof with more tension and anxiety; my heart won't bear it. So please, for both our sakes, don't do this."

Keaton tried to process what she had said, but it was blotchy in his mind, and he found it hard not to think of her sexually, especially when his eyes caught a glimpse of her breasts through her ripped nightgown. Keaton's barely conscious self tried tirelessly to fight through the effects of the ecstasy though virtually unbearable.

"And what does the other side of you want?" He garbled in response to Lia's beseech.

"The other side of me wants to be ravished by the unintoxicated you. The me that is madly in love with you doesn't care that you are motivated by liquid courage. However, I'm still a respectable woman, and that side has to consider the repercussions if this should happen while you are intoxicated."

Keaton kissed her again, and this time with a burning desire, a longing his body and mind could not ignore no matter how hard he tried. The ecstasy may have heightened the yearning, but that didn't mean it wasn't there all along. The more he kissed her, the more aroused they became, and soon his hand was running from her breast down her stomach finding its way between her thighs. Her pelvis rose from the bed, immediate reaction to his touch; Keaton took the cue to ravish her. He was gentle, though intoxicated, and Lia gasped at his every soothing stroke.

He was inside her, and she was entirely at his mercy but torn, for her body consented, but her mind did not. She groped him as the war ensued within her, pulling him in yet pushing him away.

"Keaton, please—please stop."

"Listen to your body," he whispered as his strokes got sharper and more profound.

For a moment, she went utterly numb, her consciousness had left her, and she laid there catatonic in an unreal state of mind. Her psyche went in and out of mindful reality; she was experiencing wild, ravenous sex, yet not in the way she had envisioned it.

As Keaton neared orgasm, his eyes met Lia's; with tears streaming down her cheeks, she looked into his eyes in silence and shallow breathing as sweet spasm ran through her. Keaton raptures in a jerking twitch, falling to the side of her, almost lifeless he passes out.

Lia painfully swallows the lump that had built up in her throat, that had rendered her aphonic after her climax. Scared to believe what had happened, she rolled from the bed, wrapping herself with the fragments of her nightgown.

She locked herself in the bathroom, falling to the floor in a muffled wail. A part of her was terrified, more so because of the surging, spiraling sensations through her body and mind. She had two opposing feelings simultaneously towards Keaton and what transpired. And so, she directed the anger at herself for having fallen for him so hard to the point of ambivalence.

CHAPTER 37

When the sun rays began beaming through the escapes of the drapes in Lia's bedroom, Keaton woke up fuzzy and nauseated. He pulled his hands down his face taking in a deep breath to ease the feeling. His eyes open, and he hazily scanned the room, noticing strange things. Soon the shocking realization ripped through him. He looked down on the bed with gaping eyes, further reinforcing he was not inside his bedroom.

He sprung from the bed in dread, his hands holding the sides of his head, his mouth wide open, elevated heartbeat, and rising temperature. Bits of memory from the recent hours flashed through his mind like a blaring stampede. He squeezed his hands to his forehead to slow the zipping jumble of reflections, and that's when it happened—a vivid recollection of his misdeed. His hands covering his mouth, he became dumbstruck, mindlessly stuttering,

"No, no, God no. Please let it not be true." He scanned the room again, this time for Lia; catching a glimpse of his reflection in the bedroom mirror, he realized his nakedness. He searched for his trousers in a scurry, which he found on the floor to the right of the bed. He pulled them on after two failed attempts to get his foot in the trousers' leg, not being able to think straight, overcome with guilt, worry, and panic. He rushed to the balcony, then to the bathroom, but Lia is not there. In a sprint, he dashed out the door screaming her name.

"Lia! Lia!"

Downstairs, he searched all the rooms, the kitchen, the porch, all the time asking the staff he met if they had seen Lia, who all responded that they hadn't seen her. He left the backyard garden, back into the house, rushing upstairs where he banged on his mother's bedroom door. Celia opened the door with a baffled look on her face.

"Keaton? What is it? Why are you breaking the door?"

"Mom, please tell me you have seen Lia."

Celia noticed the frantic look in his eyes and trembling hands; he looked scared to death.

"No, I haven't seen her. I have been in the garden since 7:00 a.m. and only returned to my room a few minutes ago. It's now 9:00 a.m.; perhaps she is still in her room. We were up late last night; she may have slept in."

Keaton held his head as feverish anxiety set in. "She's not in her bedroom; I was there…."

"You are scaring me." Celia gasped, adopting Keaton's panic. "Did something happen? Did you check the rest of the house, the grounds? Have you checked with the staff or her driver? Did you call her cell?"

"Her cell?" Keaton mumbled inaudibly, rushing off to find his phone. He rang her phone, pacing the hallway. Her phone rang without an answer for the first two calls and then went straight to voicemail for every call after that.

"How could I have done this." He rambled, pacing; he tossed the phone, shattering it on the wall.

“Get a hold of yourself!” Celia yelled, frightened by the noise and his inexplicit behavior.

“Can you please tell me what’s going on? Why are you looking for Lia in such alarm? Talk to me!”

“I fucked up mom, this time, I really fucked up.”

“Keaton! —language. What do you mean? Did you two fight?”

“I don’t know how it happened. I don’t even remember going into her bedroom when I came home….” He had a confused look on his face, trying hard to recollect the fragmented memories racing through his mind.

“Wait…” said Celia, looking closer at Keaton, “Did you spend the night with Lia?”

Keaton stopped pacing and looked at his mom. “Seems I did, but not intentionally, I must have been drunk when I returned. I can’t remember clearly but from the memory flashes. I did something to her, and now she’s….” He paused, staring into space as details of what happened between him and Lia became clearer. He fell to the floor with a blank look on his face, his hands gripping the sides of his head, tears running down his face.

“Keaton, what is it?” Celia screamed, kneeling beside him.

“I hurt her mom; I did. I swear I didn’t mean to—I….”

Celia held him, confused at what he was saying. “How did you hurt her? What did you do?”

Keaton looked into her eyes, his filled with guilt and remorse. He broke down, laying his head on her chest and clutching at her hands in a grunting wail.

Celia tried to make sense of the situation in her head as she held Keaton. *He spent the night with Lia, and now she is missing; while Keaton is nervous, panicked, and apologetic. What in heavens happened last night?*

Then her eyes widened as the only thing that made sense flashed across her thought. *Oh God,* she thought, looking at Keaton.

"Keaton, did you—did you force yourself on Lia?" She asked reluctantly. Nervous to hear the answer. Keaton's cries deepened in the pit of his stomach as he buried his head on her chest.

"Oh God, Keaton, how could you—how...." Celia's hands started to tremble; her body wracked with trepidation.

"Keaton—look at me," Celia said, lifting his head from her chest. "Are you sure this is what happened?"

"Mom—I think so."

"Oh God, we have to find Lia; you need to check her room, see if she left anything, a note, something. I'll check my phone to see if she texted me. You need to fix this!"

Celia got up from the floor and rushed to her bedroom to find her phone. Keaton ran back to Lia's bedroom to look for anything that could suggest where she had gone.

In Lia's bedroom, Keaton swiped at his eyes to clear the blur of his tears. He stopped in the middle of the bedroom and took a deep breath, trying to calm himself. His eyes scanned the room. A few seconds in, he saw an open notebook on the nightstand to the side of the bed he woke from earlier. He rushed over to it and grabbed the notebook. Indeed, it was a written note Lia had scribbled before she left. The pages were visibly damp from drops of her tears, bleeding the ink on the more saturated parts. Keaton's heart leaped; his eyes glued to the pages with hands shaking he read the note:

They say love makes you do crazy things, and now I have proven it. Keaton, I have lost myself for you. My dignity, my will, it is all gone.

It became clear tonight that I was no longer in control of myself or my emotions when I allowed you to take advantage of me. If you are reading this, you might have sobered up, realized what happened, and probably already regretted it. But believe me, no one regrets it more than I do. Not because you were intoxicated, not because it wasn't entirely consensual, but because I allowed it to happen.

My love for you has shrouded my ability to make judgments on what is right and wrong. Tonight, I was ambivalent towards your actions, torn—a part of me knew what you were doing was wrong, but my love for you allowed it anyway. I am so far gone that I have sat and knowingly let myself get hurt and used by you repeatedly.

Though it might be too late, I realize now that I do not belong in your world. I have no place in your heart because Katie occupies it. I am sorry that we both got trapped in this marriage, I am sorry that I wanted more, I am sorry for wanting love out of a contract that was always meant for business.

Maybe I am the one at fault; maybe my love for you was to fill a void, an emptiness inside. Whatever it is, it's over now. I have accepted my fate. We were never meant to be together. You said it yourself; "all you wanted was to marry the girl of your dreams—to build your future with Katie, then I showed up and messed it up for you." And for that, I am sorry, I will do my best to fix it.

I have returned home where I belong, and don't worry; my leaving won't affect the contract; I am not that petty. I will send you the signed divorced papers at the end of the year and relinquish full ownership of the shares.

However, I will no longer accept the incentives promised to SANCORP in the contract. SANCORP will not agree to sole manufacturing rights of TrueTek's biotech products for the European Market, nor will we take the shares promised in ownership of the newly built facilities. I think this is fitting as SANCORP will no longer be in partnership with TrueTek. This decision will take effect the moment I sign the divorce agreement.

Please don't take my cutting ties between SANCORP and TrueTek as vengeance or being petty. It is far from that. I am doing it for my sanity; a clean break from you is the only way forward for me if I am to heal and get over you.

After this, I hope you can pick up where you left off with Katie, and I wish you all the best. She is a lucky girl, and some part of me still envy her. But the reality is apparent; I need to move on.

Take care of yourself and say goodbye to mom for me; this is not how I wanted it to be. I genuinely love her as a mother and always will. I hope she can forgive me for leaving this way.

I have written too much already, so goodbye Keaton, I will always love you.

Lia.

CHAPTER 38

Celia came into Lia's room some minutes later to find Keaton on the floor to the left of the bed in tears, clutching the notebook in his hand.

"Keaton, what is it? Did Lia leave something?"

Keaton raised the notebook to Celia, who took it in a hurry. Her eyes moved in fits across the page, speed reading as her countenance swiftly saddened. She looked down on Keaton with a mixture of infuriation and pity as her eyes became glossy from emerging tears.

"You are sitting here looking pitiful, full of remorse. Can you imagine the pain that Lia is in because of your actions? You need to get up off your ass, find her and make it right."

Keaton sniffled, raising his head from its low-hanging position. "But she's gone; it's there in the note; she is returning home."

"And what difference does it make!" Celia asserted, "If you need to get on the plane and go find her, that's precisely what you'll do. I warned you that the indecisiveness of your feelings toward Lia would be destructive. Now have you seen it?"

"Mom, I swear, I would have never consciously harmed Lia. I had to have been inebriated."

"I know you wouldn't, but whether you were drunk is beside the point. Alcohol only motivated your actions, heightening emotions that were already there. Now can you honestly tell me this time that you are not in love with Lia?"

Keaton paused, looking at his mother with wet red eyes. "I am, I am in love with her…."

"Then go do what needs to be done, find Lia and let her know how you feel. You can't leave her hurting, having the wrong impression of you for the rest of her life. I raised you better than that. Now get up, get ready and find her. I will reach out to my contact at the airport to find out if Lia has already left the country. The plane is on standby should you need to depart today. I already spoke to Lucas, he will be by shortly with a new phone, and he'll take care of your meetings and reschedule your work obligations until this is sorted."

Keaton rose sharply from the floor, looked at his mom with agreeing eyes, and left the bedroom. Celia immediately got on the phone, making contacts to guide Keaton's next move.

Not long after, Celia met Keaton in his bedroom to update him with the information she had received. Keaton was ready and had a small bag packed to leave for Norway that evening if he had to.

"Mom, what is it?" he eagerly asked as Celia made her way into his bedroom. "What did you find?"

"Lia is booked on the next flight to Norway, which departs in thirty minutes. You won't get to her before she leaves, so you need to go now. I have spoken to Sebastian; he and his co-pilot will have the plane ready for take-off when you get to the airport. And before I forget, here, she handed him a new cellphone. Lucas dropped this off a few minutes ago. It's already updated with your iCloud backup, so all your contacts should be there.

Keaton moved closer to her and took the phone, pulling her into an embrace. "Thanks, mom," he whispered. "I promise I'll make it right."

"I am holding you to that; now go. Go bring back my daughter-in-law."

They gave each other a parting smile, and Keaton left the room, transported to the airport by Jaxen. On the drive, Keaton checked his phone and saw an email notification from Chad.

Hey, I have been calling and can't reach your phone. Call me when you get this.

Without hesitation, he rang Chad. "Chad, it's Keaton; what's up? You asked me to call?"

"Keaton, thank God," Chad replied on the other end. "Are you ok, is…?"

"Well, sort of, I am actually on my way to the airport; I am leaving for Norway to go find Lia."

"What do you mean wasn't she living at your place? What happened?"

"It's a long story. Let's just say I messed up. I might have been drunk when I returned home last night, and I did something inexplicable. Now Lia is gone."

"Oh fuck," shrieked Chad, "I was hoping this didn't happen."

"What do you mean?" Keaton asked with a worried expression.

"Keaton, I tried to call you shortly after you left the lounge—Trent drugged your shot with liquid ecstasy. I had a feeling something was wrong when you started feeling anxious and sweating. So, I confronted Trent after you left, and he admitted putting ecstasy in your parting shot."

"Why would he do that? What the fuck is wrong with him! Does he take pleasure fucking up other people's lives? Do you know the damage his stupidity caused? I swear to God I am going to kill him!"

"Keaton, calm down; I know you are mad. What Trent did is inexcusable, and he deserves your wrath. He wanted you to sleep with Lia to settle on your feelings for her, but he went about it wrong. I will deal with Trent. You take care of things on your end and keep me posted, let me know when you find her. If you need me to explain to her what happened at the lounge that led to this, I will. Anything to fix it."

Keaton took a deep breath to calm himself before responding to Chad. "OK, I'll keep you posted, and when you speak to Trent, tell him to stay away from me because if he crosses my path, I won't be responsible for what I may do to him."

Keaton hung up without a last word from Chad. He took Trent's action as a personal affront; it made his blood boil.

The Next Day

With an almost eight-hour flight, Keaton arrived in Oslo, Norway the following day, and in less than an hour after landing, he was on his way to Lia's home address. But like being caught in a blizzard with no clear-cut way out, seeing Lia was just as difficult. He stated his name at the gates security system to request entry and was immediately rejected. Shortly after, two of Lia's home security guards came to escort him from the gate, communicating in no uncertain terms that Lia would not see him and requested he leave at once.

He pulled his hand from the security's grip, screaming into the entry system

"Lia, I know you are in there, and I will keep coming back until you see me. We need to talk about this—I am sorry."

He left that day without putting up a fight, but he was back the next day and the day after that. On day three, he slept outside her gate the entire night, against his mother's plea for him to return to the hotel. He insisted on staying there. The following morning a black Mercedes-Benz C-Class drove out of Lia's complex, having caught a glimpse of Lia Keaton hopelessly banged on the left rear window begging her to open the door. The car sped away, knocking him to the asphalt.

He sat up in the spot he fell, broken and disheartened more so because he could only think of how much he must have hurt her for her to treat him that way. He had planned on staying there until her car returned, and so he got up and sat in front of the gate, determined that she would either have to see him or run him over. Then his phone rang.

"Mom,"

"Keaton, you will never guess who just showed up at the door."

"Mom, I am not in the mood for guessing games. Just tell me who."

"Katie...."

Keaton's mouth dropped, his face riddled with questions and concern. His heart near collapsed; he froze and became speechless. In his silence, Celia answered his unspoken questions.

"She showed up this morning, said she received a text message to meet you here urgently."

"A text message from me? I didn't send Katie a text message. When did she say she received it?"

"Four days ago, the same day you left for Norway."

"Mom, I never sent her a text message to meet me; why would I?"

"If you didn't, then who did? She knew how to get here and who to call. Apparently, she contacted Jaxen on her arrival, and he brought her here."

"Where is she now?" Keaton asked, rising from his seated position to a worrying pace.

"I've set her up in the guest room. Before we go any further, tell me, how are things going with Lia? Have you seen her yet?"

"No, not entirely," Keaton replied, downhearted. "This morning, she left the house in a chauffeured car; I tried to get her attention, hoping she would stop, but that was futile. I have been between SANCORP and her home, but I haven't had any luck. She is determined not to see me. So, I am not leaving here until she returns. I'll stay in front of the gate; she's going to have to run me over."

"Don't you say that!" Celia asserted, "I am anxious for you to clarify things with her, but not if you'll be in harm's way. These past four days, you have been outside her gate every day; you even slept there. I am sure she has heard your plea and knows it's sincere. Maybe she just needs some time. Why don't you return, give her some space, let her come around on her own time?"

"And what if she never comes around. What if I leave now and never hear from her again?"

"Keaton, honestly, I don't know what's going to happen, but you can't stay there forever. Besides, you need to return to sort things out with Katie, let her know where you stand. After that, we can decide on a new approach to see Lia."

"Mom, I will return but only after tonight. I need to wait here until Lia's car returns; I'll make one last attempt to see her before I leave, and if I fail, I will return tomorrow."

"OK, I'll settle Katie until you return. I told her you have traveled, so I'll let her know you may return tomorrow. Please be careful; you are all I have left in this world. I don't know what I would do if anything happened to you."

"I'll be fine, mom. See you soon."

When Keaton hung up, a disconcerting feeling overcame him, like his world was crashing down. It has to be Lia who texted Katie, he thought. He downloaded his text message back-up, and there it was, sent four days ago, *Sunday, October 27th, 2019, at 5:00 a.m.*

Lia, he asserted in thought. *She sent it; she must have accessed my phone when I passed out.* Then he recalled parts of the letter

Lia had left, saying sorry that the marriage had messed up his future with Katie and that she would 'do her best to fix it.'

"So that's what she meant when she wrote she would do her best to fix it," He whispered to himself. He sat back down in front of Lia's gate, his body flopped in mental and physical exhaustion, overwhelmed with more burden than he could bear. If he saw Lia, how would he convince her now that he was just as in love with her as she was in love with him? And what about Katie? How would he tell Katie he was now in love with Lia without crushing her heart?

There was no escaping it; in the end, someone would get hurt, and now it seemed he had unintentionally hurt both of them. In thought, he questioned his predicament and blamed himself. *Is this my fate?*

CHAPTER 39

Nightfall came, and Lia's car never returned, leaving Keaton cold and helpless once again sleeping outside her gate. Lia conveyed a message to him through one of her home security guards at daybreak that she would not return until Keaton returned to New York. With no alternative, a broken heart, and diminished will, Keaton boarded his private jet that afternoon set for New York.

When Keaton arrived home the following day, he dragged himself from the car and lumbered to the house. His head was pounding, weak from lack of nutrition, dehydrated and downtrodden. Celia met him in the main hall, and she was distraught by his appearance. She took him in her arms, noticing his dispiritedness and the emptiness in his eyes, wishing she could take on his burden, if even for a moment.

"Don't worry about it." She said, comforting him. "We will continue to try; let's take it one step at a time." Keaton nodded, resting his head on her shoulders.

"Where is Katie?" He asked, lifting his head in a hurry as the daunting realization waltz through his memory, reminding him that she was there.

"She is outside by the pool." Celia replied, "She has settled in comfortably since she arrived."

"Thanks, mom; I need to see her. We'll talk more later?"

"Yes, of course, go see her."

Keaton pecked her on the cheek and left the room, heading to the pool. At first glance, all he saw from his angle was the back of her head on a lounge chair by the pool, and instantaneously, a cold shiver ran through his body, and he found himself frozen a few meters behind her. Like deja vu, he had a knot in his throat and a heavy heart, just as when he had to tell her about his arranged marriage. Now he had another confession, and once again, he was terrified, scared to hurt her.

As if she could feel his presence, she got up from the lounge chair and looked behind her. Her eyes lit up like the sky on the 4th of July. And that gleaming smile he can never forget formed excitedly across her face, a smile that makes everyone in the room happy, the smile that's comforting, serene, and warms the heart.

"*Bébé!*" She screamed, running into his arms. "*Mon Dieu*, I've missed you." She wrapped her arms around his waist and hoisted herself on tippy toes, pushing her face closer to his, waiting for that reunited, explosive, mind-blowing kiss.

But it never came.

Keaton stared into her eyes, his arms stiff at his sides, a compassionate yet passive look in his eyes. Of course, he missed her too, but he had never planned on losing that part of himself to Lia, the part Katie once illuminated—his heart.

Katie released her arms and stepped back a bit, saying nothing, just looking back into his eyes, for she knew that was not her Keaton. His silence, his expression, and his stance were nothing short of apathetic.

"Are you going to talk to me about it?" She stated, her expression reflexive.

Keaton swallowed, knowing Katie had always been in sync with his emotions; he could tell she already knew his feelings had changed. Riddled with confusion, he questioned how was she standing in his presence, and he did not feel that excitement and admiration that once made him come alive?

"Why did you ask me here?" She questioned, "Your mom wouldn't tell me anything, only that you traveled, and you would make things clear on your return. Your text message said you needed me urgently, now I am here, and you look like this; what exactly is going on?"

Keaton brought both his hands together, fidgeting his fingers.

"Can we go inside?" He asked in a subtle tone masking his nervousness. Katie searched his eyes with hers, and like intuition, she detected his uneasiness. She wondered if something had gone terribly wrong, was he in trouble.

"Sure, let me grab my phone." She walked back to the lounge chair, grabbed her phone and coverup, and together, they walked side by side back to the house.

Inside his bedroom, Keaton asked Katie to sit. She gazed around at first, admiring his bedroom and subtle thoughts ran through her mind of the reality of his wealth. It was one thing to hear about it, but to experience just a tiny fragment of it, she was more and more intrigued and a bit intimidated.

She sat at the edge of the bed, resting her phone and coverup beside her, giving him her undivided attention. He was still fidgeting with his fingers, having no clue how to begin. Katie felt his trepidation; she had experienced it before, which made her anxiety level rise, for she knew something terrifying was coming.

"Start with the text message," she nudged, "Is something wrong? Why did you need me to get here so urgent?"

Keaton composed himself, taking a shallow breath before responding.

"Katie, I didn't send you that text message; Lia did."

Katie's brows knitted, her expression showed questions and confusion.

"Why would she send me an SOS text message to get here from your phone?"

Keaton hesitated in his response, uttering a series of nonsensical stutters before forming a meaningful sentence. "Lia left; she returned to Norway five days ago." Katie's confusion was peaking, "What do you mean, I thought the contract was till the end of the year?"

"It is, but something happened. I made an unforgivable mistake, causing her to leave. She sent you that text message without my knowledge because she hoped you'd return to take your rightful place in my heart."

"So—?" Katie said, pausing for a beat, trying to figure out the connection between Lia's leaving, Keaton's reservation towards her, and what she knew about the contract. "...does this mean you will still lose the shares? the company....?"

"It's not like that anymore; Lia will keep her end of the agreement until completion. It's just...."

"It's just what?" Katie asked with much impatience. "I don't get it, Lia left—OK, but you won't be losing the shares nor your company, so why the long face? Shouldn't you be happy? You never wanted the marriage, so why does it seem that there is more going on?"

Before he could respond, Katie released a barely audible snicker, her expression revealing her sudden epiphany. "Let me guess; you have fallen in love with her?" Katie's words, the accuracy, and the clarity in her tone sent chills down his spine, reinforcing his own truth—his reality. Making him question if his love for Lia was that obvious that everyone else had realized it and accepted it long before he did. His mom, friends, business partners, and colleagues, and now Katie had figured it out in seconds. He now realized he was the only one at odds with his feelings for Lia; it's like he had been wearing his emotions on a stamp across his forehead all this time for the world to see.

He looked at Katie, unable to lie to her but at the same time apprehensive about hurting her. His hesitation and unintentional silence spoke volumes, confirming her assumption. She got up from her seated position and walked closer to him until she was less than an inch in front of him, looking up into his eyes.

"Don't I deserve the truth?" She demanded, her eyes holding his focus. "I need to hear it from your mouth. Did you fall in love with her?"

Keaton closed and opened his eyes in a sort of slow-motion blink as her words tugged at his heart.

Katie looked more agitated as the seconds ticked on.

"Katie, I am so sorry, you are right—I have fallen in love with her."

"I see," Katie said softly, nodding her head, slowly backing away from him.

"How long have you known that you were in love with her?"

"Katie, please...."

"How long, Keaton!"

"Please, just sit back down, and I'll tell you everything." He begged. Keaton walked towards her, sat her down on his bedroom couch, and sat beside her. Katie kept her head straight, not looking at him, pressing her shaking hands into her lap to still them.

Keaton took a deep breath and started from the top, in detail, highlighting the beginning of his feelings for Lia during their collaboration on project Globo. He explained to Katie specifics of the intimate intricacy that happened between him and Lia the night he returned from sub-Saharan Africa, noting that night as the genesis of his emotional conflict.

He described the ordeals and emotional roller-coaster that followed, leading to his dire mistake unintentionally hurting Lia on the night of his birthday, further clarifying why Lia had left. The more he revealed, the more painful it became to witness the effects of his confession on Katie. Once again, he was ripping her heart from her chest for the same woman in a different circumstance.

He ended his confession explaining why Lia sent her the

text message, clarifying that he was not on a business trip but had gone after Lia having realized he was in love with her.

"That's everything." He stuttered, "That's how it happened. He tried to hold Katie's hands as she sat in silence, suppressing her cries but unable to hide the tears streaming down her face.

She pushed her hands deeper into her lap between her legs, her head hung. In her mind, she was screaming; *I don't want to be touched, comforted, or hear the word sorry. I just want to disappear from here like ashes in the wind.*

"Please say something," he pleaded. Trying to touch her, Katie shifted her body from him, and he withdrew his hand.

"Katie, I know you hate me right now, and you have every right to be. I have betrayed our love, and I hate myself for it. I never planned for any of this to happen. Scream at me if you need to, hit me if you have to, please just say something—anything. I am deeply sorry."

The word sorry was a trigger, stirring a wave of anger deep within her, which seemed to dry the reservoir supplying her tears because instantaneously, they stopped flowing. She dried the remnants from her cheeks, turning to face him.

"You don't deserve me." She asserted, "You don't deserve my tears." An emerging smile formed on her face like the sun clearing darkened clouds after a rainy day.

Keaton looked back at her, confused by her expression, but he dared not ask why; *she needed to vent,* he thought, *just let her.*

"You know, while I was in Greece with my family, my mom asked after you, why she hadn't seen you around for such a long time. She was worried that everything was not well with our relationship. I couldn't lie to her, so I told her of our arrangement, about your arranged marriage, and you know what she told me?

"She told me that my true love would never choose anything over me, no matter the circumstance. I didn't want to believe her, but you know what? she was right. The truth is, you made your choice the day you left me in France to get married to Lia, no matter the reason, no matter what was at stake. We were never meant to be together; it took two years before I accepted your courtship, and when we finally fell in love, in less than a year of being together, your father passes, and out of the blue, you get stuck in a pre-arranged marriage agreement. I agreed to wait for you despite the pain, with a broken heart, and in less than two months of our forever after, where we can finally be together, you fall in love with the enemy. Don't you see, fate is against us; we are not meant to be. My father once told me that in life, some peo ple come into our lives as placeholders, only for a short time, and when the right one comes along, the universe will create circumstances to shift that placeholder out of your life for the right person to take their place. I was in high school then, so I never understood what he meant. But now I know; I was your placeholder, the time has come for me to leave, and as hard as it is for me to accept, I have to, the universe has spoken. You know what's funny? Lia left because she thought I was your true love, but looking at you now, it is clear you are no longer in love with me. Our spark has left your eyes. There's not even a glimmer left. Lia was so wrong; I am not the one, she is—she is your destiny.

I'll return to France tomorrow; I hope you do get to be with her, and I wish you both all the best in your future together."

Katie got up from the couch and kissed Keaton on the forehead, then looked engagingly into his eyes and said, "I won't hold any grudges. It just wasn't meant to be." She slipped the ring off her finger, took his hand, and placed it in the center of his palm, closing his fingers over it.

"Katie…."

She shook her head in slow motion, stopping him before he could say anything else.

"Keaton, you know I am right, so let's not make this any harder than it needs to be. I'll make returning flight arrangements, and I'd appreciate it if Jaxen could take me to the airport tomorrow." She gave him a tight-lipped smile and left his room.

Keaton watched her leave until the door was closed behind her. He looked down at the ring in the palm of his hand and memories of their time together—their love played a slide show through his mind causing him to break down in tears.

"God is this how you meant for my life to be? Because if it is, then either it's a sick joke or punishment for something I did. How could you give me everything I have ever hoped for ... being in love with Katie, only to make me fall for another, then rip them both away from me at the same time? What have I done to deserve this?" he cried, cowering his head into his palms.

CHAPTER 40

After Katie returned to France, Keaton spent the remaining two months of the marriage contract, back and forth between New York and Norway, determined to find Lia, eager for her forgiveness, desperate to confess his love to her. Still, he had no luck. On his last trip, he discovered that Lia was no longer living at the only address he knew, and her uncle was no longer accommodating his nuisances which made finding her even more grueling.

On the eve of the new year, having just returned from Norway after unsuccessfully camping outside SANCORP for over a week, Keaton was sitting in his home study when Celia came rushing in with a FedEx envelope.

"Keaton, look! The couriers just dropped this off; it's from Lia," she shouted, running over to his desk.

With much urgency, Keaton got up from behind the desk, promptly taking the envelope and tearing the closing seal from the opening. He pulled the documents from the envelope and began to scan through, luster slowly drained from his face and his eyes became somber.

"What is it?" Celia asked impatiently

"It's the divorce documents; Lia has signed them requesting my signature to make our separation official."

"Let me see," Celia said; taking the documents, she carefully scanned through them page by page; when she got to the last page, she saw a smaller letter-sized envelope attached to the back page with a paper clip, with the words 'Read me' written on the front of the envelope.

"Keaton, look, there's a letter," she said, handing him the envelope. Keaton hurriedly took the letter, opened it, and began to read:

Hi Keaton,

I hope by now you have sorted things out with Katie to rebuild your future together. Forgive me for texting her without your knowledge; I had to try to fix it. I couldn't allow our marriage to break another woman's heart as it did mine.

As you can see, I have signed the divorce papers, and once you sign them, the contract is complete; you can get married to Katie and move on with your life.

These past months ever since I left New York, I have done everything possible to get over you, and I am still trying. I refused to see you when you came looking for me because I am still weak to you.

Though I know you were only trying to find me to apologize, I am not strong enough to face you without bearing my weakness. My broken heart needs healing, and that will never happen if we stay in touch. My love for you has consumed me to the point that I am sure I would never be able to let go or walk away if I see you again.

For a long time, I have been angry at you for not reciprocating my love; however, now that I have had time to think with an unbiased view, I have accepted the fact that love cannot be forced. So, what if I love you? It means nothing if you don't feel the same way—if your heart belongs to another and that's no fault of yours, I get that now; it is what it is.

Leaving is the hardest thing I have ever done, but it was the right thing to do so you can be with the one you love.

I might not have ended this contract with a happily ever after with you, but I believe I still won because you have given me one of the best gifts a woman could ever need. I will always have a part of you with this gift, and I am at peace with that.

Now, I hold no grudges, there's no need to look for me, no need for apologetic regrets because we were both responsible for what happened, and with the blessing that came out of it, I can never look at it in a negative light ever again.

I have left Oslo, Norway, and I don't plan on returning anytime soon. I want to start a life with this blessing in another part of Europe, somewhere verdant that blends the old with the new for a wholesome adventure.

So, here's to starting over in our rightful futures, to fate and new beginnings. May this separation serve as an emblem, as the day we both finally get to be free. No more living the lives everyone else wants us to live; from now on, may our happiness be coined with our own hands, may we follow our own direction.

Take care of yourself, Keaton, and take care of mom.

Love always,

Lia

Keaton's hands shook, a paralyzed expression on his face. Soon the letter fell from his hand; he stood fixed in the same spot, barely breathing.

"What is it, what did the letter say?" Celia asked, petrified by his appearance.

"Mom, I think. I think Lia is—she is…."

"She's what, Keaton? What?"

Still frozen in shock, an elevated heartbeat, and the sudden heat overtaking his body, Keaton could hardly breathe, let alone find words to speak. Celia swiftly picked the letter up from the floor and read it at lightning speed, soon realizing what Keaton was trying to say.

"Oh, dear God, she's pregnant." Celia covered her mouth with her free hand, her eyes welling with tears.

"Keaton, she's pregnant. Are you hearing me? She's pregnant." Celia yelled, smiling through her tears.

Keaton didn't speak because he couldn't, but he managed to move, grabbing his phone from the desk running out of the study.

"Where are you going?" Celia shouted at his back

"I've got to find her mom. I won't stop till I do." He shouted back, dashing out the door.

Celia looked at the letter again, a wave of joy and sadness gushing through her; in her heart, Lia was and would always be her daughter-in-law. Now Lia was carrying her grandchild but didn't want to be found. Like Keaton, Celia's heart broke; she wished he had accepted that fate brought Lia to him earlier. *Is it too late,* she thought, *will I ever see them again—will I get to be a part of this child's life?*

"God, please let Keaton find her," she whispered in tears, looking up in a wistful prayer, pressing the letter against her heart.

CHAPTER 41

Two Years Later: Bern, Switzerland

Keaton exited the corporate head office of ZenTMED, the new Swiss company TrueTek partnered with for manufacturing its biotech products for the European market. With the dissolving of the partnership with SANCORP at the end of he and Lia's marriage contract two years ago, Keaton had just taken the step in the last few months to reinstate a new European partner.

Since he received Lia's letter two years ago, finding that she was pregnant, he spared no expense or resources to locate her, but without success. Lia being just as affluent as he is, ensured she was never found.

But he never gave up, and he never signed the divorce papers, for, in his heart, she was his wife. He wore the ring she gave him on their wedding day ever since and still traveled all over Europe to the verdant areas searching for her, promising himself he would never stop until the day he died. He could never visit any part of Europe without thinking of her or reliving their time together.

Keaton felt a great sense of anxiety every time he was in another part of Europe, and today was no different. His hands trembled ever so slightly as he exited the building, his eyes scanning around the outdoors with a longing hope that fate would one day let him run into Lia. He stared across the street at the luscious viridescent park scattered with children, echoes of cheerful play and gleeful giggles. A warm feeling surged through him, and he thought about what his child might look like now. Was his son or daughter playing in a park somewhere, and what he would give to see his child's smile, to see Lia's smile once again.

"Jaxen, I think I'm going to sit in the park for a while. You can wait for me in the car."

"Sure, Sir," Jaxen replied, communicating Keaton's wishes to the rest of his security team through his earpiece.

Keaton walked across the street and sat on a bench in the park, viewing the playground's splash pad. Watching the children play, splashing around, and having fun brought him such joy and a sense of well-being. A smile of enjoyment formed across his face, and he had the feeling that he could sit there forever.

"Keaton, don't you run to that splash pad. You are not wearing a bathing suit. Keaton, stop!" The sound came from the left of him, and for a second, he wondered if he had heard right or was he imagining things? But then he was sure he had heard his name, and in reflex, he began looking in the direction he heard it. And that's when he saw the back of a lady with a similar frame and hair as Lia chasing after a little boy who was happily giggling, running towards the splash pad.

Without a second thought, Keaton sprung up from the bench and rushed towards them, and within inches of them, he stopped frozen in his track. The lady he saw had caught the little boy she was chasing. Like the slow dramatic turn in movies, she had turned, he was now looking at her face to face—Lia.

Without words, their emotional reunion spoke volumes through the soul connection of their eyes. At that moment, Keaton's entire being was fragrant in a sweet release; the relief, the chance for joy was once again in front of him—Lia and his son, stealing his breath and the heat from his skin.

"Keaton?" Lia gasped, looking at him wide-eyed, in shock, clutching her son in her arms.

Keaton stepped closer to her, so close he could hear her heartbeat, their eyes swelling with tears. He folded his hands around Lia's back, drawing her in. He could feel her body shake, he looked into her eyes and looked at the boy she clutched in her arm, and it broke him. Keaton pulled them into his arms, locked in the strength of a long-anticipated hug, bawling for the missed time he would never make back, both crying to release the tension of two long years.

Lia pulled her head back and wiped her tears, her eyes overflowing with more relief than her heart could hold. Keaton noshes her with his eyes, running his fingers through her hair as if he couldn't quite believe he was not in a dream.

He kissed her face sweet and gentle, tasting her tears. Lia tried to speak, but all she could do was cry.

"Don't ever leave me again." Keaton croaked. Planting kisses all over her face once more before folding them into his arms.

Keaton pulled back, taking the child from Lia's arms, melting into his heavenly opalescent eyes.

"He's my son, isn't he?" He croaked.

"Yes," Lia sobbed, nodding her head, swiping at her eyes.

Torrents of tears flowed down Keaton's face as he wrapped his son in his arms, shuddering uncontrollably. Something inside of him snapped like brittle glass, with shards tearing through his gut and heart and all he wanted to do was hold them close, never to let them go.

"Hi," Keaton said to his son in a high-pitch baby voice, his eyes gleaming with tears, "I am Keaton, your father."

"My name is Keaton, too, and I am two years old." The little boy replied with a joyous look on his face melting Keaton's heart like butter against the sun.

"Lia, I am so sorry; I tried looking for you all these years—I tried."

"I know you did," she sobbed. "I just wanted you to be happy; I never wanted you to feel obligated to me because of our son."

"But I have not been happy. Ever since you left, I have been miserable. Not a day went by that I hadn't thought about you. It's my fault that I lost you—both of you because I was too stupid to admit how I felt, and before I knew it, it was too late. Lia, I love you. I am so in love with you. I prayed every day for the past two years, begging God to let me see you again if only to tell you how much I love you. I know I am late, but I promise you if you give me another chance, I'll spend the rest of my life making it up to you. Please, can we start over?"

Lia looked back at him confused. Inside she was screaming 'yes!' but she had to know.

"What about Katie, isn't she the one?"

"No, Katie and I parted ways the day I returned from Norway, a few days after you had left. I told her everything, and we parted amicably. She's married now and doing well. And, I have never stopped searching for you. See," he said, raising his left hand showing her the ring.

"I have never taken it off; the reason I never signed the divorce papers no matter how much pressure I received from your lawyers is that I couldn't let you go. Somehow, the knowledge of being legally married to you, whether or not I could find you, gave me faith and kept me sane over the years. Lia, you're my only wife, the love of my life, and I would have died a lonesome man if I never saw you again."

Tears rolled unchecked, tears neither of them wiped away, for, after so many years and with much-misplaced guilt, it was warranted.

Keaton pulled her into his arm, balancing his son in the other. With shallow breath through continuous sobs, he asserted in a plea, "I have lost you once, and I will not lose you again; please give me another chance, please."

Lia nodded, "Ja—Ja," a yes that came out in croaking wails.

"Yes!" she said again emphatically.

In the moment, Keaton held both of them in a never-ending embrace, thanking God for answering his prayers, for he was content that even if the world came to an end that second, he would have died the happiest man alive.

EPILOGUE

One Year Later: Oslo, Norway

On a summery afternoon at their mansion west of Oslo, a heavily pregnant Lia exited at the back of the main house with a pitcher of lemonade in her hand. She walked onto the grassy lawn of their backyard, leading to a breathtaking, pebble infinity pool with blending sea views, where Keaton and three-year-old Keaton Jr are having an exciting floatie race.

"Come on, guys, it's time for lunch," Lia gushed, smiling at them.

"Let's go, buddy; it's time for lunch," Keaton said, lifting his son out of the pool.

He kissed Lia on the forehead, lovingly rubbing her tummy before bending down to speak to his unborn child.

"How is my princess today?" He whispered with pure delight in his eyes. "I can't wait to meet you, only one more month, and you're here."

"I need her out already," Lia smiled. "Let's go; lunch will be in the garden today."

Keaton rose and pecked her on the lips, gazing into her eyes. As it has been ever since they reunited, their heartbeats naturally synchronized, emanating a love that would last forever.

"Let me take that," Keaton beamed, taking the pitcher, and holding his son's hand as they walked towards the garden.

"When is mom going to be here?" Lia asked, one hand supporting her waist.

"Next week," Keaton replied. "You know she's been working to restructure the charities to represent both TrueTek and SANCORP since our merger. She should be in the final stages; I'll have her here before the baby is born—I promise."

"I need her like yesterday," Lia snickered.

Keaton laughed, "I'll see what I can do."

"Yay, grandma is coming!" Little Keaton said gleefully, swinging onto his father's hand.

"Yeah, buddy, Grandma will be here soon. I know you miss her."

"Grandma brings the best gifts!" He yelled in excitement.

They all giggled, walking into the distance into a happily ever after—devised by fate.

The End

About the Author

Avagaye is an indie author with a sunflower ambivert personality. When she isn't writing contemporary love stories, or fascinating children's books, she can be found binge watching historical K-dramas with her husband, and creating momentous adventures with their four-year old son.

Avagaye's journey into writing started instinctively, wanting to turn her childhood dream and her love for storytelling into a reality. What began as wishful fulfillment of a dream has become incredibly fulfilling. Now she can't imagine herself doing anything else.

Avagaye writes with a passion to create fictional worlds that her readers never want to leave, and characters that her readers love and hate to love.

She lives by the quote: "Always be yourself, express yourself, have faith in yourself, do not go out and look for a successful personality and duplicate it." —Bruce Lee.

Adult Books

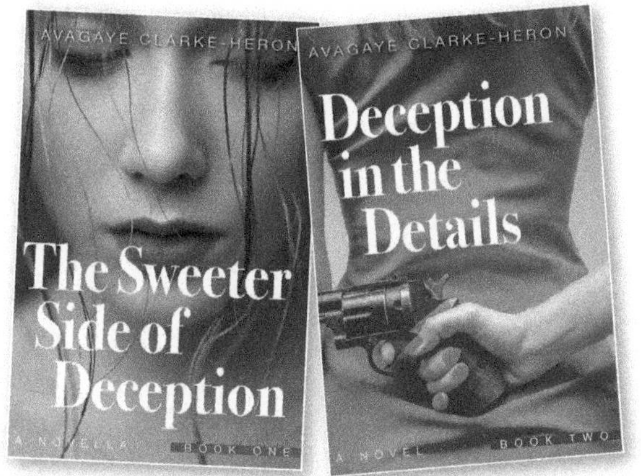

9781732403420 Paperback

9781732403482 Paperback

Children's Books

9780982963012 Hardcover
9781732403406 Paperback

9781732403468 Hardcover
9781732403451 Paperback

Connect with Avagaye and stay updated.

CPSIA information can be obtained
at www.ICGtesting.com
Printed in the USA
LVHW011130200222
711571LV00002B/21